— A Novel —

SHATTERED PIECES

The Redemptive Love Series

Playing recklessly with love is a dangerous game.

DORIS H. DANCY

Lightning Fast Book Publishing, LLC

www.lfbookpublishing.com

ISBN: 979-8-9852917-9-7

CONTENTS

DEDICATION

To my Mom, Mrs. Mildred B. Hodge

She is, and always will be, the angel on my shoulder. I miss you still and will never forget our many talks, shopping sprees, movie experiences, hours of laughter, and moments when you wiped my tears away. I will forever remember the many sacrifices you made to nudge me toward the person I am today, but most of all, Mom, thank you for giving me, Jesus.

Without God, all of our efforts turn to ashes
And our sunrise into the darkest of nights.
Without Him, life is a meaningless drama
In which the decisive scenes are missing.

Dr. Martin Luther King, Jr.

ACKNOWLEDGMENTS

There is absolutely no way that this novel would be published without the help of my Lord and Savior Jesus Christ. I thank Him for His mercy, His grace, and His favor. I am most grateful for the Lord in my life and all of the blessings and opportunities that He affords me daily.

To my loving husband, Willie, what would I do without you? You are my inspiration and my motivation to be all that God wants me to be. You have supported me in every step of this journey with your attention and your willingness to be by my side. I thank God for making this fantastic loving connection so many years ago. I love you more and more with each passing day.

To my daughters, Monica Dancy-Hayes and Tara Dancy Abaya, thank you for your unwavering love. I so much appreciate the respect that you show me daily. Thank you for your positive criticism and your willingness to stop your busy schedules to help. Monica, you went through my pages with a fine-tooth comb helping me see what was in keeping with my characters and when they were falling off the rails. You helped me write passages that were difficult for me, and you were so patient. Tara, I thank you for being there for me in my hours of discouragement always knowing just the right thing to say to a mother and father who gave you Jesus. I am grateful for your paying special attention to my original quotes and giving me honest feedback. You helped with my technology, my photos, and whatever else I threw at you at the last minute. I cannot thank you both enough for being the daughters I prayed that you would be.

To my sister-in-law, Elesta Dancy White, you are the best Beta reader I could ask for and there are no words to express adequately my gratitude for your help. Your comments were extremely helpful in moving my characters and plot forward. I thank you for the time that you have given to me ~ an unrefundable gift.

To my outstanding friends, Mrs. Joyce A.R.Weeks and the Rev. Barbara Dudley: You are always there beside me in so many different ways, supporting me in whatever God puts in my hand. Joyce, God has blessed me with your love and friendship for many years and you continue to demonstrate your loyalty to me in a multiplicity of ways. No matter what I am involved with, you are there encouraging, helping, and giving me your beautiful loving smile. You continually walk that extra mile that never fails to benefit me immensely. I am forever grateful for your Godly friendship. Barbara, the thing that makes you so special to me is the closeness that we share with Almighty God. You are there to pray for and with me, study the Word with me, and help me keep My Lord front and center in my life. You have pushed me toward what God has asked me to do, and you never fail to lend me the helping hand I need to get it done. Thank you both.

To my Pastor, The Reverend Dr. Oretha P. Cross, members and friends of St. Paul AME Church, Newport News, thank you for your outstanding support in all that I do. You have purchased my novels and given me kind words of encouragement. Because my church family means so much to me, there is nothing that I will do without your being front and center in whatever it is that God asks of me. Your loyalty has been unflinching, and I am forever grateful for the opportunities you have given me, the kind words that you have spoken to and about me, the events that you have attended, the help at events you have given, and the many words that you have read of my writings. I am most grateful for your standing beside me as I walk this path that is lighted by Our Lord and Savior, Jesus Christ helping me be obedient to His voice. I am humbled by your support and forever grateful to you all.

Thank you to my webmaster, Tracye McLean, who is always listening to God and doing all that she can to make my projects excellent. She will forever be an outstanding part of my life.

Thank you to Matthew C. Horne of *Lightning Fast Book Publishing, LLC* for your consistent excellence, your unwavering attention to my projects, and your friendship. You are an awesome leader who will continue to grow closer and closer to God as you implement the plans He has for you.

To every teacher who has ever taught me anything, I say thank you. Without your dedication, patience, and love, none of this would be possible.

Lastly, but by no means least, thank you to my readers who have purchased all of my novels, commented to me at book clubs, on Facebook, and Amazon, in blogs, on the radio, on hub pages, and in person.

You all have been faithful to me every step of the way and I am, and always will be humbled and most grateful. Thank you.

With Love,

Doris

PROLOGUE

Sometimes an end is the best chance for a beginning.

"Ahhhhhhhhhhhhhhhhhhhhhhhhhhhhhhhhhhhhh!" My scream startles the night. It's gut wrenching, loud but hoarse, choking but clear, and it disturbs the very depth of my soul. My body bolts upright, and the sweat is profuse. I'm soaked. My mind is a panoramic movie zooming pass the cramped three- room hot box, pass the filthy wall in the kitchen I faced on one leg for hours, pass the tall muscular man standing ready with the belt raised or the hot iron threatening. My inner camera pans pass the mice gnawing my feet, pass the aching hunger knots in my stomach, pass old bone breaks, urine smells, rotting food, sore bruises, ...pass... pass...pass...my Mom.

At first, I don't know where I am, and then in a flash, my mind propels me out of the darkness of my past and back to my present. I take a deep breath. I'm safe. I'm back. I feel a joy inside me realizing that it is just my nightmare resurfacing again. It is no longer real. What I know, however, is an unwelcomed visit from my brother, Chad, would be enough to cause a tidal wave of bad memories to attack me again.

Momentarily, I sit in a cold silence hearing only the quick breaths I take. I feel around in the darkness for S.G. I know he's on the nightstand next to the bed where he rests every night. I search for him in my despair, find him, grab him, bring him to me, and clutch him tightly against my chest. I close my eyes in gratitude, and I feel my lips moving soundlessly, like in a prayer. He's the only comforting thing in my world at the moment, my smooth beautiful rock from the river that I've kept hidden and safe since I was seven years old. He's mine...all mine. At first, he is my pet, then my toy, then my lucky piece, now my **S**aving **G**race, my S.G. He has grown up with me. His smoothness calms me enough to talk, so I reach for the phone, and punch in number one, and wait for Angel to answer.

"Zack?" She sounds hoarse and sleepy... a good sound... a sexy sound.

"It's late. You have to let me go, Zack. You can't keep calling me like this. I'm not coming back this time." She takes an exasperated breath, and then I hear the anxiety in her voice. She knows me, and she's wondering what is the real reason I called.

Zack, what's wrong?"

"Nothing baby." My voice is smooth, and I try for sexy, but I don't quite make it. I push on. "You know me. I just needed to hear your sweet voice."

"At two in the morning, Zack?" She still sounds sleepy but sarcastic now.

"Ah man! I'm sorry. I didn't check the clock. I was just missing you, and I had to hear your voice."

"Well, you need to remember to check the clock. I have a very early appointment in the morning. Models can't have bags under their eyes, and, besides, I don't need you calling me. I've got to try to get over you. Anyway, why are you roaming around in that big apartment at this hour in the morning when you have to go to work too?" I feel her hesitation, hear the deep sigh, and I know she has figured it out.

"It happened again didn't it, Zack? Tell me the truth." There is a change in her tone, one of concern as the realization hits her. I'm quiet, but my silence is enough to answer her question. There is a rustling of her covers, and I know she's slipping down into a more comfortable position to spend some quiet time talking me down from what she has seen happen to me at least five times in the darkness of night.

"Have you seen a doctor yet, Zack?"

"No."

"Why not, Baby?"

"Because... because I don't need some stranger poking around in the recesses of my brain trying to fix me. That's why."

"Zack, this is going to keep happening until you get the help you need. There is nothing wrong with getting help. Heck, I see my shrink twice a week." She laughs and I know she's just playing and trying to lighten my mood. The last thing Angel needs is a shrink. Her family raised her with a love that I cannot even imagine.

"Look, I don't ... I don't want to talk about doctors and my needing help."

"So, what do you want to talk about at two in the morning, the nightmare?"

"No, not at all. How about we talk about what you have on right now," I suggest, capturing my sexy.

"Zack, I've told you a hundred times, I don't play phone games. You're waking me up in the middle of the night when I have to get up early, and you want me to play phone games. You're such a selfish jerk. That's why I'm not in your bed right now."

"Hmm," I smile my slick smile and slowly lick my lips. "I know I'm a jerk, and now you know it so let's move on. What are you wearing sexy lady?" I ask leaning on my pillow. I prop my head up with one hand and let her hear the voice I know usually drives her crazy.

"You know what, Zack? Whatever it is I'm wearing, I'm about to go back to sleep in it. Goodnight."

This time, the voice fails me, and the click of the phone assures me just how much it fails me.

"These stupid nightmares cut my game," I mutter in a silence that surrounds me and hits me like a ton of bricks. I can't be alone right now. This is not a good time, and Angel knows that better than almost anyone except Derek who lived with me at Harvard for seven years. I exhale an exasperatingly loud sigh and whine in my anger, "Why did she hang up in my face?" The fear will resurface, the sweat will return, and the visions of yesteryear will not disappear even when I hold on tightly to my rock. So, I file through other rescue possibilities in my mind, and my thoughts land on Summer who is always willing to help me out, in whatever way I need her. I know she wants more from me too, but I'm certain that if I had it to give, she would not be on the receiving end. I know I need a woman like Angel who can read me and take no prisoners. The two of us could have worked if I hadn't been so sure she wouldn't leave me. I misjudged her patience and her willingness to take whatever pain I inflicted on her. She stopped playing my game and totally cut me out of her love life.

After I call Summer, my friend with benefits, I jump in the shower to wash away the evidence of my fear, change into my black silk pj pants and leave my chest bare. Summer likes that. I quickly change the sheets and comforter on my bed, light some scented candles, put on some smooth jazz, and wait for the doorbell. When I hear it, I rush to the door, and she leans in and thoroughly kisses me. She's wearing a coat that screams that's all there is. It's belted tightly around her tiny waist and the wide lapels do nothing to cover the plunging neckline. I won't lie. I'm excited.

She slightly shoves me backward into the living room, kicks the door shut and I unbuckle her belt for the grand reveal.

"You like?" she mummers.

"No, I love."

She slips off the coat, and we move together into the bedroom without stopping the kiss that is sending me into another world far away from haunting dreams.

"Take your time, Angel," I mutter.

"Angel? You don't mean that, Baby. If Angel could do this, I wouldn't be here."

I start to lie my way out of calling the wrong name, but I can't because her mouth is too busy on mine to bother wasting that kind of time. It's obvious that she could care less what name I call her, so for the rest of the night it's on, and I'm able to put on the mask and she doesn't have a clue what is behind it. I romance her, love her, and for a moment, I make her feel like she is my queen just because I need her to be with me right now. I can't even think that she might leave me. During the night, there are no problems. In the early morning, we have drifted into that sleep where both a blissful glow and serenity encompass the two of us.

The doorbell startles me awake, and for a minute, I don't believe it's really ringing, and then I hear it again. I grab my jeans and stumble to the door. Looking through the peephole, I see her full beauty and my heart sinks.

"Open the door, Zack. I hear you." Angel's voice is loud and demanding.

I don't say anything at first as I try to come up with a solution to get me out of this mess, knowing full well there isn't one. So, I take a deep breath, brace myself, and slowly peek out of the door. In a second, she pushes the door open and breezes past me in all of her beauty. She's gorgeous and smells divine. I am immediately reminded why her profession is modeling, and what I have lost.

"I thought you said you weren't coming back," I say closing the door.

"I wasn't, but I couldn't get your sorry tail out of my mind after you called last night, so I'm here to check on you. You sounded horrible on the phone then, but how are you now?" She puts her hand to my forehead like I'm five years old with a fever or something.

"I'm fine, Baby. You didn't need to come," I mutter slowly trying to wring the sweat from my hands.

"What's wrong with you. You look nervous. Are you sure you're all right?"

That's when it happens. Summer coughs. Angel hears her, and we both look at each other. Silence stands between us while Recognition screams. Angel's mouth is slightly open, her eyes find mine, and we both turn at the same time to see Summer leaning against the door wearing just my shirt. It is a very heavy moment, but Angel is so secure that she still manages to find her voice.

"I'm sorry. I ... I didn't know you had company. I'll see you," she utters moving toward the door, but Summer's response stops her. At the sound of a mocking tone, Angel halts her steps, but doesn't turn around.

"I wouldn't call me company. I'd say more like ah... roommate. I've been here for a while doing some very special things to help a very special friend. You know? Right, baby?"

I turn toward the voice, and I can feel the cold, hard stare in my own eyes. "Summer, you don't want to do this." My voice is quiet, but dead serious.

"Angel, don't go," I gasp. I reach for her arm and at the same time turn to face Summer. "Summer was just about to leave. Right, Summer?"

Angel quickly interrupts, shaking her head "No, Zack. You keep playing house." Pausing for just a moment, making sure her words are clear, leaving no question on her stance, she continues. "I think I'm finally getting a clear picture. I've been fooling only myself. This is the same mistake I made some years ago with another guy just like you. I fall in love, but you guys just use that to your advantage.

11

Well, I'm tired of being used, and secretly thinking that we can have something between us...that you really do care about me... or that you can change. I get the picture now, Zack. It's perfectly clear...picture perfect!" She opens the door, and I try to stop her. Her look stops me in my tracks. I can feel the iciness of her stare penetrating the very essence of my soul. Breaking her gaze simply gives me a momentary lapse from the effects of her coldness, so I follow her outside. I don't want her to leave me. I don't want this to be the end of us.

"Ange, baby. I'm sorry." My voice is an anguished plea. I feel desperate, ashamed, and afraid.

"Why, Zack? You love playing games with people's lives. Foolish me. At one point, I thought we were beginning to have something real...something meaningful. When I saw that we weren't, I left. Somehow, I thought that might be enough to wake you up. Ha! The joke's on me."

In my heart I know what she's saying has truth to it, but how, after what she's seen, do I make her see that what she walked in on was nothing more than an act of convenience. Summer means nothing to me.

"I don't know what to say."

"It's ok, Zack. You don't have to say anything. It's all on me, so I'll say it. I'm done."

I feel the walls closing all around me, and that makes my heart pound. I look around for a way out, but there is none. Somewhere in the recesses of my mind, I hear the sound of shattering glass, and I wonder what it all means.

"You're done? What does that mean?" I ask with some agitation.

"I'll tell you what. I'm going to leave you with your ah ... room-mate, and maybe the two of you can figure it out. You know the saying: 'Two heads are better than one.'"

I feel her hurt, and she leaves me feeling foolish, sad, and speechless. I watch her get into her car, fasten the seatbelt, and drive away in the New York morning light. This is a scene I hadn't counted on, and I know the one I'm about to have with Summer is going to be worst. I take a deep breath, open the door, and I see her still standing in the same spot only now my shirt is pooled around her feet on the floor.

"Come here, Baby." Summer moves towards me seductively, with her arms ready to surround me.

"You need to get dressed and leave." I make no attempt to move toward her or spare her feelings.

"Leave? After everything I've done for you? I came over here in the middle of the night, Clown, and helped you out. You're kidding, right?"

"Summer get your clothes on, and get out of my house." Closing my eyes for a brief moment, my left hand finds its way to my face, squeezing that space at the apex of my nose, releasing the tension building between my eyes. My carefully controlled rage is breaking free. I need her to hear me. She is standing looking at me like she can't believe what I just said so I make it clear to her naked self.

"NOW!" I scream. I see her flinch, and the loudness of my voice is all it takes for her to believe me.

I wait impatiently for Summer to gather all of her things and leave before I dial Angel, but she doesn't answer. I dial again, and it rings again and again. I dial a third time...a fourth... a fifth, and finally she picks up.

"Would you please stop calling me, Zack? There is absolutely nothing else to say."

"I'm sorry." My voice is a whisper because I don't want it to break, and I feel the tears burning my eyes so I know the possibility is great.

"Zack, you're always sorry. How about we just recognize that, accept that, and move on."

"Baby, I don't want to move on without you."

"Really?" I respond with heavy sarcasm. "Yes, you do. Zack, you move on every time you invite one of those bimbos into your life, every time you choose to hurt me, and every time you act like you forget that you care about me."

I sigh loudly because I don't want to hear this.

"You know, there's something my Mom used to tell me when I was growing up. She used to say that if you decide to do something wrong, own it because the consequences will be yours alone. So, you need to own this. I know we're just friends, but in this last year, I made the mistake of thinking it was building into something a lot more. I know you, Zack, so it was foolish of me to think that. The first time I ever saw you when you came by my house with Derek looking for Arianna, you had PLAYER written all over you. I knew it then, and I sure know it now. Nothing with you is ever going to change, is it?"

I take a deep breath, but I say nothing. I feel like a kid being scolded by an adult.

"I made the mistake of trying to believe your words and ignore your actions, so I own this and the consequences that go with it. I'll admit it: My heart, right now is g- breaking... you tell me with everything you do that I mean absolutely nothing to you, and I'm a repeat offender. I've done the same thing with you that I did with Shawn. When he left me, I thought I would die, but I didn't then and I won't now. What I know is that I have to really learn something this time. I want so badly to be really loved that I give too much too soon. I admit that. I keep asking myself when am I going to learn that sex is just a byproduct. It NEVER holds a man. You give this nonrefundable gift too soon, and you cry tears of regret a lot later. So, now I cry."

"You don't have to cry, Angel. You mean everything to me. I admit that I have some major problems, but you're really what I need."

"Well, if that's true, why do you have a "roommate" before I can blink my eye? ...before my scent is out of your house?"

"I don't. I had the nightmare, and I couldn't be alone so I called Summer. That's the truth."

"So, she's a babysitter?"

"OK. I deserve that, but, where are you? I want to come over."

"I don't think so. I don't want to keep getting disappointed, so let's just leave it alone. I'll talk with you later."

"Angel, tell me. Are you at your apartment or are you leaving town?"

"You don't deserve to know my plans. I just stopped by this morning to check on you. You take care of yourself, Zack, because that's what I'm going to do for myself."

I hear the dial tone before I can respond, and for the first time in my life, a woman makes me cry.

~ Zack's Journey ~

1

NEW BEGINNINGS

God has a way of giving us unexpected golden gifts
when we least expect them.

I know I'm singing far too loudly, and tremendously off key. No one would be able to recognize this song if I were singing by myself, but my clap is on target.

"Zack, stop singing above everyone else. You don't even know this song."

"I do, Derek. My grandma taught me this song a long time ago.

"No, she did not," he whispers emphatically. "This is a new song by Hezekiah Walker, and your grandma never heard of him cause she was way ahead of his time. Now stop embarrassing me."

I keep singing, *Every Praise* because that's all I can understand from the choir. When the song is over, everyone is either seated or standing and still praising the Lord.

"Hallelujah! Praise the Lord!" the people shout. That's what almost everybody is doing so I join in too.

"Zack, sit down. You don't know what you're doing."

"Why did you bring me to church if you don't want me to do what everyone else is doing?"

"Cause you don't know what you're doing."

I can tell that Arianna is trying to stop laughing, or hide the fact that she is. During the prayer, I see Derek attempting to keep an eye on me, so I act like my eyes are closed, but the girl next to Arianna has caught my attention, and I want to know who she is.

"D," I whisper. "Who is that next to Arianna?"

"Shh. It's prayer time, man. Stop talking."

"Who is she?" I insist.

"Jazmin Grant. Now stop talking."

"Jazmin Grant. Do you know her?"

"Yes, now stop talking, and listen to the prayer," he whispers with his teeth clenched to try to look like he's not talking. I wait and listen, but I'm impatient, and the prayer is too long for me. "Tell her my name, D. Tell her," I whisper and nudge him hard, but he keeps his eyes closed and keeps pretending that he's listening to the prayer. When the preacher finally says "Amen," I think now he'll tell her my name, but they sing another song, a quiet song. The program says it's a chant, and D is singing it so I have to wait some more. When the chant is over, I see Jazmin raise her head and glance my way, and I give her a little wave, a wink, and a smile. She doesn't wave back, but I see her smile to herself, and look down at her hands.

20

Near the end of the sermon, the preacher is almost screaming and making a funny sound in his throat. I see Jazmin stand up and wave her hand in the air. She's saying something to the preacher. I don't understand what she's saying, but I do understand how good she looks. I let my eyes wash over her and guess that she's about 5'6 with beautiful smooth skin. I notice her tiny waistline and her cute short haircut. Her suit is a pale pink and the skirt is just above her knees. From the side, I can tell that her eyes are big, brown, and beautiful, shaded by very long gorgeous natural eyelashes. They are nothing that you buy in a store. These are natural, all hers. With her hand in the air, I see her manicured nails and her slender fingers with only one ring which has NO real significance so I know she's free, and I can't wait to meet her after church.

After the last prayer, everyone is filing out of the pews, and I touch Arianna on her arm.

"Ari, D won't help me out, but don't let Jazmin get away. Introduce us." Ari just starts laughing again.

"Zack, that girl is way out of your league, so leave her alone." D's eyes have that determined look when he means business, but I ignore that as usual.

"What? I don't understand that, D. What do you mean she's out of my league," I ask making sure that Jazmin is still nearby, and I haven't missed my opportunity to meet this beautiful lady. I see her stop to talk with some other guy, and I see her touch his shoulder and laugh.

"She's a nice, quiet, talented young lady who doesn't deserve to be hurt, or get caught up in your drama, so leave her alone, and NO, I will not introduce her to you. She's way out of your league, man. I'm telling you. Leave her alone. It hasn't been a good six months since Angel left your behind. Take a break!"

"Ok, be like that. It just means I activate Plan B."

"What the heck is Plan B?"

"Watch and weep, Brother," I answer sarcastically.

In the crowd, I see Jazmin moving slowly toward me so I stop and wait for her to catch up. I feel D pulling my jacket, but I will not be moved.

"Hi, Jazmin is it?"

"Yes, it is. ...and you are?"

"Zack. Zack Belford." We're walking out of the church together now, and she stops to shake the hand of the preacher, and I do the same. Going down the steps I take the opportunity to hold her at her elbow to make sure she doesn't fall.

"Thank you, Zack. It was nice meeting you."

"Take my word for it, the pleasure is all mine. I hope to see you again very soon." My words come slowly, my voice is low and sexy, and I know she does not miss the second wink of the day or the smile. I see her lower her eyes, and I notice a very shy smile take over her beautiful lips. I also see a very deep dimple that makes me want to touch her face, but I don't dare. It's way too soon even for me. She gives me a little wave, and I see her walk to a silver convertible BMW and drive away.

Back at the cottage, all I can talk about is Jazmin, but D won't give me any insight other than the fact that she is an extremely talented artist with a small downtown studio. She loves photography and was graduated from the University of Virginia two years ago. She has been doing a little work for Ari off and on with the models, and he does tell me that Ari loves her work, that her photos are unique and add a special flair to the clothing. Other than that, D says I have no need to know more. Since this is a short little weekend visit, I don't have time to mess around with D and his protection measures if I want to get to know this girl, so I have to come up with a different plan. I decide to try to get Ari to open up more and, *ahh*, the magic works. I saunter into the kitchen, away from D, and strike up what must appear to be a very casual conversation.

"So, you say that Jazmin has a flair with the camera, huh?" I ask nonchalantly standing at the window staring out pretending to look at the ocean.

"Yeah, she really does. Her photos are all so very unique. There are no two that I could say are alike or even close to being alike. She's one of those persons who dares to be different, Zack, and that makes her work extra special."

Ari is busy cutting up veggies for our salad and doesn't seem to realize my motives, so I push on.

"Do you have any of her work here? I'd love to see exactly what you mean. It's hard for me to figure out how she's different unless I actually see her work. You know what I mean?" I casually turn and look at Ari, and she looks back at me.

"Yeah, I know exactly what you mean. Look at the picture we have hanging on the wall in the hallway. She took that."

BINGO!!!

I can barely keep my feet from skipping down the hall. I am so impatient to know this girl, but I manage to control myself so Ari won't get like D and think she's out of my league. I mosey down the hallway and take the picture off the wall and examine it closely. It is all that they have said. It's unique and immediately draws me into it. I can't take my eyes away. The lady doesn't look like a model at all, but rather an elegant woman captured in a significant moment in time. She is seated at an angle on a contemporary white sofa. Her red dress fits perfectly with its skirt spread flawlessly over her crossed legs. It flows down, slightly touching the black and white checkered floor beneath her bare feet that peek out. While her red shoes are cast aside close by, her folded hands rest demurely in her lap helping to speak nonverbally of a sort of austerity, class, and beauty. The scene depicts a dichotomy of what is both harsh and dulcet; it captures the light, and seems completely undisturbed by an incongruous fly that buzzes too close to her exquisiteness. Her coal black eyes are startling and follow me wherever I might stand. The setting, the colors, the angles, the lighting and shading are things expertly done, and I can already see what a special person Jazmin Grant must be to create something so different, so beautiful, and so daringly mysterious. I turn the picture over, and I can't believe my luck. There must be a God who is rewarding me for my one visit to church today.

There, on the back of the photo, is a card with the name JazArt, two phone numbers, and addresses for one studio in Virginia and one in New York City. I lift the card from the back and slip it into my pocket. I know that tomorrow there will definitely be a call from New York to order some JazArt and just as sure as I know my name, soon there will be a visit to the Big Apple from the artist, herself, the creator of *The Secrets of Lady Rouge.*

—⁓—

Work is long and hard, and today my staff continues to get on my nerves. One of our projects is near its end, and it just seems that things are not falling into place like they should. I actually get into an argument with my assistant for not making the calls that would have closed our deal a week ago. Everything was set. All he had to do was close. I did it myself today and completed everything with everyone happy in less than ten minutes. I don't cope well with people who have little or no creativity and drive.

Now I'm irritated again because this traffic is crawling, and I want to get home to make the call that I have been thinking about all day. I didn't want to call while I was at work because I want nothing to interrupt my flow when I get Jazmin on the phone. I make a decision to relax as soon as I get home so I won't be in such a foul mood when I talk with her.

Finally, my high rise is in sight. I park my car and talk to myself.

You can't go too fast with this girl, I caution myself. *D already thinks that she's out of your league, whatever that means, but it doesn't sound good for me.*

I keep telling myself to be careful.

"Don't move too fast. Kill the old lines. Watch the sexy voice thing," I mutter aloud. "She's a church girl, and she might think that's too forward." I take a deep breath.

"Breath Zack...breath," I mumble.

I take the elevator to the Penthouse, throw my keys in the basket at the door, and take off my suit coat. I pour myself a glass of wine, take a big swallow, put on a little jazz, and relax in my favorite chair. I play around with my Rubik cube just to check that my awesome skills are still intact and ready to crush any next opponent. Satisfied that all is well and no one can come close to beating my time, I place it carefully back in its rightful place, grab my cell, and slowly dial her number. I feel my heart pick up its beat, and I'm nervous. This girl is "out of my league." On ring three, I hear her soft sweet voice, and my heart skips a beat.

"Hello?"

"Hello, Jazmin?"

"Yes?"

"This is Zack Belford. I met you yesterday in church. Remember?"

"Sure, I do. How are you?"

"Fine, now that I hear your sweet sexy voice again."

"Hmm."

"Too fast, Z," I mentally check myself. The hmm response is a caution. *Take it easy. This girl is real class, and you sure don't want to blow your chance by being too aggressive. D has already said ten times at least that she's out of your league, and you don't want him to be right.*

"I wanted a chance to talk with you yesterday, but you seemed to be in a hurry. Were you?"

"Not really. I was just on my way home."

"So... where exactly is home? Virginia?"

"Sometimes it's Virginia, and sometimes it's New York."

"New York?"

"Yes, I'm originally from New York. My parents live about an hour away from the city, but I have art studios in both New York City and here in the Tidewater area. Right now, I'm working out of Virginia, but in about two weeks, I have my first art exhibition at one of the galleries in New York. I'll be back in the city next week to make some last- minute arrangements. The gallery owner is going to show me how my art will be presented. He says that I can make some minor changes then, but I wouldn't dare question his judgment at this point. I'm just excited about the exhibition, whether I sell anything this time around or not."

"That sounds very exciting for you, and I'm sure you'll sell something."

"I'm not sure if I will or not and right now, I don't much care as long as I'm received well."

"Well, when money is involved, I don't think I could have your attitude. I would not only want to sell, I would want to sell big," I chuckle.

"Well, this is my first exhibition. New artists almost never sell big or even expect to the first time around. I'm not that well known yet, but Erick Gardo, the gallery owner, loves my work and my drive so he's giving me this awesome opportunity," she gushes. "He says that I'm unique and a risk- taker."

"Is he on the up and up?"

"What do you mean?"

"Well, does he expect anything for this 'awesome opportunity?'"

"No, just my loyalty to the art and a consistent production of my best work. Why would you say something like that?"

"Please forget I said anything." I rush on knowing that I have already misspoken. "That was just one of my thoughtless comments. I'm sorry. Listen, I can't believe you live in New York," I remark changing the subject as quickly as possible. "I live in New York too. I was just visiting D, I mean, Derek and Arianna for the weekend. Do you think I could come to that show of yours?"

"I'd love to have you there, Zack. Give me your address. I'll send you all of the information, and I'll look forward to seeing you."

"That's a deal, and now I can guarantee that you will sell at least one piece. I saw one of your artistic photos at Derek's and I am quite intrigued by your work."

I hear her giggle a little, and I give her my address. I think to myself that it might be a good idea to stop the conversation at that. I don't want to mess this up, but I do dare one more thing.

"When you get in town, give me a call to let me know that you're here."

"Hmm...maybe. We'll see."

"Yes, we will. Good night, Jazmin. You take good care of you, all right?"

"I will. Good night, Zack."

When I hang up the phone, I can't believe my luck. She actually lives in New York. I wonder if she has her own place or if she commutes to her parents' home in the suburbs. I had already decided that if I needed to visit her in Virginia, it would only take about forty-five minutes in the air, but it seems that's not necessary at all.

With purpose, I allow Erick Gardo to skip around in my brain for a second, and hope that he doesn't have any plans for cozying up to Jazmin. That could end badly for him. I spend about two more minutes thinking about our phone conversation before I notice the romantic jazz sounds in the background and decide to call Summer over for a nightcap. No need to waste a perfectly good night. That's just not my style, and Summer is always willing no matter the time of night or how infrequent the calls. I dial the number and wait for a great night.

2

GALLERY OF ART

Sometimes in the midst of meeting a stranger there is that profound moment when we know the joy of making a lasting friend.

Two weeks seem to drag on, and there are no calls from Jazmin to let me know if she's in New York or not. A call to Derek to get a simple home telephone number is a total fail. All I get is a half hour lecture on my past behavior and a plea to "just leave the girl alone." However, I did get an exquisite invitation to the gallery exhibition in the mail, and I know it starts tonight at 7:30, and you can believe that I will be there.

Winding my way through traffic, I have time to think about this new girl in my life, well sort of in my life. At least, in my mind, she's in my life. I think about her big brown eyes with those unbelievable long eyelashes. I try to think if I have ever seen anyone with real eyelashes that long. I remember her tiny waistline, and that pixie hair cut that makes her oval face have a playful look...a happy face. And who could ever forget those deep dimples that grace her cheeks when she smiles.

At home, I turn on my jazz, get a small drink of wine just to relax, and jump into the shower. I walk into my closet and pull out one of my many tuxedoes. This one is my most expensive one, and I think it exudes the idea of money. When I check myself out in my full-length mirror, I know that I look extremely good, but I also know that for some reason, I'm a bit nervous.

When I enter the gallery, I see what I don't want to see...a number of people who know me, and won't want me to have anything to do with Jazmin Grant. People are chatting in groups, some viewing the art and discussing its beauty, but in the center of the room, I see Nina Wellington, Derek's mom, standing with Derek, Arianna and Jazmin. Derek spots me first, and then all of their eyes fall on me. I quickly put on my mask of a smile and move over to them.

"Good Evening." The silence in this circle is deafening, but Jazmin saves me.

"Hi, Zack. I'm so glad that you could make it," she smiles up at me with genuine enthusiasm.

"I wouldn't have missed it for the world, girl." I look directly into her eyes, and at that moment it's almost as if everyone else in the room disappears. I see up close her beauty and her eyes pull me into them. I stare momentarily, and I think the only thing that tears me away from those alluring eyes is D's voice.

"So, what's up, Z? I didn't know you would be here."

"Yeah, Jazmin was kind enough to invite me. Arianna, Mrs. Wellington, good evening, ladies. It's good to see you both." I see Arianna smile and lower her eyes, while Nina Wellington gives me the look... you know, the one that can almost kill.

"I wish I could say the same to you, young man, but I certainly cannot." Nina's voice is harsh and in it, I hear the old hates and bad memories resurface in my mind.

"Mom, stop. This is not the time or the place."

"Derek, this poor girl has no idea what she's doing inviting this gangster here."

"Excuse me?" I intervene.

"You are excused. You need to leave here right now before you start to destroy another beautiful life. Just leave Zackary."

"I was invited here, Mrs. Wellington, and I have no intention of leaving. I will, however, respect you enough to try to stay out of your presence." I walk away, and alone, I begin my tour of the unbelievable artwork on display.

After about three minutes of viewing by myself, I feel a soft tap on my shoulder. When I turn, I look down, and she is there beside me.

"Thanks for coming, Zack." She playfully pushes up against me.

"Are you sure about that, girl?" I gently push back.

"Absolutely. I would have been very disappointed if you had not come."

"Really?"

"Yes. Really. I had already checked my watch twice."

"I would have been disappointed if I hadn't come."

"I am curious though."

"About what?"

"I'm wondering why no one wants me to get to know you," she teases poking me in my chest. "Mrs. Wellington says you're a monster. So, what kind of monster are you?" She asks flirtatiously smiling up at me.

"I'm the kind of monster that can make you fall in love in a night, girl," I flirt taking the liberty of lifting her chin and kissing her cheek.

"Oh, you're the guru of unrequited love, huh?" she mutters.

"What?"

"Never mind," she giggles.

"What did D tell you?"

I see her take a deep breath. "...that I would do myself a favor if I leave you off my future guest lists."

"Huh. What great girlie advice did Arianna give you about me?"

Jazmin smiles at that as if they have some amazing secret that only the two of them will ever know. She looks up at me and scrunches up her mouth."

"What did she tell you, girl?"

"That you'll break my heart, but I'll probably enjoy the ride," she giggles and covers her mouth and almost closes her eyes in her shyness. "I can say this: I have been adequately warned."

"Hmm. I think so. Changing the subject, I had no idea you were a water colorist."

"Yes. That's my favorite medium."

"Well, I found the work I want to purchase."

"Zack, you don't have to buy anything. Everything is going quite well tonight, and all of these pieces are extremely expensive."

"No, I really do want to buy this one piece. I don't care how much it costs."

"Ok. Which one?"

"It's over here near the water fountain."

"Oh, I already know the one. That one, unfortunately, is not for sale."

"It has to be. I don't just want it; I need it."

"I'm sorry, Zack. I really can't sell that one."

"I'm sorry too. Are you *sure* you won't sell it?"

"I'm positive." I hear a tone of finality, and I decide not to push more now. I really want this piece, so I decide to try again at a more convenient time and place, if you know what I mean.

Erick Gardo approaches us smiling. He is a handsome middle-aged man with a hint of uncontrollable grey hair peeking out from a head full of medium brown strands. Everything about him is classy, so-phisticated, and elegant. He has a sort of quietness about him, but it, by no means, takes away his enthusiasm for art or his confidence in himself.

"You are quite the hit tonight, young lady. Everyone is interested in your work. I told you. You are very different." His voice is a bit hushed, and somehow I see a father figure in him that just wants the best for Jazmin.

"Erick, I want you to meet a friend of mine, Zackary Belford."

"Great to meet you, Mr. Belford."

"Zack...Call me Zack, and the pleasure is mine, Sir."

"You have quite a talented friend, Zack, and I know that she's going to go far in the art world. Jaz, there are collectors here amazed at the richness of your work. They're saying things like they can't believe the boldness of your pieces. Your work is really breaking new ground."

"That's my goal." Her eyes meet mine, and she does not look away when she continues. ". . . to always explore new territories even though there may be some pitfalls. I like taking risks and making people see something that was always there but slightly hidden from view...the enchantment is just beneath the surface and rarely visible to the casual viewer." She drops her eyes now, and I see a shy smile form as her head lowers.

"Well, you're doing that," Erick assures her, obviously missing the point that was perfectly clear to me.

During the night's event, I meet her lovely parents; I mingle and smile with Jazmin, and it is during this night that I become a significant part of her world.

In a short private meeting, Erick tells her what works are sold and at what price; she is ecstatic. As I understand it, even though a lot was not sold, there were enough pieces sold to encourage her and Erick. It seems that she has made a great showing and collectors now know her name and some of her works.

"You want to go celebrate with me tonight?" I ask, feeling the euphoria rub off on me.

"Not tonight, Zack. I'm far too tired. The excitement of all of this has worn me out, and I promised my parents I'd spend some time with them. I'll call you, later."

"You didn't call when you came in town last week," I admonish with no hint of playfulness.

"...and I never said that I would," She smiles her shy smile. "Now, I am saying that I will, but not tonight." She looks into my eyes, I wink, smile, and bend to kiss her cheek, but she moves away, gives her little wave, and disappears some place in another part of the gallery.

I step out into the night and look up at a sky filled with stars. I hear a familiar voice call to me, and it makes me happy that D and Arianna have caught up with me.

I'll admit, I am a bit disappointed about Jazmin not joining us, but D and Ari spend a little time at my place before an end comes to this almost perfect night.

—⚏—

Two days pass before my phone buzzes, and I see the face I want to see smiling back at me.

"Jazmin, hi."

"Hi, Zack. Where are you?"

"I'm downtown, having a little dinner all by myself."

"Ah, how sad, she teases. I was going to come by if you weren't too busy tonight."

"Never too busy for you, my love. What time?"

"Well, I'm just leaving my parents, and according to the address that I have, I'm about an hour from your place."

"I'll be there. Count on it."

"OK, I'll see you in a few."

The phone goes dead, and I cram the rest of my food, gulp down the last of my water, pay the bill, and dash to my car for the ten-minute drive to the penthouse. I take a quick shower, dress in casual black slacks, a gray collarless casual shirt, my gold chain and black loafers. I light a few candles, turn up Kenny G, chill some expensive wine, and wait.

When the doorbell rings, I check myself in a mirror, and open the door to one gorgeous sight. Leaning up against the door jam, I see her dressed in metallic silver denim skinny jeans with a matching jacket, a black top that slightly exposes her flat tummy, silver high heels, a tiny cross around her neck, and a pair of dangling earrings that set off her pixie hair.

"Hey, you," Her smile lights up her face showing her beautiful white straight teeth that I swear had to have braces on them for the entire length of middle school. I take a deep breath.

"Hi. Don't stand out there, girl. Come on in."

Her light, expensive perfume wafts through the room as she passes me and goes to stand in front of the glass wall that almost surrounds us. Looking out at the beauty of the New York skyline, I see her suck in her breath, and I know she already sees far more than I.

"Wow, Zack. I would love to paint this scene."

"What? Really? That, instead of this?" I joke pointing to myself.

"Well, that too," she laughs.

"Have a seat. Would you like something to drink after your long drive?"

"Water is fine."

"Water? I have some great wine here. Would you like that instead?"

"No, I just do water, tea and a little soda now and then."

"Then water it will be." I put in some ice, a dash of lemon and bringing it to her gives me my first real chance to get up close and personal. Standing close to her, I suck in my breath. "Do you have any idea how gorgeous you are, girl?"

"I don't know about that, but I do get a glimpse of me very day," she laughs. "and I don't think I see what you see right now." I take the glass from her hand, circle her waist, and look deeply into those unbelievable eyes. "I don't think I have ever seen eyelashes as long as yours."

"...And I don't think I have ever seen a guy who moves as fast as you," she smiles pushing out of my grasp, picking up her water, and getting some space between us.

"Tell me about yourself, Zack. How did you meet Derek and Arianna?" she asks looking out at the night.

Needless to say, that story takes me quite a while to tell, but we talk about a lot of things even though I'm careful to skirt around things like how I hurt Derek so deeply, the drama I caused with Morgan, and my chaotic sorry past life. Everything I tell her is the truth. I just omit a lot of details. I talk about Harvard, my job on Wall Street, and how I found this awesome Penthouse apartment. We talk about jazz and our favorite artists, how she's lived a lifetime in love with art, her back and forth trips from New York to Virginia, photography, and some of her future plans. Somewhere during the conversations and personal discoveries about each other, we find ourselves sitting cross-legged beside each other on the floor snacking on popcorn, chips, grape soda, and laughing hysterically at a TV movie. It is just plain clean fun, an unusual night for me. It is very different, but, surprisingly, almost like magic. The night passes incredibly fast, and when she checks the time on her phone, it's already 2:00 AM.

"Gosh, I had no idea it was so late. What's that saying? 'Time flies when you're having fun.' I guess I was having a lot of fun."

"I know I am, present tense," I comment helping her up from the floor. Somewhere during the night, *I can't believe I didn't notice,* she relaxed and took off her jacket. Now, I am standing close to her with those metallic skinny jeans clinging to her and her little black top showing me her perfect body. Well, lest I waste any more time, I put my arms around her shoulders as we walk toward the door that is far too close. Standing in front of it, I circle her waist and drink in those eyes again.

"Zack, you really know how to entertain a girl, and make her lose track of time."

"Hmm. You haven't seen a thing yet, girl."

"I bet," she laughs. "Well, I had a *really* good time tonight."

"Me too. When can I see you again?" I ask lightly touching her chin. "Well, I'm here for a month. So just give me a call."

"Count on it." I lean over for a kiss, and she turns just in time for me to touch her cheek with my lips. I linger there for a moment, and she breaks the embrace, turns toward the door, and waits for me to open it. I reach around her, and unlatch the door. She moves through it to the hallway, and turns to face me. I lean up against the door and wait to hear whatever she is hesitating to say. I see her take a deep breath.

"Zack?" Her voice is almost a whisper.

"Yes." My eyes are asking her to stay.

"Let's take this slowly, ok? ...Friends?"

"Friends. Good friends," I wink and smile. I watch her walk to the elevator, look back at me, and disappear through the doors. I close my door and realize that this is the first date that I have ever had where I didn't end up in bed with someone, usually someone I don't even really know. While I clean up what's left of the food and drinks, I try to decide if the end of my evening is good or bad, and since I don't get a clear answer, I go to bed alone wondering if I've just met my first real challenge.

3

THE SHOOT

True friendships wear no masks.

I wake slowly, and out of my sleep, it dawns on me that it's Saturday, and I have two days off. I roll over, throw the covers back, sit on the side of my bed, and smile to myself. I'm thinking about the girl who got away last night. I glance at my watch and see that it's a little after six. The day is just breaking. I go into the bathroom and clean up, throw on my workout clothes and head out for my morning run. Outside, the fall air is crisp...pleasant, and I do a few stretches before I start my run. It always amazes me to see how many people are already into their busy day when I whiz pass, but, after all, this is the city that never sleeps. I wind my way through the streets and see dogs being walked, other runners, people on their way to work and sidewalk venders set up for coffee, pastries and other goodies. My mind drifts back to Jazmin, and I wonder what she's doing this morning. What will her day be like? Most importantly, would she allow me to be in it with her so soon after our first little date? I decide to give her a call and see.

Back at my apartment, I shower and dress. I have this odd feeling of exhilaration for some reason. I guess it's the expectation of something new in my life. Since I don't usually give girls a second thought after one date, this is new territory for me. I sit at the bar, grab a cup of coffee and a slice of banana nut bread, my favorite. I see that sweet, shy face in my mind. I mentally see how she slowly lowers those long eyelashes of hers, cocks her head to the side, and looks back up at me. I smile to myself. *She's gorgeous.* I decide that it's late enough to call, so I dial her number.

"Hello, Zack."

"Hey, girl. What's up? You busy?"

"Not yet."

"Do you have plans, today?"

"Hmm, I do, kind of. I have a new camera, and I want to see what it can do. I'm going to take some random shots today, and see what I can do with them."

"May I go?"

"Sure, if you want. I'm going to three different sites, and it'll be fun having someone else along for the ride."

"Should I meet you some place?"

"No, why don't I pick you up, and that way we won't have to go to the trouble of parking two cars. Besides, we'll get a chance to talk more."

"Sounds good."

"All right. I'll see you in about an hour."

"Great. I'll meet you out front." I slide my phone off, clean up my dishes, and decide to change my clothes just in case she wants to take a few shots of me. I want to look really good. I put on a pair of very expensive black slacks, a red V-neck sweater, my gold chain, gold bracelet and black loafers. When I check myself out in the mirror, I smile my million-dollar smile, and brag to myself that I know models that don't look this good. I check out my perfectly trimmed beard, grab my sunshades, and head for the elevator. I push the button and the door opens on a scene that I absolutely detest. The surprise makes me quickly suck in my breath, and my heart automatically sets itself to a pounding unsteady beat. My oldest brother, Chad, is leaning against the back wall of the elevator with his arms spread and a tooth-pick dangling from his mouth. He's wearing that cynical grin that I absolutely hate.

"Going somewhere baby brother?" His words are slow and threatening.

"What do you want?" I spit out in my sudden anger.

"Maybe just a simple hello and a smile from my rich little baby brother. Maybe that's what I want."

He steps out of the elevator, and I make an attempt to dash in and push the button, but as usual, he is quicker, stronger, and more determined.

"You wouldn't try to leave me out here in this cold hallway all by myself without a key to that comfortable apartment, would you?

Would you do that to someone paying you a friendly visit? Come on, stay a while, baby bro. What's the rush?"

"Chad, what do you want?"

"Hmm... What do I want? What do I always want from you, little Bro? Two things... I want money and a lot of it, and I want you to admit that you owe me whatever I want. You owe me whatever I demand from you cause you took everything from me, Little Bro. Everything that happened to me is your fault, and I'm waiting for the day that you admit what you did to me. Until then Zack, you're mine baby and you're going to pay my way to wherever I want to go, and right now, I want a better place. Why should I live like dirt while you lavish in luxury? Look at this place. I want to live like this, and I could have if it hadn't been for you."

"Look man, I'm on my way out. We can talk about this later."

"You still don't get it." His laughter is sardonic as he starts to light his cigarette.

"Put that out, Man. This is a no smoking zone."

"Huh! ...no smoke zone. You're funny." He chuckles on his every word.

He lights the cigarette, draws hard on it, and blows the smoke in my face. My first thought is of Jazmin and how I don't want my clothes smelling like his nasty cigarette, and my second thought is I need to get rid of him as fast as I can. He doesn't really make me as nervous as he used to, just angry and helpless which makes me angrier. I sigh loudly and feel exasperated.

"How am I supposed to get you an apartment right now?"

"Oh, you don't have to worry about that. I already have one waiting for me. I just need the cash for the deposit and the rent money."

"How much is this place, and where is it?"

He pulls out a piece of paper with an address and an enormous figure. "This is what you need to pay, Bro."

"Look, I don't carry that kind of cash around. I'll take care of it. Don't worry about it."

"Oh, I'm not worried. That's for you to do. If this isn't paid by tomorrow, I'll be back with my suitcases to move in here with you, Little Bro. Understand? You shouldn't have done what you did and none of this would've been necessary. I would have had my own education, my own money, my own job and you could have been out of my life, but you messed all that up."

"Chad, I'll talk to you tomorrow."

"Make sure you do. Fifth Avenue, Bro. No later than three."

He steps backward into the elevator, draws hard again on his cigarette, drops it to the glistening floor, smashes it under his shoe all without taking his eyes from me once.

"No smoke zone. You kill me, Little Bro," he chuckles.

The door closes and he's gone. I take a deep breath and try to compose myself; I try to stop my hands from shaking and my heart from beating like some African drum. I walk to the opposite end of the hall and take the other elevator, one without the odor of smoke. Before I reach the bottom floor, I have to shake the images of that fateful day from my mind again, the Day of Horrors that Chad refuses to allow me to forget. I have to shut out the dirty kitchen, the smell of blood, the taste of fear, the sounds of hysteria, and the sight of me at age seven and her at thirty-seven.

Out in the brilliant sunlight, I check to see if Chad is still lurking, but I see Jazmin instead. My heart skips a beat, and I feel light again. I walk quickly to her car, get in, and worry if my clothes smell like smoke.

"Hey pretty lady." I smile and touch her cheek.

"Hey you. What took you so long? I thought I was going to get a ticket sitting out here under a 'No Parking' sign."

"Why did you do that?" I chuckle.

"I wasn't sure where you might come out so I wanted to be where you could see me."

"Well, let's go before all of your efforts are for nothing."

We drive through the city, find a parking space on a side street and walk to Central Park. The walk is refreshing and lightens my mood. Momentarily, I actually forget about Chad and all of his mess. Walking together, I find a way to take Jazmin's hand, and I love holding it. Somehow, I feel a sense of comfort in her touch, and in her presence, I have a kind of peace, like the world can be all right if you're with the right people, at the right time, and in the right place. In this moment, I feel carefree, almost happy like the stars are aligning for me.

In the park, Jazmin seems to snap everything in sight. I am directed to sit under a majestic tree with the beauty of its golden leaves embracing me, shadowing me, playing shade games with me as sunlight dances a whimsical dance through the vacant spaces. I am told to stand this way, then that way, hold my chin up, put my hands in my pockets, take my hands out of my pockets, put my hands here, then there, like this, smile, don't smile, act sexy, act naughty, lean on the tree with one hand touching it and the other on my waist.

We leave and drive to the beach. We walk barefoot in the sand, and she snaps pictures of everything, of anything, but somehow even then I know whatever the camera catches will be beyond beautiful, beyond alluring, beyond simply a picture of one of the best days of my life.

During the day, I find out that she has her own apartment in the city. She paints during the day working on a collection that she says will knock us all off our socks. I learn that she is juggling two studios, a small one in Virginia where she has an assistant, a contract working with Arianna's models, and she takes time, like today, to feed another passion of hers: photography. In the lateness of the evening, we find ourselves wrapped in a romantic scene in the charming Boathouse Restaurant on the lakefront looking at each other over a candlelight dinner. In the glow of the soft light and backdrop of the water, I see her loveliness, her innocence, her inner happiness and most of all that something mysterious that keeps drawing me to her. When I make her laugh, I see her eyes sparkle in the light's reflection, and when she looks down in her shyness, I notice again those long alluring eyelashes that may be my undoing. I look at her intently across the table.

"Jazmin, may I call you Jaz? I hope so because I love that name. I love the sound of it. To me, it's perfect for you, and it reminds me of my musical passion." I wink and smile. It's my first attempt with her to be just a little sexy.

"I love it, too. When I came up with the name *JazArt*, it seemed perfect for me, because I like Jazz so much. So yes, I would love for you to call me Jaz." She smiles taking my hand in hers and looking at me with those beautiful brown eyes.

"Zack, I love spending time with you. You do something other people can't seem to do for me."

I feel her slightly tighten the grasp of my hand.

"Well, what in the world is that, girl?" I inquire, sincerely interested rubbing the top of her hands and looking deeply into her eyes.

"You make me relax. Sometimes I feel uptight when I'm around people, especially people I don't really know, but you have this knack of making me feel comfortable in your presence. You're not judging everything I do or expecting perfection of some sort from me. I can just be me, which is unusual. Last night we just ate popcorn, drank soda, and laughed like crazy. You didn't expect me to have this air of sophistication the whole time like my parents seem to expect. And today, it's just me with you having fun doing the things that I enjoy the most.

She pauses, then continues.

"You're not expecting me to be something special or do something special. You don't care if the pictures are good or all throw away trash. You just accept me for me. You don't tell me to stop being shy, or stop giggling, or expect me to know something that you know like the back of your hand when I have no idea about it. I guess the word is accepting. See, look how much I talk with you. I never talk this much with anyone, and I certainly don't tell them this much of my inner thoughts, this much of how I feel inside. I usually just push all of this down to a secret place in my heart, and become the Jazmin they want me to be, not the Jaz I really am and long to be."

I'm sitting across from this beautiful woman quietly watching her, and listening to her bare her heart and compliment me which is quite a rarity. I feel my stillness. I'm aware of my fingers: two are resting on my left cheek, my thumb under my chin and the others curled around my mouth. My eyes barely move from her mouth. I see her allow her words to spill over like a flood—like they've been bottled up inside of her for years, and finally there's this magical moment when she can let them out of their cage, and for the first time those words and feelings take flight and they're free. She's free—at least for the moment. I'm looking at her intently, feeling a strange sense of jealousy wash over me. I'm wondering when I will be able to feel that kind of freedom and just be me. When will I be able to retire my mask and show my real face? And when it does happen, will it be with her? Will I be able, one day, to trust her enough so she can be the one to give me my magical moment of liberty?

The night wears on, and I learn quite a bit about this amazing woman in front of me as she realizes this new found freedom. Eventually, we find our way back to my apartment, and she parks again under the "No Parking" sign.

"Jaz, I have two parking spaces. One is outside right over there and one is in the parking garage. Park your car over there, and come in with me. I don't want to say goodnight just yet."

She looks in my eyes, and I lean over and brush her lips. *Take it slowly, Zack. Don't frighten her.*

"Zack, I think you could be very special to me, but I don't know that yet. I had a wonderful time last night and today. Can that be enough for you right now?"

51

I take her hand in mine and feel something that I have NEVER felt before. I kiss her hand. I feel something new and different; I feel a sense of veracity in the kiss. The feeling is strange, but it feels good. I look into her eyes.

"Jaz, you're. . .you're very different from any lady I've ever known, so for right now, yes, it's enough."

I kiss her hand again and look at her.

"You sure about this?" I wink.

She giggles and lightly slaps at my arm. "Yes, get out of my car before I change my mind. I'm sure about this."

Our day and night together end, and as I walk toward the high rise alone, I look up at the stars, and in the September sky I recognize something that has fascinated me since the fifth grade—something I never forgot. I see both the big and little dipper, and I stop, stare at them, and with my eyes, I draw an imaginary line to connect the two. They seem exceptionally bright tonight, and they both seem to let each star wink at me to make me smile. Somewhere in this gigantic universe, with all of its mysteries, a little something changed in me tonight: As miniscule as it may be, I still feel it, can almost touch it, and I know that it happened and is captured inside my heart.

4

MAKING A CHANGE

Anger disguises common sense and dismisses the common touch.

Up in the penthouse, I feel lonesome. I'm just not used to returning home alone. I turn on some Jazz, pour myself a small glass of wine and sit for a moment thinking about the day. If Chad had not come, and if Jaz had stayed with me, this day would have been perfect. I scroll through the contacts on my phone and try to decide whom to invite over tonight, but something about that just doesn't feel right for me at the moment. Instead, I dial Jaz.

"Hi, you home yet?"

"Yes, I just walked in, all safe and sound." Her voice is bright and upbeat.

"Great, I was just checking to make sure. I enjoyed my day with my favorite photographer."

". . . and I enjoyed my day with my favorite model," she giggles.

"Favorite?"

"I'd say so."

"Are you sure about that, girl?"

"For the moment."

"Oh, it's like that, huh?—for the moment? So, if I'm your favorite, even for the moment, why didn't you come up with me?"

"Cause I don't play games, Zack and I know that you do."

"Girl, you don't know anything about me."

"And that's why I'm at home right now and not there. Remember, I've been warned—several times," she giggles.

"Hmm. That you have. Look, changing the subject: how about going with me tomorrow."

"Where? Church?"

"Naw, not this time. I'm running over to Jersey to see my Giants, and I'd love it if you were with me. A few of the guys I work with are bringing their wives, girlfriends, whatever, you know. We have a private suite waiting for us, booze, great food—the works. Come go with me. You'll have fun."

"Really? You want a little church girl who doesn't drink booze and knows very little about football to go with you to a Giants' game in your special little suite?"

"Yep, I do. I'm a great teacher, and maybe I can continue my talent for relaxing you," I chuckle at this double meaning of my statement. "What do you say?"

"Hmm..." She takes a deep breath. "Sure, why not."

"Great. Give me an address and I'll pick you up around seven."

I get the address, finish off the evening with a little more small talk, and say goodnight. I make a short call to solidify Chad's apartment because I can't take the chance of him trying to move in with me. After I do the pay- by-phone thing, I prepare for bed, and drift off to sleep letting my mind dance around the joy of anticipating another day with Jaz and the excitement of being at MetLife with friends and my awesome Giants. Half way between sleep and awake, I wonder what's changing inside of me. Why don't I have someone in my bed with me tonight?

I open my eyes to sunlight filtering through my blinds, and my heart skips a beat when I think about what I have planned for the day. A smile crosses my lips, and I lick them just anticipating the day and maybe the night. I shower and dress in what I call my New York Giants' uniform. The reflection in my full-length mirror tells me that my jeans are a perfect match for my royal blue script hoodie, and even this causal, I look great. I grab my keys from the basket at the door and ride the elevator down to my red convertible 911 Carrera Cabriolet.

In less than ten minutes, I'm standing at Jaz's door. I ring the bell and wait. When she opens the door, she actually takes my breath away. Standing in front of me grinning, she is dressed in jeans, a short red cutoff top and a little jean jacket that sparkles almost as bright as her gorgeous eyes. Her pixie hair cut is perfectly accented with little diamond stud earrings. Her make-up is flawless, and she smells divine. She catches me off guard, and for a moment I can't speak, but I quickly recover and manage a weak, "Hi."

"Wow, girl. I don't know if I can take you out with company. Somebody might steal you from me. We might have to stay here."

"Come in, silly," she laughs. Let me grab my purse, and I'm ready to go."

She comes back with a small red wallet size shoulder purse, and I can't help myself any longer. I risk everything. I move over in front of her and take her in my arms. I look into her eyes and she lowers them and looks back up at me. I touch her face and cup her chin and slowly bring her lips to mine, and the kiss is slow, sweet, and harmless. I pull her even closer to me and kiss her again, this time with more passion, and I feel her positive response.

"Friends, right?" I wink and smile at her.

"Yeah, good friends." She smiles that shy smile that drives me a little crazy.

"Be careful. We might miss the game."

"I won't let that happen," she giggles.

"You sure about that, Babe?

"Very."

I lean in and kiss her again, but this time she slightly pushes on my chest to break my embrace.

"I think we should go before we're late."

"Ah, it's only about a forty-five minute drive so I don't think we have to worry about being late. Actually, there is no real time schedule on us."

"Well, it is if we want to beat the crowds and see the whole game."

"The crowd's not going the same way that we're going. As far as the game is concerned, we have some extra time. We get to go into a private entrance so you see, we can take our time."

"No, we can't, Casanova. Let's go," she insists pulling me toward the door.

The ride to Rutherford is calm and fairly easy. When we arrive, both of us can feel the thrill of the crowds, and we are immediately swept up in the excitement. There is so much going on at once that it's virtually impossible to take it all in, but a sweep of our eyes over the area clearly spells exhilaration. We find our way to our private suite and the other guys and their guests are already in place mixing drinks, sampling the smorgasbord of delicious looking food, chatting, and of course, watching the preliminaries. I can tell that Jaz is trying to feel at ease with my friends, and she manages to impress me with her responses to their questions and comments. No shyness in sight. Everybody is upbeat, and I look out at the enormous crowds gathering below and move over to one of the TVs. We take a seat, and I look over at this gorgeous woman next to me and put my arm around her shoulders. I feel this strange sense of pride with her next to me.

"Having fun?"

"Yes, I am. I've never been to a NFL game before so everything is new to me."

I reach for her hand and bring it to my lips and immediately turn back to the TV.

"Hey Zack, you want something to drink?" Matt calls. "Thanks, man. I'll get us something during the game."

"Jazmin, what about you?"

"No, Matt. I'll wait for Zack."

"Suit yourself. I hope something is left when you two decide you're hungry," he laughs.

Jaz and I sit and talk. I explain some little things about the game, and she asks as many questions as her limited knowledge will allow. At one point, she gets up and looks out at the crowd below us, and then I see her talking with Brett's fiancée, Lauren, about her *NFL Fanicure*, a new nail trend that I suppose is now all the rave for our lady fans. When the game begins, I lose track of everything that is going on except the drinks, the food, and Manning having the game of his life. Our little party has multiple opportunities to erupt with cheers, shouts, and hand slaps all around. I am caught up in the total excitement of what I see is going to be a comfortable win for us since the score is 31-17 in the fourth quarter with less than a minute to go. At the end of what I consider a great game, I look around for Jaz and find her standing over in a corner giggling with Matt. To me, he's standing far too close to her, and then I see him touch her bare waist, lean over, and whisper in her ear. At that point, I lose it. I saunter over to where they are standing, pull Jaz to me, and look Matt directly in his eyes.

"Man, you need to pump your brakes." My voice is quiet, but I am seething inside. The suite disappears for me, and there are only the three of us present in my view. I see Matt roll his eyes, and Jaz looks up at me seemingly a bit confused.

"We were just talking, man," he smirks.

"Like I said, you need to pump your brakes." My voice is quiet, and my words come slowly and emphatically.

"Your lady is an artist, and I *own* some of her artwork, so we were just talking about that."

"And that conversation necessitated your touching her waist and whispering in her ear, right?" I ask, stepping close to him.

He is looking around me now finding her eyes instead. "Listen Jazmin, maybe we can finish our conversation at a later date, uninterrupted," Matt remarks with a wink as he emphasizes "uninterrupted."

Before I can think, before I can even begin to restrain myself, my fist finds a direct shot to his left eye, and he reels from the blow and stumbles to the floor. Using the loose cloth of his jersey, I grab him up off the floor with one hand, swing him around, and with both hands and a lot of force, I slam him to the floor again. Standing over him, I hear my breath coming fast and hard.

"Like I said, you need to pump your brakes." I glance around me, and the suite that has been filled with cheers, laughter, and camaraderie is now still, quiet, and filled with inquisitive stares. I step over Matt still on the floor, grab Jazmin's hand aggressively, and leave the room.

Outside, I am furious, but quiet. I try to calm myself as we walk to the car. Well, she runs trying to keep up. We get in, and we ride back to New York City in total silence.

After about forty or fifty minutes, the car comes to an abrupt halt directly in front of Jaz's door. I see her turn and look at me. Instinctively, I know that tears are in her eyes, and I sense her sadness, but I can't bring myself to look at her or let her off the hook. This kind of thing just doesn't happen to me, and I can't let it happen again.

I nervously tap the steering wheel, and look straight ahead. I know that my mouth is pretty tight and balled because I want her to know how furious I still am. In my peripheral vision, I see her hand move to the door handle. She's given up talking to me. However, as fast as I see her motion to leave, I am equally as fast snapping the automatic locks on. The click seems louder than ever. Even it seems to have an aggressiveness that speaks volumes. Her head turns quickly toward me at this startling sound, and this time I look at her. I open my mouth to speak, and I want the words to come out slowly and emphatically. I want her to know how hurt I am, but instead my anger takes over, and I have no control. I feel my hands balled and sweat inside the ball. My eyes blink far faster than normal, and heat oozes from my brow.

"How could you do this? What were you thinking? Do you honestly think that was okay? How did you think I would feel looking around and finding you hold up in a corner with some other guy? I just don't understand what your thoughts were, Jazmin? Do you think even now that that little performance doesn't hurt me or embarrass me? Is this the REAL you, the kind of girl you *really* are?" I am even madder now, and I want to hurt her back so I go in for the kill. "Is this something you do all the time—act like some Little Miss Shy Church Princess and then turn into some kind of tease? Is this what you do? 'If it is, I don't want it, I don't need it, and I don't need you.'"

I stop long enough to see a tear slide down her face, drop, and form a wet spot on the blueness of her jeans. She turns her head toward the window, rests her arm on the edge of it, and runs her fingers through her short dark brown hair. After a second or two, she turns her head, and looks at me.

"Zack, I'm sorry. We were just talking. I'm sorry if you see that as wrong, but you can't have that much control over me. I am who I am, and I don't plan to change. I will be free to talk with whomever I please, whenever I please. If you can't deal with that, then you can't deal with me. I will say, however, whether you know it or not, you already mean a lot to me. Our friendship is important to me, and I hope you can believe that. You made something out of nothing tonight, Zack, and I feel like I may not be able to convince you that this was nothing to worry about. I was not trying to disrespect you. We were just. . . talking.

"Well, I didn't like it. Just so you know, I have a major problem with him looking around me to you and talking about finishing your conversation uninterrupted," I snap.

"That was wrong, but I can't control him, and you can't smack down every guy that talks with me."

I soften a bit and take her hand in mine. "Sorry about the smack down, but if I take you someplace, Jaz, I want to know that your attention is on me, and that you are not looking around for someone else."

"I can assure you that I wasn't. Matt came over when I was talking to a couple of the ladies, and when they left us alone it ended with Matt and me talking about art. That's all."

I lean over and cup her chin, and gently cover her lips with mine.

"Friends again?" I ask looking directly into her beautiful eyes. My voice is soft and sexy.

"You tell me. I never stopped being your friend."

61

"Friends," I whisper close to her mouth, and seal the word with a soft kiss. . . the kind that I hope will make her want more of me.

"Good night, Zack. I'll see you soon."

"Promise?"

"Yes, I do."

I get out, and walk around the car and open her door. I reach inside to steady her and bring her body close to mine. Standing close in the cool night air, I feel her heart beat, and I like the feeling. It's a steady beat that makes me draw her closer. There's something different about this girl, but I can't really put my finger on it. However, whatever it is, I like it a lot. Her touch comforts me, and I can't recall ever feeling this before. I take a deep breath and feel her rest her head on my shoulder. I have this strange sense of relief and even a stranger sense of euphoria.

With my eyes closed, my senses seem even more alert, and I notice everything: how relaxed I feel with Jaz's arms around my shoulders, the soft sweet smell of her breath, her mild perfume, the gentleness of her hands on my neck, her tiny waist and the soft, smooth feel of her bare skin beneath my hands. She seems so small and vulnerable. I know that my normal self would never let this opportunity pass, but with Jaz, I'm not sure of her vulnerability, and I can't take the chance of being wrong. She stood up to me even in my fury, and at the same time offered an apology for hurting me. Feeling the comfort of her in my arms, I want a lot more than I plan to ask for at the moment, but still my lips tease and kiss her passionately. It is by no mean my idea of the ultimate, but for a lady they say is "out of my league," it will have to do for the moment.

"Good night, baby," I say close to her lips with a wink and a slight smile. She looks up at me, holds her gaze, and lets her hands slowly move down my arms to my hands. She holds them both in front of us.

"Good night, friend," she says covering one of my hands with hers as if to seal a pact.

With that we walk the few paces to the door arm in arm. I take her key, unlock the door, and push it open. I kiss the tip of her nose, and she touches my face, smiles shyly, and disappears inside.

~ Jazmin ~

5

GETTING TO KNOW YOU

Ignoring RED FLAGS is the introduction
to self-inflicted pain and sorrow.

I shut the door behind me, lean up against it, inhale slowly and deeply, and then exhale loudly. I close my eyes for a second and hear Derek's voice in my head. *Be careful, Jazmin. Zack can hurt you badly, and walk away unscathed.* I push away from the door, toss my purse on the sofa as I pass, and head straight for my bedroom. I want to undress and get in bed, but all of a sudden, I'm just too tired. Instead, I sit on the side of the bed for what I think is going to be a moment or two. I fall back and cover my eyes with my arm to protect me from the soft lamplight washing over me.

Zack made tonight very hard, and I'm wondering if he will make many of my nights hard if I keep down this path with him. Despite my common sense, warnings from my close friends, and the prover-bial red flags waving with ferocity in my face, I still don't want this friendship to end. I still don't want to think that I can't talk with him again, see him again, and feel free to even love him if that is where it all leads. Silently, I do what I always do when things seem far beyond my capabilities. Lying in the stillness of my room, I pray that God will lead me to do the right thing. Somehow, I don't feel good about this new friendship, but is that God telling me to back away or is it just my own fear of the unknown—my fear to take a risk? Maybe it's just my own insecurities helped on by Derek, Arianna, and Nina Wellington's voices in my head: *He can be ruthless. He's a charmer who's hard to resist, but he stings. He's no good. Leave him alone. You're too good for him.*

In the quietness of my bedroom, behind my shaded eyes, I think about our day together. I think about the excitement of its beginning, but also in my mind's eye, I vividly see Matt struggling to get up from that unnecessary swift and powerful blow to his head. I recall the tight grip on my wrist, the jerking motion that pulled me toward the door, and the deafening fifty- minute silence that brought me home. I feel the sting of his words in the barrage of questions that he gives me no time to answer. I hear the tremor of my weak voice in apology despite the fact that I defy being told with whom I can speak at any given time. However, the rigid contradiction is that I am, at the same time, yielding to the allure of his seductive voice, submitting to the tenderness of his touch on my skin, and even now, in my solitude, automatically reacting to the playfulness of his teasing kisses. Lying here now, alone, I take a deep breath, and beg my God to tell me what to do.

The phone startles me back to reality, and I dig it out of my jean pocket and see Zack's smiling face. The call surprises me. I can't help noticing that my heart skips a beat, and electric shocks propel butter-flies to flight.

"Hello."

"Hey, girl. You in bed yet?"

"No. Not quite." I can barely hear him. "Are you?" "Nooo." He draws the word out in a provocative whisper.

There is a long pause. "I miss you already, girl. You want to come over?" He is using his sleepy voice, but I know that's the last thing he is. . . sleepy.

His voice is drawing me to him—making me want to feel his gentle touch, and finish those teasing kisses he started, but my sanity kicks in just in time, and I know I've got to change this mood, now.

"Zack, you're crazy. No, I don't want to come over. I don't answer booty calls," I laugh. *I've got to lighten the mood, and take the controls from him.*

"Well, that's not what it is, baby," he whispers seductively.

"What is it then?" My voice is a little loud and playful.

"Hmm! It's just me being lonesome and not feeling like sitting around in an empty apartment. It's an innocent call to a friend."

"And Zack, if I believe that, sell me that bridge you built all by yourself with your own blood, sweat, and tears," I giggle.

"See girl, you like to play. You drive a hard bargain." *That voice is killing me.*

Despite the fact that his voice is low, enticing, and sexy, I certainly know better than to fall into this trap. To keep my good common sense in full control, to heed the words of my father every time I went out with a guy in high school, and to obey the voices of caution from my recent friends, I know I have to get off of this phone. If I linger too long, I see myself grabbing that purse and dashing out to Never-Never Land.

"Look, Zack, I'm not coming over, and I have to get up early tomorrow. I want to stop by a chapel to say a few prayers since I missed church today. Do you want to come with me?"

"Oh yeah. That's right. You're the little church girl. No wonder."

"No wonder what?"

"Nothing. You all are just different, you know, more cautious."

"Do you want to go with me in the morning?"

"Naw, not this time, Baby. Maybe sometime in the near future."

"Not to push, but why wait? I'm only going to stop by to say a few prayers of praise before work."

"I just don't think I'm up for that scene tomorrow, but I'll go with you one day."

"Is that a promise?"

"See, I told you. You drive a hard bargain, but yes, Jaz, it's a promise."

"Well, I'm back in Virginia after tomorrow so you're off the hook for the near future."

"See you take my heart and then leave me for Virginia."

"Zack, I don't have your heart, and you know it," I giggle.

"No, I don't know it. Look how I reacted with Matt. I flattened that dude cause he was touching you. How long will you be in Virginia?"

"Not long this time. I have a new manager there who is quite good, but I do have to check in now and then. I'll be back to my main studio in a few weeks, about a month."

"That long, huh?"

"I'll be back before you can deck Matt again," I laugh.

"You're funny. If I see him, I might have to take care of him again tomorrow."

I giggle at his craziness. "Good night, Zack."

"Wait," he rushes to say. "Can we spend the evening together tomorrow? After all you are leaving me again."

"Sure, I don't see why not. I'd like that. I'll call you when I'm home."

"All right. Now...if you change your mind about tonight, Baby, just come on over. No need to call ahead."

"Good night, Zack.

"Hugs and kisses to my best girl. Good night." I hear a slight chuckle in his voice just before the click.

I know he's playing with me. I'm his new challenge, and he's playing to win. On the other hand, I'm caught in this infatuation net, and I hope not headed for a fall. If he wins, does that mean I lose?

I undress, and prepare for bed. When I slide under the covers, the sheets are cool and comforting, and the memory of Zack's voice over the phone and the hum of the heater lull me into a blissful sleep.

Drifting off, I feel the smile on my face, and I can barely wait for tomorrow evening.

—◊—

My morning is quieting and thoughtful, and the visit to the chapel brings me a sense of peacefulness. I ask God for direction and pray that in my own way, I don't ignore His decisions about the direction my life should take. At work, the day seems to drag, maybe because I check the time at least every thirty minutes. Just before twelve, when my phones buzzes, and I see Zack's face on the screen, my mouth moves into this automatic grin that I'm sure he can hear in my hello.

"I'm leaving now, Baby. Can you?"

"Zack, it's lunch time. It's kind of early to leave."

"Not when you can't wait any longer to see someone. Come on, babe. Meet me now. After all, you are the boss.

"But the boss will be gone for a month so I need to get a few things in order."

"I need some time. Come on, J. Meet me."

"All right. You know I can't really resist you. I'll see you in an hour."

"That's what I'm talking about. See you in a few." "Bye"

The traffic is crowded, but at least Zack doesn't live that far, and I probably need this time to compose myself. He makes me a little nervous and a little intimidated, but I want to see him as much as he wants to see me. After all, the next month is going to be filled with work, work, work, and the joy of every woman's life: annual check-ups. Ugh!

I pull into the parking garage, check my hair in the mirror and take the elevator to the top floor. At the door, I take a deep breath and ring the bell. The door opens, and standing there in all of his allure, he takes my breath away. *Wow! What a man.* In one sweep of my eyes, I see it all. He's casually dressed in black slacks, a light blue V-neck sweater, and a gorgeous gold chain that holds my eyes at his neck. He's barefoot and smells masculine and wonderful. Soft jazz plays throughout the house and behind him, I see a table set for two.

"Hey beautiful." He winks, and a slight smile crawls across his face as he takes my hand and places his charismatic greeting on my right cheek.

"Hey," is all I can muster. He gently pulls me inside, and I hear the door close quietly behind me. He holds me now in his strong arms, and I can feel the strength of his embrace. I look into his eyes; he's looking in mine, and he touches my lips with his thumb, and I kiss it as it lingers. He pulls me closer and kisses my forehead, then my cheek and my neck, and then he finds his way to my lips, and I melt in his arms. His kisses are soft, gentle, and filled with passion.

"Hungry?" He whispers close to my mouth. "I fixed lunch for us."

"Good," I mummer as I initiate another kiss.

He takes my hand and kisses the back of it and leads me to a table that makes me wonder if he set it.

"Did you do this?" I ask surveying the setting.

"Yes, I learned how to set a table in college. D taught me. He taught me all about the different forks and how to set a table for elegance. He used to tease me about never needing such a skill. Well, I need it today for this beautiful, elegant, special woman in front of me."

Zack pulls out a seat for me and serves me a tossed salad with an array of dressings from which to choose; all of them are displayed in silver cups attached to a rotational bottom platform. Nice touch. After the salad, he pulls out club sandwiches on a decorative tray that are so pretty that I don't believe he made them until he shows me the crumbs from the toaster, the packaging from the meat, and the left-over veggies in the fridge. We laugh a lot and I admire his incredible cooking skills.

"How did you learn to make such a beautiful and delicious lunch?"

"Well, when you live alone, and there's no one around to help, you get hungry and learn to fend for yourself. D and I did a lot of experimenting and both of us can cook pretty well. We watched a lot of cooking shows on TV. I still watch them, and I know I can fix food better than Derek, but then, I can do most things better than Derek, but that's a whole other subject," he teases. "He just didn't take the whole thing as seriously as I did. Silver Spoon didn't think he would need it very often, and he doesn't." We both laugh a little and enjoy our meal together.

I see that Zack is a little obsessed about the clean- up. He doesn't stop until every dish is washed, every appliance he used clean, and ev-erything put away in its correct place. I help, but I see that he's doing what I do over so I stop, sit, and just watch him.

"I have a surprise for you."

"You do?" I ask. "What is it?"

"Go look in my bedroom on the bed."

"What are you trying to pull, Zack?"

"Nothing. I'll stay here. You go and look."

"Where is your bedroom?"

"Well, that's a question I've never heard before. It's down the hall, first door on your right," he laughs.

"You think you're so funny."

"No, that's honest."

I get up and smack at him. He dodges still laughing, and I walk down the hallway and open the first door on my right. When I enter, I'm speechless. The glass wall reveals a view of New York City that is incredible, and the room is decorated to the nines. The colors are a soft beige and white. The carpet is fluffy and immaculately white, and it's almost like stepping into the clouds. The bed is queen size and is covered in beige, brown, and white with a mixture of different size pillows. Off from the bedroom is a bath with colors that match the bedroom—only there are accent pieces in turquoise. Everything is beautiful, perfect, and clean to a fault. On the bed, I see a long black evening gown, beautiful black lingerie, very expensive Louis Vuitton red sole black high heels, a black evening purse and what appears to be a small teardrop diamond necklace with matching earrings. All still have the price tags on them. I pick up the necklace and hear Zack at the door.

"Do you like it?" He's leaning up against the door jam and his voice is low, quiet, and sexy. *Ahh... he's so gorgeous. I want this man.*

"Zack, what are you doing?"

"Well, I want to take my angel to a Jazz concert tonight, but I didn't want you to leave and go home for anything, so I had these things brought over for you this morning. I left the tags on because I didn't want you to think that I have a closet full of female clothes on hand," he chuckles. He comes over and circles my waist, and lightly kisses me on my cheek.

"I told you, you are already very special to me. I've never met a lady like you, and I just want to do things to make you happy."

"I'm speechless, Zack. All of this is beautiful, and I appreciate the idea, but I can't take these things. It's too much."

"Not to me, it's not." It's the first time I've ever bought a girl anything." He picks up the necklace from the bed, turns my back to him, and clasps it around my neck. He turns me back to face him and looks me in my eyes. For that moment, I know that I am seeing something that Zack never shows anyone. There is no mask. He is present in front of me.

"Please don't fight me on this, Jaz. In my world, where so much has been bad, where so much has been taken from me, baby, you are my beautiful angel—my saving grace. You're something good that's come into my life. Let me love you," he whispers close to my ear, and touches my face. "Put these things on for me, and let me take you out and show you a great time before you leave again. Give me something good to think about while you're gone. There's no catch to this. I'm not asking for anything in return except your happiness."

"Well, when you put it that way. . . Ok, but you have to go out while I change."

"I have to change too, and my things are in here," he smiles playing with my face.

"Well, let me change someplace else."

He shows me a room across the hall and it is equally beautiful. The only thing missing is the New York view. We both change and when I step out of the room I hear a loud whistle, and I see Zack with a huge grin on his handsome face.

The night is magical and perfect; the concert of smooth jazz is mesmerizing, relaxing and we both enjoy every minute of it. At the end of the night, I come up to get my things, and he asks me to stay. I say an emphatic no. He takes me in his arms, and for ten minutes we say good night, and in those ten minutes, I realize without a doubt, I will come back to this man whatever the risks.

~ Zack ~

6

A Friend Indeed

Fear ties tight knots and almost dares the mind to attempt escape.

With Jazmin in Virginia for a month, my life is dull, and nothing seems to move me out of a slight depression. I throw myself into my work that is paying off huge dividends that promise me a big promotion, and the biggest monetary bonus of my life for sure, but that still does not hide her face in my sleep or stop sweet memories from invading my mind all day long. I miss holding her even though she has just started allowing me to be that intimate. Kissing and holding are all that she has permitted, but I miss that. I'll admit, I've had a few ladies over to spend the night since she's been gone, but even the magic of that is not the same now, and I just want to see my Jaz. For the first two weeks, we talk on the phone a lot, Skype a lot, send texts and all of that, but for the last week, I haven't been able to reach her but once, and even then, she was different—distant. I can't quite put my finger on the real difference, but I know she was not the same.

Now, I'm beginning to worry, so I have to risk calling Derek and getting a lecture from him, hearing the same line over and over. *Leave the girl alone, Zack. She's out of your league. She's out of your league.* However, despite having to go through a stupid long boring lecture about my past history, I dial his number anyway. I have to know where she is, and why she is no longer communicating with me.

"Good Morning, Brollen and Brollen Law. How may I direct your call?"

"This is Zachary Belford, calling from Wall Street for Attorney Wellington."

"One moment, please."

"Hey, Zee! What's up?"

"Not much, D. Sorry to call you at work, but I'm a little worried."

"Jazmin, right?"

"Yeah. Where is she?"

"You know, ordinarily, I wouldn't tell you a thing about her because you know how I feel about your hooking up with her, but something is wrong, and we can't get it out of her. After she finally told us it wasn't about you, Ari and I were actually going to call you tonight. I think you need to come and see about her."

"What happened?"

"We don't know. All we know is she's not coming to work, not answering her calls, and she's hold up in her condo and won't answer the door. When Ari finally got in once, she was in bed doing a lot of crying. Ari says that she was a mess, but still, she wouldn't talk to her at all. She did admit it didn't have anything to do with you—that you guys were fine. Ari stayed as long as she would allow her to, but in about a half hour she asked her to leave. She says she'll be ok, but that's all we could get. Can you come and see about her?"

"I'm there, man. I'll be there in a couple of hours if I can get my friend's private plane. If not, I'll take a commercial or drive down myself. In any event, I'll see you today or tonight. Thanks, man. Later."

I dial Mike to see if his plane is available, and if he will allow me to use it. I tell him the situation and immediately he arranges for me to leave as soon as possible. I dash home to pack a few things when the doorbell rings. I look through the peek hole and see Chad. This is the last thing I need right now. I take a deep breath and reluctantly open the door.

"Hey, Little Bro," he says pushing his way in.

"Hey yourself. What's up?"

"Nothing much. I called your job, and they said you were here, so I thought to myself, "Self, you ought to just drop in on his day off. Maybe the two of us can have a nice little friendly visit, maybe even a picnic, or something family like, you know," he chuckles.

"Sorry to disappoint," I say heading back to my bedroom. "I'm about to catch a flight in about an hour, so I don't have time for a friendly chat, picnics, or family visits with you."

"Flight? Where you going?"

"Oh, my job didn't tell you they were sending me on an emergency trip to save the world?" I ask throwing a few things in my overnight.

"No, they didn't tell me that. No joke, where you going?"

"I'm going to save the world, and you need to get out of my way so I can be on time for my flight," I say zipping up my garment bag. I dash in the bathroom and hurriedly throw my toiletries together, zip the bag, and move back into the bedroom.

"Look man, I need some cash," he mumbles following me.

"Get a job."

"I don't need a job. You have a job, and I have you." Chad puts his foot out in front of me, and I almost trip. "Just give me the cash, man, that I wouldn't be asking for if—

"I know 'if it wasn't for you stealing my life," I mock his stupid voice.

"I'm not playing with you, Zack. I need some money, and you're not leaving here in one piece if I don't get it."

I look at this no- good brother of mine, take out my wallet, and throw all the bills I have at his feet. I grab my bags, open the door, and wait for him to pick up the cash. When he gets to the door, he slams it shut, and sucker punches me hard in the gut.

"Don't ever, as long as I let you live, do that again, Little Bro."

He opens the door, and leaves me in a ball gagging on the floor.

I manage to get up, and sit down for a moment to push my breakfast back down to my stomach, and hate myself for having to wipe the tears that I feel moving down my cheeks. Sitting alone in the quietness, my mind flashes on an eighteen-year- old Chad shielding me from the blood- splattered kitchen, pushing me out of our three-room filthy house and yelling at me to hide. In my mind, I see him getting me up every morning, helping me get dressed for school and waiting at the bus stop with me until I am safely on my way. I see him bending over my homework with me and yelling at me for not understanding something I read. I hear the anger in his voice through the years, the disappointment of his failures while he helps me and manages my other brothers from a distance. I push these thoughts away now. My breakfast is back in its rightful place, and the pain from the unexpected blow to my midriff has subsided. I pick up my bags, make my way to the elevator and put my mind on Jazmin, my angel with a broken wing.

—ᴍ—

The flight is very short, but serene, and D is there when we land to take me to his cottage. I'm nervous and can't figure out what could possibly be wrong with my angel. I take a few minutes to put my things down and call Arianna at work, and she tells me basically the same thing that Derek told me on the phone. I get directions to Jaz's condo on a hideaway beach, and Derek lends me one of his cars for the complicated route to her place.

At the door, I ring the bell at first, but I don't hear a sound other than the waves coming off of the ocean.

"Jaz, it's me. Zack. Open the door." Still, I hear only the lapping of waves.

"Jazmin, I know you're in there." No sound. "Open the door."

I hear a slight rustling, but there is no attempt to let me in so I forget the bell and bang my fist on the door as hard as I can.

"Jaz, open up!" I'm yelling now. "I'm not playing. I'll break this door down if you don't open it. What's wrong with you, girl?"

I hear the lock give way, and she opens it slightly. It's just enough for her to peek out.

"Zack, just leave me alone." Her voice sounds weak—exhausted, like she's near her last breath. Her face is sad and swollen.

"Girl, I'm not about to leave you alone, and I'm not playing. I've left my job in the middle of a huge project that we are about to close on that will make us millions, borrowed a private plane, flew here from New York on a minute's notice, borrowed D's car, and had to wrap around trying to find this secluded beach all because I'm so worried about you. All of a sudden you can't pick up a phone and open your mouth to tell somebody what's going on with you? Let me in, J. I'm telling you now, I'm not playing."

She hesitates, but moves aside, and I go in and quietly close the door. She looks so small and helpless. I see her swollen eyes, her almost lifeless body, and I slowly unfold her arms, carefully bring her to me, and the dam breaks. Her cry is soft, but it's a hard cry like it's coming from an inner place hard to touch. She's shaking in my arms, and my tears fall because of her. I just hold her at first. We say nothing, and when she is spent, we simply stand slightly swaying, holding tightly to each other. She breaks the silence.

"Did you really borrow a plane to come to me?"

"Yes, I did," I answer against her hair.

"You know people with private planes?"

"Obviously, yes, I do, and a lot of them." I kiss the top of her head, and we keep our swaying rhythm, but I push back slightly and try to look in her eyes, but she won't let me so I pull her to me and keep holding her.

"Would you really have knocked my door down if I didn't open it?" she asks against my chest.

I gently push her out, hold her face up to me with both of my hands, and look in her eyes. "Yes."

"Really?"

"Yes. I'm worried about you." I feel her snuggle closer to me, tighten her arms around my neck, take a deep breath, and exhale loudly.

"Talk to me, baby," I whisper against her ear. "Tell me what's wrong."

"I can't."

"You can't or you won't." I ask against her hair.

"I'm scared, Zack."

"Scared of what, angel? I'm here now. You don't have to be scared. I'll take care of you."

"But you can't."

"I can't if you don't tell me what it is. Let's sit down, and you tell me what's wrong. If somebody is bothering you, you let me know. You know I can take care of that."

"I wish it were that simple."

We move over to a nearby love seat and sit down. I take her hands in mine, and I see her sneak a glance at me.

"What's scaring my angel?" I hold her face up to mine so that I can see her beautiful eyes and search them for whatever I can find.

"Doctors." She lowers her eyes and then her head. "Doctors?" I lift her chin to look at me.

I see her take a very deep breath. "Zack, I . . . I had a check-up scheduled when I got here and everything was fine until one of the doctors called and said he found something suspicious in one of my breasts, and they had to run more tests."

"Did they run the tests?"

"Yes.

"So, what do the tests show?"

"I don't know. My appointment is tomorrow. That's when they plan to tell me."

"So, you don't really know if anything is wrong or not. Right?"

"Right, but they did more tests, and I looked up a lot of stuff on the Internet."

"Jaz, the Internet cannot diagnose your condition, and what the doctors have said doesn't mean anything is wrong. They're just checking to make sure. They saw something, and they wanted to check it out. That's all."

"On the Internet it says—"

I interrupt her. "The Internet knows nothing about you, and you are not a doctor so you can't give yourself a valid prognosis. You're scaring yourself to death for nothing, angel.

"Zack, I'm just twenty-five years old with my whole life ahead of me. I don't want to lose my life or my breasts."

"Jazmin, you are not going to lose either."

"You don't know that."

"I know about as much as you know, and no one has told you anything at this point."

She sits up and looks directly in my eyes as if she will be able to see something important when she makes her next statement.

"Men love breasts, Zack, and you're not going to love me if I don't have any."

"You've never even made out with me, girl, so how do you know what I love? Maybe I don't love breasts at all. Maybe I love legs. Are your legs all right?" I try to take a playful peek.

"Yes, my legs are fine," she answers pulling her robe over them more securely.

For the first time since I entered her home, she laughs and playfully hits at me.

"You know you love breasts, Zack."

"Not if you don't have any. Take my word for it, girl, I'll find something on you to love. I have no problem with that."

"What man doesn't like breasts?"

"Well, maybe I'm an anomaly. Maybe I like fingers and toes. You have no idea what I like, and, might I add, seemingly not too anxious to find out." I pull her close to me, and I feel her exhale. She smells wonderful, and I inhale the sweet smell of her and both of us relax.

"You know what I think?" I say against her hair.

"What do you think, Zack?"

"I can't believe I'm saying this, but I think you should get out of this beautiful, sexy lingerie that makes you look so gorgeous, put on some jeans and a shirt and let's go out and get something to eat together, unless you want to get dressed and cook for me."

"I don't feel up to it."

"Why because you're the genius with an Internet prognosis that's killing you off in a day or two?" I laugh.

"No, silly. I know I won't go in a day or two," she smiles.

"Girl, go get dressed. We're out of here for a minute."

She leaves my arms, and I hear the shower running, and it gives me the first opportunity to look around at this beautiful condo. It is definitely the home of an artist and photographer with its contemporary lines, high ceilings, and glass walls. It's beautiful, and the colors grab my attention. They are stunningly bright, friendly, and artistic. They seem to serve as accents to this amazing view of the ocean. I notice the seaside motif with the lighthouses, statues of seagulls, shells, and little boats placed here and there. I pick up a boat, turn it over in my hands, and bad memories slam inside my mind. I put it back in its rightful place and push the memory back to its dark hole.

I survey the room again and notice a few things out of place, and when I walk to the kitchen, I see a couple of paper plates on the counter, some half- eaten pizza, a dirty glass, and some cups in the sink. I clean everything and pick up a few papers and medical books in the bedroom, make the bed, and wait in the living room for my angel with the slightly injured wing.

I hear her finish her shower and get dressed. When she comes into the living room, she looks transformed. She's dressed in black slacks, and a black sweater with pearl snowflakes at the neckline. She has on black heels, small diamond stud earrings, and the diamond necklace daintily near the top of her breasts. She looks absolutely exquisite. *Wow! She's stunning!* I walk over to her and take her in my arms.

"Jaz . . . Jaz . . ." I hesitate. "Let me kiss you the way I want to kiss you? May I?" I ask looking directly in her beautiful eyes.

"I don't know. How is that?"

"Let me show you," I whisper in her ear. The passion in the kiss is unmistakable. It speaks of a growing love, fulfillment to erase moments of emptiness caused by an absent lover, and the joy of finally being close enough to touch once more. It is a kiss that communicates for both of us the beginning of something very special at a time that we both need to feel special, needed, and wanted: *her,* for what doctors may say tomorrow, and *me,* for the secret consuming guilt that rides my back daily—a guilt that Chad refuses to allow me to relinquish or at least share since I was only seven on the Day of Horrors—the day when disaster struck. *What could I do?*

"I think I needed that kiss, Zack," she whispers breathlessly against my chest.

"I know I did," I say as I kiss her nose and pull her tightly to me. "Let's get out of here."

She directs me to the beautiful *Fisherman's Pier Restaurant* not far from her condo. When we drive up, I see that it has at least three floors and the sides facing the ocean are all glass. I hear the music piped outside and know already that this is a good place to be right now. Inside, Jaz requests what she calls her usual: seating on the third floor, ocean side.

"Yes, Miss Grant, right this way."

We are escorted to our seats and the view is outstanding. Even in the nightlight, I see the caps of the waves, and the stars in the October sky are bright and beautiful. There is a calmness that surrounds us that only comes in special places and this is, indeed, one of those places.

We chat awhile and when the waiter comes to take our order, I ask what's good and Jazmin gives me great suggestions. The food is delicious and after we eat, we sit with coffee in a small somewhat private lounge area and talk.

"I'm so glad you came to see about me, Zack."

"Why didn't you call me and tell me what was going on instead of going through all of this alone? You know I would have come."

"I was so scared."

"You don't have to be anymore. I'll be right here with you no matter what the doctors say. I won't let you go through this alone."

"Have you ever been scared, Zack? Do you know how I feel right now?"

"Yeah, I know exactly what fear is like. It happened to me once, but I had someone to help me."

"When was that?"

Hmm. I'll tell you, but I'll admit up front, it's hard for me to talk about." I take her hand in mine and hold it to my cheek. "I was seven years old, and my grandma came to take care of us."

"Where were your parents?"

I hear myself snatch a breath at the word *parents*. "That's a longer harder story that I'm really not ready to share, but I will tell you about my grandma. I remember her first night there. She was sitting in my father's lounge chair in front of his TV, but the TV was off. I peeked in the door, and she saw me. I remember that she held out her hand to me and said, "Come here, baby. Come talk to Grandma." I smile remembering that moment. "I remember that I didn't move at first, and I started to leave the door, but she called me again. She said, "Zachary, come here, baby. Come and talk to your Grandma." Her voice was so quiet, Jaz. I could hear the love in it. I was so scared, not of her, but what I thought was going to happen to me. It was a horrible day. So many bad things had happened that day. I went to her, and she hugged me, and she sat me in her lap, and I started to cry. Jaz, I was so scared, but I remember that was the first of many times she sang to me about a Rock."

"A rock?"

"Yeah, she was hugging me and singing to me about a rock that night."

I'm rubbing Jaz's hand softly and almost absentmindedly on my face, and for some reason, the touch is reminding me even more of Grandma. My voice sounds low and even distant to me, and it is as if only Jazmin and I are in this place.

"She used to talk a lot about that Rock. She would tell me to always stay close to the Rock—that He would protect me, shelter me, and when I was scare He would hide me. One day I went on a hunt for my own rock, and I found it down by a river, and I still have it to this day. We had a lot of long talks about the Rock. She would always say, 'Hoooold tight to the Rock, Baby. Neeeeever let the Rock go 'cause He won't let you go.' Hmm . . . *I feel a smile on my lips.* "People say that when someone dies, you soon forget their voice. I

93

still remember her voice. I can still hear her sound." Even though I know that Jaz is sitting so close to me, and I know that I'm holding her hand, I feel that I'm traveling back in time and space, and I can even smell my grandma's perfume. It's almost like she's sitting at the table with us.

"She died when I was twelve, and I looked all over her room for her Rock, but I couldn't find it. I couldn't find it, Jaz. I looked hard for it, so I got another one, a special one, a pretty one. It was smooth; it felt good. When no one was looking, I hid it in her casket before they sealed her up. I didn't want her to go without her Rock. I wanted to find hers so she could have it with her. She loved it so much, but she never showed it to me. I guess she kept it in her own special hiding place, and she didn't want anyone to find it and take it from her. I looked everywhere in her room for it, but it wasn't there. I caught a bus one day, and I went to the cemetery all by myself. I sat at her grave, and I tried to sing the song she used to sing to me about her Rock, but I couldn't remember it all. I still can't. I wish I could. All I remember is '...the solid Rock I stand—' I was crying sitting by her grave; She always said I was smart. I didn't want her to know I had forgotten the words to her song, so I kept repeating what I could remember;—the Solid Rock I stand—'"

"On Christ," Jaz whispers. I know she didn't want to bring me abruptly back from the place where I had traveled.

"That's it! On Christ, the solid Rock I stand..."

". . . all other ground . . . "Jazmin murmurs and smiles like she's remembering something.

". . . is sinking sand. That was her song about the Rock. That's it. You know it, too."

I see Jazmin lower her head a bit, and I see a tear fall.

"What?"

"Zack, did you ever hear her talk about Jesus?"

"Yes, but she talked more about the Rock."

"Zack, the Rock is Jesus. She was telling you to depend always on Jesus, that He will always protect you, shelter you, and guide you. Anything else you depend on is sinking sand. She was talking about Jesus, Zack."

We sit quietly for a moment, and I ponder what Jazmin has told me. Jesus is the Rock who guides, protects and hides you. Everything else is sinking sand. *Hmm...Interesting.*

"You know, Zack, I know why God sent you to me today. He had to remind me that He is here with me. I got so caught up in my fear that I wasn't thinking about God. I was thinking about me. So, thank you for reminding me to stand on the Solid Rock."

"In that area, I don't know what I'm talking about, Jaz."

"No, but your grandma did, and you repeated enough of what she said that it reminded me that God will never leave us or forsake us. We just have to trust that He is always near."

I kiss her hand and smile. I'm still not real sure what I've done to help her, but whatever it is, I'm glad.

"...feeling better?"

". . . much better. Your grandma helped me like she helped you."

95

"That's good. Do you feel like going to speak with D and Ari? We don't have to stay long, but they're very worried about you. I'm sure they would love to see you looking all beautiful like you do now."

She smiles that shy smile of hers and I'm so happy to see it.

"Sure. I'll go by for a minute, but please don't make me stay long. I'm really not up to it, and I do have my appointment in the morning."

"Deal. We'll just go by for a moment, and then I'll take you home."

"Are you going to stay with me tonight?'

"Do you want me to stay with you?"

"Yes, but upstairs in the guest bedroom."

"I wouldn't think of staying anywhere else, girl," I laugh.

"Yes, you would," she giggles and hits at me.

I kiss her lightly on the cheek, and we gather our things and head to the car.

The evening is still early and the wind off of the ocean has a bit of a sting to it so I wrap my jacket around my angel, and I feel her shiver as I get her to the car. We drive to the Wellington's and at the door I see her take a rather fearful look at me.

"It's going to be all right, baby," I assure her. I can tell that she doesn't want to tell too much, but I feel that we have to tell them something so they won't continue to worry. Derek comes to the door and welcomes us inside.

"Jasmin!" Ari rushes over to hug her. "How are you?"

"I'm fine. Zack helped me a lot."

"You guys come have a seat. Can I get you anything?"

"No, we ate already. We just came by for a minute to let you see that Jaz is all right. Everything's going to be fine."

That's when I noticed Ari.

"You got a bun in the oven, girl? You about to make me an uncle?" I grin.

"Yes, and we're so happy about this. We can't wait."

"Look at you, man. You're about to be a Daddy. Now that's something." I grin and hug my friend in congratulations.

"We hadn't told anybody yet so I'm glad that you two are the first to know." Derek is beaming and goes over and puts his arms around his wife. I look at my Jaz to see how she's reacting, and I see a big grin on her face, but I'm beginning to know her, and I can see that the grin does not reach her eyes. I know she's happy for our friends, but I also know she's wondering if this will ever happen to her.

Arianna and Jaz move over to another area of the room, and I can tell that Jaz is telling her about the appointment she has in the morning. While they talk privately, D manages to make me angry, and I cut our visit even shorter than originally intended.

"You coming back here tonight?"

"No, I think I need to stay with Jaz."

"Well, you know better than I do that she's been through a lot lately, so man go easy. Don't try to get her in a bed with you tonight. Give her a break."

"D, you don't know what you're talking about."

"Yes, I do. I know you. All I'm saying is the girl has been through a lot, and you need to give her a break. Maybe you need to come back here tonight."

"Maybe you need to mind your own business. I know what I'm doing. I got her out of bed, dressed, out of her house, and over here, didn't I? According to you, she wouldn't stop crying for days. Is she crying now? No. So, does that look like I'm trying to hurt her?"

"No, but you can't help yourself sometimes. You always have to win and conquer somebody no matter what. I told you a long time ago that this girl is out of your league, and you need to help her right now but not take advantage of her."

"You know what, Derek? "

"What?"

"You need to realize that in life people change sometimes, and everything is not always as it seems. I know how fragile Jazmin is right now, more than you do, so for you to suggest that I might do anything to hurt her is an insult to me. Give me credit for a little sense, man."

I am totally exasperated with him, and I need to leave before I deck his butt. I can't take the chance of upsetting Arianna. After all, she's carrying this fool's baby.

"Show me where my things are, and let me go. I'll bring your car back as soon as I can."

I see him take a deep exasperated breath, walk to the back of the house, and return with my bags. Jazmin takes this as a clue to get ready to leave, and I see her hug Arianna goodbye. At the door, I congratulate the two new parents again, and we tell them goodnight.

Back at Jazmin's, I assure her again that all is well. I tell her to go to bed and get mentally prepared for her appointment in the morning. I find my way upstairs to her beautiful, but girly guest bedroom. During the night, I toss and turn a lot worrying about the outcome of her tests, and how I can help her if things don't go in her favor. I lie awake for hours hoping that all will be well for my angel. I think of my grandma, and I fall into a fitful sleep murmuring, "On Christ, the Solid Rock I stand. All other ground is sinking sand."

7

LIFE'S TESTS

True friendship is always on call and answers at a moment's notice.

At five, my body clock wakes me, and I lie still, allowing myself a moment to adjust my mind to where I am and what I may have to do in this day. To keep worry at bay, I clean up a bit, and throw on my workout clothes for a quick run down the beach. I peek in and see that Jaz is still asleep. My short run, as always, helps me. The early morning air is chilly and refreshing, and the beach is serene and beautiful. I see the sun slightly peeking over the horizon, and I can already tell that this is going to be a beautiful autumn day; I just have no idea what it will bring for my angel and me, so I whisper my line aloud in the rhythm of my paces... *On Christ the solid Rock I stand. All other ground is sinking sand.*

When I return to the condo, Jaz is still asleep so I put on some coffee and while there is not much in her fridge, I've learned a long time ago how to make a meal out of practically nothing, so I'm good.

I find some eggs, an onion, some bell pepper, a smidgen of milk, a half carton of juice, some old cheese and three strips of bacon. For me, a gold mine. I search around and find great fixings for morning romance. I set the table with one artificial rose, three tea lights, china and gold flatware. I whip up omelets, pour two cups of coffee, two glasses of juice and place my omelets on the plates with decorative squiggles of hot sauce. Just as I complete my masterpiece, my angel enters the kitchen.

"Oh, I see how it's going to be," I tease.

"What?" she smiles a shy sleepy smile.

"I get up early, finish the breakfast, and you make a grand entrance just in time to sit down to share my scrumptious meal."

"That's the plan," she giggles and sides up to me. I take her in my arms and lightly kiss her on the cheek and the tip of her nose just before I find her lips.

"Sit down, My Lady. Your breakfast awaits." I bow at the waist, and she laughs and playfully slaps at me as I pull out her seat.

"I could get use to this," she smiles.

"So could I with a little something added here and there," I reply laughing and taking my seat.

She gets the point but ignores me with a roll of her eyes. Just as I'm about to dig in to my masterpiece, my angel does what angels do, and begins a prayer of gratitude for the food, for the day, and to my surprise, for me. That makes me smile, and something jumps in my heart. I have no idea what that is, but it feels like pain and joy all at the same time. Weird.

She volunteers to clean up the dishes, but I will have none of it. Besides, I see some spots that need some extra attention, and this is my opportunity so I send her out to dress so I can clean things the way I like them—sparkling. When I finish, the stove takes on a look of newness that I don't think it has seen since it was new. There are no longer smudges on the glass surface and the oven is perfect. The stainless- steel sink glitters in the sunlight coming through the window, and everything is in its proper place.

I dash upstairs, shower, and dress in a pair of black slacks, gray shirt, black sweater, my black socks and patent leather shoes. I put on my gold bracelet, grab my gray leather jacket, black and gray scarf, and go downstairs to wait for Jaz. At the foot of the stairs, I see her slowly pacing back and forth. At first, she doesn't notice me, but when she does, I see the worried look in her eyes. I don't say anything nor does she. I simply take her in my arms and hold her for a moment.

"You know this is going to be all right, don't you," I ask holding her so that I can see her eyes.

"Yes, I do. I just want to be whole for you."

"You will be. However, you are, baby, it will be whole for me. Okay?"

"Okay."

In the car, I see her wrap and unwrap her fingers so I place my hands over hers for a moment, and glance at her.

"Jaz, it's going to be all right.

"I know, but I'm still nervous."

We check in at the doctor's office and sit for what seems like hours, but in reality, it's ten minutes before the nurse comes to the door.

"Miss Jazmin Grant?"

We both jump in our nervousness and stand.

"Right this way. The doctor will see you in his office. The office is large and decorated with family pictures. We see his two children smiling and he and his wife are playing ball with them. There is another framed picture on the wall of a child's drawing, and Jaz says that there is great potential in that.

"Zack, do you think I'll ever have a family?"

"Jaz, don't be silly. Of course, you will." I tickle her under her chin and smile. "...with or without breasts. They are just not that important," I try to assure her.

She doesn't answer me, but I can see a very slight smile on her lips.

"Jazmin, take my hands." She reaches for them, and I look in her eyes. "Say this with me: On Christ—"

"—the Solid Rock I stand. All other ground is sinking sand." We smile and I hug her, and at that moment the doctor enters. He looks to be in his late thirties or early forties with a friendly smile. For some reason, I stand. I have no idea why. I guess I'm more nervous than I think I am. I feel a little foolish, but I quickly introduce myself, shake his hand, and take my seat again.

"Miss Grant, I know this has been a long time for you, so I'll get right to the point. The news is good."

Jaz takes a quick look at me, and I take her hand in mine.

"You have two tiny cysts that are both benign. They're what we call micro cysts. They're too small to feel, but they can be seen during imaging tests. We picked them up during your mammogram and thought they might just be cysts, but we weren't sure, so we checked them out more closely and everything is fine."

"Do I need to get rid of them, Doctor?"

"No, not at all. Yours don't require any treatment. However, if you see that they're growing or changing, getting larger or painful or otherwise uncomfortable, come back and see me right away, and we can drain them. I'll instruct my nurse to give you some additional information to take with you and read, but at this point there is absolutely nothing to worry about. A lot of times these cysts totally disappear after menopause, but you have a long time before that happens," he smiles.

We both stand and thank the doctor. "Wait here for a moment, and I'll have my nurse come in with the papers and the sheets you need to check out before you leave. You two have a great day."

I shake his hand again.

"We will, Doc."

"You take good care of this special lady, young man."

"I will." When the doctor leaves, we jump together in each other's arms and hug like crazy. We're laughing, smiling, jumping, and kissing. It's hard to describe the relief, the joy, the freedom that showers down all at once. The nurse comes in and we are slightly embarrassed, but she joins in our little celebration with a hardy handshake and well wishes. She gives us the papers to read and the checkout sheets.

In the car, we celebrate again. We bounce in our seats, we laugh, we kiss, and then my angel does what angels do: We pray a thanksgiving prayer. I'll admit, my eyes were not closed. I don't take my eyes from her as she prays, and I see her sincerity, I feel the power of her words, and I'm amazed. I'll admit, I'm also a bit confused about this God we are praying to, but to clear up all of my confusion and lack of knowledge will take a while, and this is Jaz's moment.

"Let's really celebrate," I blurt out in my excitement.

"How? What do you want to do?"

"Do you swim?"

"Yes, I love to swim."

"Let's go swimming. There's so much freedom to swimming, and I think both of us feel so free right now, and I never leave home without my swimming trunks."

We go back to the condo, pick up swimwear and go to the Wellness Center at the Channing House of Design. When we get inside, no one else is there and it's perfect. I dive in the water first and Jaz follows me giggling. As soon as she gets in the water, I splash her, she splashes me back, and takes off with "you can't catch me."

"In your dreams, girl. You're a piece of cake," I brag as I race pass, splashing her with my powerful strokes.

"I'll race you back," she calls out and immediately turns and starts in the opposite direction. I whirl around, and she is close to the end, but not close enough. I take the challenge and still pass her with the advantage she gave herself. At the end, I take her hands and together we dip down in the refreshing water, and I kiss her beneath the surface. We explode up to the surface gasping for air, laughing, and choking a bit. I hug my angel in the water, and playfully tousle her flat short hair.

"Stop, crazy man!" she shouts.

"Make me, crazy girl," and I tousle her hair again and take off down the pool.

My kick is powerful, but I still feel her trying to close in on me so I slow down to be caught just to see what she plans to do. At my side, she grabs my head and tries to dunk it under the water, but my baldhead is slick and I wrestle out of her grip, take her at her waist and toss her over. She bounces up.

"You're gonna pay for that," she laughs.

"How? How?" I taunt close to her face.

"Like this." She whirls around me, jumps on my back and pounds my shoulders from behind. I try to shake her off, but she has some kind of death grip on me, and she won't budge. She keeps pounding my shoulders and yelling something stupid like "Hi-Ho Silver." Finally, we are laughing so hard that she loses her grip and falls back into the water, and I splash her continuously until she takes off down the pool. We play, we laugh, and we have a great time. Out of the water, we look like raisins or dried prunes.

We dress, run by Arianna's office, tell her the great news and take off for lunch at the Fisherman's Pier. It is a fantastic day, but all good things do come to an end, and I have to get back to New York and help my team and the Senior Project Managers put the finishing touches on our multi-million- dollar project that went through like a charm. At the restaurant, I receive a text from one of my bosses with balloons, stars, celebration banners, and a note that says, "*Hoping all is well with you and your friend. Hurry home. You deserve to be a part of this great event!*"

At the condo, I pack my things, call ahead for my private flight back, and check in with D to let him know everything with Jaz is fine, and I'm leaving and making arrangements for him to get his car. Jaz meets me at the foot of the steps, and I take her in my arms. It's hard to say goodbye to this girl, and I can't really figure that out yet. I'm the love 'em and leave 'em kind of guy, but for some reason, this is very different.

"When are you coming home?" I ask playing in her hair.

"Soon, I promise. I don't know the exact date, but soon. I miss you already."

"I miss you more."

"Zack, thank you for...."

"No, don't thank me," I interrupt. "There is nothing to thank me for. I did what I needed to do when you care about someone. I'm sure you would do the same for me."

"Yes, I would."

"Well, I have to get out of here. I had a great time, and you take care of you," I whisper in her ear.

"You do the same, and congratulations again on your team's success."

"Thank you, angel." I take her hand in mine and kiss her fingers. "See, I told you: I'm a fingers and toes man," I joke and she smiles.

"Well, when the time comes, you might add a few other things to your

list."

"I'm sure. If you let me, I might be able to feel those old mean cysts." I wink and smother her for five minutes with longing kisses and reluctant goodbye hugs.

On the plane, I lean my head back, and I'm fast asleep before the take off, and an unusual sense of peace surrounds me.

Back in New York, I make a few calls to my bosses and team, and things are even better than I thought. Our success is huge, and our bosses couldn't be happier with the part that we played. My team is riding high, and life is good. Before I know it, my condo is filled with people congratulating the team and telling us what geniuses we are. I have no idea how this happened, but all of my girls are here, the champagne is flowing, and I can't stop smiling. All of this equals money, money, money and more money, and I couldn't be happier.

I see Summer looking absolutely beautiful standing in the corner alone sipping her drink. I causally move over to her.

"Hi, baby. How are you?"

"I wasn't good. I've been missing you."

"Well we can fix that," I say landing a light kiss on her lips.

"Tonight?"

"Of course, tonight. Why wait, girl?"

"Where have you been, Zack? I've been calling."

"Have you, now? I had to take a little trip, but I'm back now, and you don't have to miss me one more second. Who put this little shindig together?"

"Carl made the calls as soon as we knew you were coming home."

"Well, I'm glad someone called you. You look good, baby."

"Why didn't you call and tell me you were leaving town, Zack? I was worried."

"It was an emergency trip, baby."

"You couldn't call when you got there?"

"I could have, but as you know, I didn't. I'm not on any kind of leash with you, Summer, so don't try to put me on one. We enjoy our little special arrangement so let's not complicate things. I'm here now, and I'm fine. We don't want to mess up our night together, okay, baby?"

I wrap my arms around her waist and pull her to me, but something doesn't seem right. I try to ignore the feeling and once she kisses me, it becomes a little easier, but Jaz is still in the back of my mind. At the end of the night, when all the guests are gone, I clean up the mess they made, and Summer and I make up for lost time.

In the morning, I leave her asleep in my bed. I shower, dress, and head out for my office feeling like I have the world by a string, and however I decide to pull them, it all belongs to me, and everything is under my control.

~ Jazmin ~

8

UNCERTAIN TIMES

Warnings wave persistently, and try desperately to be recognized.

Ihave never known an elevator to take this long to get to the top floor. Realistically, I know that it makes it to the top in less than a minute, but right now it seems that it's taking a lifetime. I'm so anxious to see Zack. It's been two weeks since I kissed him, two weeks since I looked into what he calls his baby browns, and two weeks since I've felt his strong arms encircle me and give me that sly smile that makes me melt into him even though I'm playing the hard- to- get game.

Finally, the elevator opens, and I walk the few paces to his door. I want to surprise him so I don't call and tell him that I'm leaving Virginia today, nor do I call to say I'm coming to see him early tonight. I shift the weight of the beautifully wrapped gift under my arm and smile to myself just before I ring the bell. When the door opens, I'm grinning all ready, and my mouth is shaped to say surprise, but I get the surprise instead. It's not Zack who opens the door. Rather, standing in front of me is a pretty girl, tall, with long flowing dark brown hair. She is dressed in a very short wrap showing her thighs, legs, and most of her breasts. Once she sees me, she folds her arms, leans up against the door jam, looks me up and down, and pops her gum hard.

"Yeah? You lost?"

"No," I reply quietly. "Is Zack here?"

"Hmm...who's asking?"

"Can you just get Zack and tell him that Jazmin wants to see him?"

"Obviously, Jazmin, he's not here." She's looking at the gift now and chewing her gum even harder. "Look, whatever your name is, Zack isn't here right now, and when he does get here, he won't have time for visitors. Take my word for it, Sweetheart. So, I suggest you forget all about your little reunion and gift exchange 'cause I got this covered."

"I see." I hesitate briefly and the girl in the door feels it necessary to make herself very clear. "Look, I don't have a clue why you think Zack wants to see you, but I can assure you that he does not. Like I said, I got this. Summer has this covered."

She unfolds her arms, steps back, stares at me while playing with the gum in her mouth and never takes her eyes from mine until she slams the door in my face. I am shaking, and at first, I have no idea what my next step should be. I walk to the elevator, push the button and let it take me back to the lobby, and then I make a decision.

I dig my cell out of my pocket and because I'm so nervous, I almost drop it. When I get a firm grip, I punch in Zack's number.

"Hey, Babe." He sounds excited.

"Hi Zack. Where are you now?" I hear the contrasting sadness in my own voice.

"I had to work late so I'm still at my office."

"Is it all right if I come by for a minute?"

"Most definitely. I didn't know you were coming back today, but I'll be here. Are you all right? You sound sad. Is everything all right?"

"I'm fine," I lie. "I'll see you in a few."

The drive to his office seems long, and my thoughts are everywhere.

How does this man really feel about me? More importantly, how do I really feel about him? How could he have some other woman staying with him after all we've shared? We've made no commitments to each other, but my reality is staring me in the face. My heart hurts, even though it has no real right to hurt, and other than a few kisses and some long hugs, I've given him no indication that we are any more than just good friends.

I park, reach for the gift, and take the elevator to the twenty-first floor. When I get off the elevator, the area seems a bit deserted, but Zack's secretary greets me and shows me to his office. The area is beautiful and so much like Zack. Everything is shiny, clean, orderly, and very decorated. Standing in the outer area, I brace myself before I turn the knob to his inner office. When he sees me, his grin is immediate and genuine, and he jumps up from his desk and attempts to take me in his arms, but I push back.

"Zack, I just left your penthouse.

"Hmm...so you met Summer."

"Not exactly. Let's say I got some specific directions from Summer. Anyway, that's not important. I just want to bring this gift to you. I know you told me not to thank you, but I have to do something to show you how much I appreciate what you did for me, so I brought you this. When you open it, if Summer doesn't want you to keep it, please, please make sure that it gets back to me intact. This is very special to me, but I want you to have it. Don't let anything happen to it. That's all I ask."

"Jaz, I don't know what Summer said to you, but I'm sorry you ran into that. I'm very sorry. I wish I had known you were coming today, and none of this would have happened, but I can assure you that nothing will happen to this beautiful gift. I don't get many, and I treasure the few that I do get. I guard them with my life," he chuckles nervously.

"Zack, you don't owe me anything, but I owe you, at least, this much. You take care of you, and I'll be seeing you."

"Wait, Jaz." He reaches for my arm. "This is not what it looks like. Summer is just a friend."

"That may be your impression, Zack, but I can assure you, it is not hers. Listen, like I said, you don't owe me anything."

I turn my back and start out of the door when I feel the tears burning my eyes. I don't want him to see them. I don't want him to feel that he owes me anything, and I don't want him to feel guilty about anything. After all, we said that we were just friends, with no benefits.

"I'll find my way out. I'll see you, Zack."

On my way down in the elevator, my tears fall silently, and there is a strange ache in my chest. Arianna's words ring loudly: *He'll break your heart, but you'll probably enjoy the ride.* Somewhere in the back of my mind, I realize that the first part of her statement is probably very true, but the last part, not so much.

~ Zack ~

9

UNCERTAIN FUTURES

When the mind can think of nothing but yesterday and tomorrow, then today gets lost in its own present place.

When Jazmin closes the door, I want to run after her and beg her to give me a chance to straighten things out, but somehow, I know that she will not be able to hear me right now. I saw the hurt in her eyes, and I heard the resignation in her voice, but what I know is that I don't want to lose her friendship, and I'll do whatever I have to in order to salvage it. She means something different to me, and I want a chance to figure out what it is. All of these feelings are so new to me, and I don't quite know what they mean. I look around my office, and for some reason, suddenly it seems empty, and all of my hard work appears to lack something extremely important. This thought is so foreign to me because the money is flowing like crazy, but there's something lacking in my life that I can't put my finger on right now, but, strangely enough, I know for sure that money can't fix it.

I look at the exquisitely wrapped gift resting against my desk, and I pick it up. It's a bit heavy. I move over to a longer glass table, and lay it there. I try to slip off the huge gold and black bow that marks the center, but it's too tight, and I realize that I will have to cut it in order to get inside. I hate cutting it. It destroys its perfection. Anyway, I find some scissors make a clean straight cut, and let the ribbon fall away. I find the source holding this beautiful golden paper together, and carefully slide my fingers underneath, and pull the paper apart without a tear. I open the box, remove the velvet covering and my eyes fall on my prize. I can't believe what I see. It's the watercolor that I wanted to purchase the night of Jaz's showing. She told me it was not for sale, and I now see that it is my special gift. I look at every detail. I run my fingers delicately across the many green shade trees in the background. They almost hide the clearness of the cerulean sky above. My eyes drink in every stroke and slowly move down to the ground where rocks, in beige sands are scattered here and there. Memory helps me hear the babbling brook and feel the coolness of its rippling water. There, center to it all, is the seven-year boy, kneeling at the water's edge fishing out his very special rock. It's a rock like Grandma's and he is holding it up toward the sun. The sparkle invades the shadows of the land and displays an unbelievable brilliance in the reflection of the sun.

Standing, looking down at a replica of that piece of my life so many years ago sends my mind reeling. My legs are suddenly weak, and I feel the tears blur my vision. How did this memory touch the mind and hands of an artist when no one was there to witness this precious moment but me?

I move across the room and sit at my desk. With my hands folded, they serve as a resting place for a head that seems too heavy now to hold itself erect. My mind drifts back to that day—he day this scene was created—the day I lost my only treasure. It was a tiny ship, the kind I dreamed would sail me away one day to a better place—a place away from nightmares and horrific memories. At seven, it was my pride and joy. I had placed it in the bathroom sink, and I splashed the water to make the waves and create the travel. I was the Captain, and they heard me shout, "All hands on deck." Chad had come running and yelled about wasting water and time, pushed me from my duty, and destroyed my ship and all the hands on deck. Sitting here now, I can hear his laughter as clear as day, and I see him slap the tiny vessel from my hands, and I hear it hit the floor. I see his foot rise and tease the destruction of my little ship. I hear my cry, "Stop, Chad," but, it's too late. I see the foot slam and what was my command, lay in shattered pieces.

I remember this very sad time for me vividly. I run from our shabby place, and cross a field with tears streaming down my face. I brush through the trees that scratch my arms, and finally come to my only place of peace—a place where sun, and sky, and water, and birds, and earth surround me in a tranquility that is otherwise unknown to me. I kneel at the water's edge and search the brook for something to own—something that will be mine—all mine and whole. Nothing about it will be broken. My eyes search the brook almost in desperation. I fish out a smooth cool rock and hold it up to the sun. The light finds the miniscule sparkles in it that shimmer in a natural beauty. I can have this. It's mine to keep. I'll think about it when Grandma talks about her Rock. When she sings about it, I'll know that I have my own secret rock. To secure it, I hide it in my little pocket until I get it back home and put it under my very small part of the mattress where it is safe. At night, when the lights are out, and I hear the sounds of sleep, I run my hand under the mattress and hold it until the morning light.

I don't know how long I sit at my desk in this memory that haunts me like so many nightmares of my childhood, but when I come back to myself, I pick up my desk phone and dial my home.

"Summer," I say in almost a whisper, "I'll be home in three hours. When I get there, I want you gone and no trace that you've been there." I give her no explanation, no time to respond, no chance to plead a case. I place the phone quietly back in its cradle, carefully pick up the painting, and leave my office.

The drive to Jaz's condo is brief, so brief in fact that I don't really have time to think about what I want to say. I think to myself that if I had a day, a week, a month, a year would I really know what to say then? Would I have a plan with this girl? She confuses the heck out of me, but what I know for sure, what I'm not confused about at all is that I don't want to lose her. I don't want to lose my angel.

I park, get out of the car, and straighten my clothes. In my nervousness, I even the length of the white scarf hanging around my neck, walk to the door, and let my shaking fingers find the bell. I hear her approach, the lock gives way, and I see the door open to me. I stand still. Our eyes meet and hold together. She's silent with a stare that shows her puffy eyes, and, glancing down, I notice the tissue slightly balled in her hand. I look in her eyes and break the silence.

"I'm sorry." My voice is a whisper.

She reaches for my hand and urges me inside. I close the door behind me quietly and reach for her. We fall into each other's arms and melt into a kiss that tells it all. The passion exudes an equal desire, but I'm careful, and mentally caution myself. *...not too fast, Zack. Don't frighten her.* I pull back and find her eyes.

"Jaz, what are we doing? What do you want from me?"

"Honesty. . . just honesty, Zack. If you have someone else, I don't want to be surprised by that. I want honesty. Can you do that?" I see a tear slide slowly down her cheek, and I wipe it away with my thumb.

"To be perfectly honest, Baby, I don't know. I want to be, but my honesty could cause me to lose the one really good person in my life—you. You're my angel, whole and perfect."

"Zack, your dishonesty can do the same thing even faster. I'm not perfect, and I don't want you to get that kind of image in your mind, but I do have parameters, dreams, and goals for my future, and I'm not willing to compromise all of that. Zack, I don't want to play games. It's simple. If you already have a girlfriend, just tell me. We can still be friends. We haven't passed that point."

"I think we have. Your tears tell me that we have. This ache in my heart when I see that I have hurt you tells me that we have. No, you don't live with me. No, we haven't made love, but there's something inside of me that you have changed, and there is something inside of you that I've changed, and we can't change it back to mere friendship. We have to admit that and see where we go from here."

I take her in my arms now and we stand in silence, feeling our hearts beat together. This is a feeling I have never felt in my life.

After these moments of comfort, Jazmin breaks the silence and moves out of my arms. "Do you want to watch a movie?"

"Sure. Do you have something to make us laugh? I think we need to laugh."

"I do. Look on the shelf and pick out something you like while I make some popcorn and something to drink."

"Sounds good."

I hear her in the kitchen, and I choose a comedy and relax in front of the TV. When she brings in the food and drink, I look at her small frame, her cute waistline, and just the whole beautiful look of her.

"Stop staring, Zack. You make me nervous doing that."

"Why? You look so good to me. Come sit in my lap for a minute." She sits and wraps her arms around my neck.

"Is *she* still there?"

"No."

"What did you do?"

I'm silent at first, and I look at her and run my hand along her back. "Let's just say, I helped her realize that she can't decide my friends, and she had to leave."

"You did that for me?"

"I did that for us."

I smile at her, and we sit together on the floor, watch the movie and enjoy our carpet picnic. We have a great time laughing at the movie and with each other. After the movie ends, our conversation tells us that we have a lot in common. We share things going on in our careers, and our talk is relaxing and comfortable. I thank her for the gorgeous painting, and while I feel like I can almost tell Jaz anything, I know I can't yet reveal the heavy traffic in my brain. I can only talk about a lot of other things that only give a cursory peep into the devastation that I have experienced during my life. It's too heavy for any quick reveal of the problems that lie deep in the recesses of my consciousness. So, we just do the basic small talk. Of course, I've taken the liberty of enjoying a few great kisses, we've hugged a lot and everything is going along fine until just before the clock strikes midnight. That's when she starts acting like she's Cinderella or something like it. She starts cleaning up and rushing me to go because she says that she has to get up early. I really don't want to go. I don't want to miss her, and I can't tell her how badly I want to feel her body next to mine. I want to feel that sense of security that only she seems to give me. We stand together in each other's arms, and I feel like I've reached a good place in my life. I hug her and smile to myself. I'm successful at work. I like what I do. I finally have some real friends, and I may, at some point, have this little church girl in love with me. Who would have thought it? Life is good, and I can't believe my luck or what Derek would say are blessings. I give her a squeeze, and we kiss. I can feel that she has advanced to another level in her passion, but I also sense that she's hesitant to go much further. I feel her hands on my chest slightly pushing me away. I look in her eyes, and move in for more of her, but her resistance is firmer, and I know what that means.

"Goodnight, Lover Boy. Will you call me when you get home?"

"Yes, I promise."

Her voice is soft, alluring and the sound of it melts me. *What is this?* All of it is so unfamiliar to me, but I like it even though it scares me a little. It takes me out of a control that I have always had. It takes my power away so much so that I know that with all of my charm, expertise, experience with women, and manipulations, Jaz is not going to let me stay, so I refuse to lose the argument by asking; however, I also decide that I'm not going home empty handed. I'm going to see a little bit about what this girl has got.

"You're something else, girl." I kiss her again and pull her as close to me as I can. "I miss you already." I hear my own voice, and I know it sounds sexy, but probably to no avail. I secretly smile at my own self- awareness.

"I miss you, too."

I kiss her neck and pull back looking into her gorgeous eyes. I trace her jaw line with my index finger and let it come to rest at her lips. She kisses my fingers and I lean in for a kiss, but I tease and draw back just slightly. I hear a soft sound come from her, and I understand that very well, so I tease more and when I can't wait any longer, I let our lips meet. The kiss is long, sensual, and hungry. I play with the back of her head and hair pushing her mouth closer and giving her everything I've got, and she gives back to me. I gently pull her head back by her hair, and I hear her soft moan again. When I look into her eyes, I see what I want to see, and we kiss again as passionately as before. When the kiss is spent, I look into her eyes again, and that's when I see them—tears.

"What's wrong, Baby?" I whisper.

You're doing it, Zack. You're doing what they said you'd do."

"What?"

128

"You're making me fall in love with you, and you're going to hurt me, and, like they say, I can't seem to help myself from falling."

She's crying now—really crying, and I pull her close to me and feel my own heart break. I know my record better than she ever will, but I don't want to hurt this girl. I want to love her, and I wish there were a book I could read or some instructions on the back of a love potion bottle, but I do have sense enough to know that this kind of knowledge comes a very different way. I just need to find the passage-way to it, and for some reason, for Jaz, I know I'll search relentlessly for it, albeit that may come in a very distant future, but somehow, deep inside myself, I know it will come.

"Baby, listen to me. I'm not going to hurt you. I'll always protect you. You're my angel. Jazmin, you're different. I've never met a girl like you, and I've never felt the things I feel with you." I wipe her tears with my thumbs and mingle the wetness on her face with the wetness of my kisses on her cheeks. I pull her as tightly to me as I can and whisper in her ear.

"Don't be scared, girl. You got a little something they never had." I smile down at her and rock her in my arms. "You just made me feel it, and I've never felt it before. I can't explain the difference, but I feel the difference. Let's just take this slowly, carefully, and not worry too much about the future. Somehow, it seems to always take care of itself. Let's just be this precious moment where our hearts beat togeth-er in an unexplainable love. Actually, that's all we can be absolutely sure about anyway."

She puts her arms around my neck and pulls me to her in a gentle kiss that says a final goodnight. Her hands slide down to my chest, and she reaches behind her and gets my white wool scarf. She puts it around my neck and adjusts it so that the sides hang perfectly.

"See," she smiles up at me. I know a little something about you. You'd never wear a scarf that doesn't hang perfectly. I just hope I don't have to mess it up and strangle you with it one day," she giggles.

"I promise you, you won't," I chuckle. She gives my scarf a little tug, releases me, walks me to the door, opens it, and stands leaning up against the jam with her arms folded from the chill of the late October night air.

"Don't forget. Call me when you get home."

"I will. I'll call as soon as I walk in. Okay? I promise." I wiggle her nose, wink, and walk to my car.

The night is clear, the air is refreshing, and the drive home is peaceful. I wonder to myself if this is what love feels like. I can't wait to get inside and call her to say goodnight again. Does love make you anxious? Does it make your heart skip beats? Do you feel some strange electricity in your stomach? More importantly, does it make you feel like you never want to live without that person being in your life? I smile to myself, and realize that whatever I'm feeling is new and good.

I decide to park in the parking garage tonight, and when the car comes to a complete stop, I reach behind me for the painting, but I hesitate because I really haven't decided if I want to hang it in my apartment or in my office. I know that I want it where I can see it clearly and often, so I leave it for now until I decide the best home for it.

I get out, and listen for the squawk that tells me the car is secure. I almost reach the elevator door that takes me up to the penthouse when I hear running, and before I can look around something hard and steel-like strikes my head. I see stars. I feel dizzy, and I feel unbelievable pain. I stagger to the floor, and I feel blood running down my face, and it is sticky on the cold hard cement floor. Steel-toed shoes kick me in my side once, twice, maybe three times. I try to roll into a ball to protect anything I can. Hands wrench the Rolex from my wrist, search my pockets and grab my wallet. I feel my hand being jerked and my diamond ring twisted from my finger. I feel a sharp piecing stab near my shoulder, the exit of a knife, and I hear voices that sound muffled and strange.

"Come on G. Man, that's enough, and leave that cell, stupid. They can trace us with it."

"Look at the rich man now. What you gonna do? Huh? Huh?"

The last thing I remember is being punched hard in the gut and my head being stomped again and again against the hard cement floor, and then nothing, nothing, nothing but blood, blackness, and loud sounds of silence.

~ Jazmin ~

10

ON CHRIST. . .

*In unexpected moments, the fragility of life nudges us
to acknowledge its reality.*

I dash in the shower so that I'll be out by the time Zack gets home
and calls me. I want to be relaxed and talk a while. I really do already miss him. Out of the shower, I put on some very comfortable
pj's and plop on the top of my bed with big, plush pillows and a
magazine to wait for my call. Another ten minutes pass, and I search
my phone for the third time to see if I missed a call when I was in the
shower, but the phone indicates that no one has called. It's been at
least forty-five minutes since he left my arms, wiggled my nose, and
winked at me. I'm beginning to worry slightly. He said he would call.
He promised. I'm getting this sinking feeling that something terrible
is wrong, but I try to dismiss it, pick up my phone, and punch in his
private number.

"It's me. You know what to do."

"Zack, Baby, where are you? You left almost an hour ago. Call me. I'm worried." It takes about fifteen minutes from my door to his and even in traffic, he should have called by now. The sinking feeling is more pronounced, and I get off the bed and pace a little back and forth. *He promised he'd call. I know he wouldn't break that promise.* I punch in his number again, and the same silly message plays back again, and the sinking feeling takes over my body. My palms are sweaty, and all of a sudden, I'm nervous beyond measure. I have this weird feeling like I hear his voice calling me, but he's not. I realize I can't keep waiting. I have to see what's going on, so I throw on some jeans, a shirt, and my jacket, grab my purse, and head over to the penthouse.

The traffic is comparatively light, but even so the cars seem to be going extremely slow. This is New York City, and I know the cars are not going slowly. This is about my speeding and really breaking the limit. I slow down a bit because I don't want to get a ticket. That will slow me down even more. I reach his place in the usual fifteen minutes, and I see that he did not park in his outside spot, so I wheel into the parking garage. I know that his inside park is just across from the north elevator so I'm making my way in that direction when my headlights fall on the white wool scarf he was wearing.

"That's odd," I mutter.

I stop the car beside the scarf, lean out, and pick it up and that is when real terror cases through my body. The scarf is splattered with blood that is still wet. I drop it back on the cement floor and race to the area where I know he parks. My heartbeat slows when I see his car is in its rightful place and everything looks normal. Now, that is when I get mad.

"I know he didn't forget to call me because that girl is still here. If they fought, and he took her back up to that penthouse to calm her down, I'm done. It's over. I've had it with him!"

I am beside myself now. I can't remember when I've been this angry, but I'm also very determined to confront him, his lies, his betrayal, his mess. No one is going to treat me like this. Here I am running around half dressed after midnight worrying about him, and he's probably snug as a bug in a rug with his booty call. No, this is not happening to me.

I circle around to Guest Parking, jump out in my anger, and almost run toward the elevator. I look inside his car and see the painting on the back seat, and I get more furious. He didn't think enough of my gift to even take it inside. I round the other cars and start toward the elevator, and that is when I see a body collapsed on the cement floor. I know the clothes well, so I know it's Zack. My heart sinks. At first, I stop in my tracks. I'm frozen there. The recognition that my Zack is lying helplessly on a cold cement floor is too much to process in a second. It takes a minute. I stare speechlessly with my hands covering my open mouth, and I stop breathing for a moment. Then reality hits me hard, and I race to him. I kneel at his side, and see blood pooling around him. His face is cut and bruised, and blood has almost covered the front of his shirt. I'm so nervous now that I can barely open my purse to get my phone, but somehow, I manage and dial 911.

"911. What is your emergency?"

"My boyfriend is badly hurt. I scream in the phone. My words are mingled with my crying, my nervousness, and my fear when I say the words that don't even make sense to me. "I don't know if he's alive or dead. I don't want to move him because I see so much blood."

"Can you tell if he's breathing? Is there a pulse?"

"I don't know!" I scream. "Please hurry." I barely hear the operator's instructions, and I try to do what she says, but I don't know what to do. I'm holding the phone to my ear, and I hear her tell me that the ambulance is on its way. It seems like an eternity kneeling over Zack and looking down on him through my tears. He is quiet, lifeless, very still and there is no resemblance to the man who held me in his arms and kissed me passionately just a few minutes ago.

I see his wallet a short distance away, pick it up, and put it in my jean pocket. Kneeling down beside him, I feel a need to be nearer, so I sit close to him on the floor. I want to put his head in my lap. I want to brush his face, and kiss his lips to make him know that everything is all right, but I know movement will hurt him even more, so I lie down in the bloody stickiness. Close to his ear, I whisper to him.

"Baby, I'm here. I'm right here. You're going to be all right. The rescue squad is on its way. You're strong, Baby. You can make it. You have to make it." In my anguish, I try to see any evidence of life . . . maybe just the rise and fall of his breathing, but there is nothing.

"I love you. Can you hear me? I love you." Somewhere inside of me, I hear my words and know that they are true. I know that I love this man lying here still and lifeless. I look at his swollen, bleeding lips that I just kissed. "You can't leave me, Babe. You can't go," I gasp brushing his bleeding face and touching his broken body. "I need you, and I know you need me. Please Zack, fight. Fight to live, Baby. It's going to be all right. I'm here. I'm here . . . right next you. I'm not going to leave you. You said you were going to protect me, and I need you to do that, Baby. I need you. Open your eyes, Zack.

"Can you open your eyes, Baby?"

The siren sounds close, and I scramble up to wave the rescue over to us. Four men jump from the screaming vehicle and begin their work immediately. They gently push me aside several times, but the good news is they find a faint pulse, and now I know Zack is still alive. They pump emergency meds, slow his bleeding, put a neck brace on him, and are in a constant communication with the hospital before they put him on a stretcher, hoist him in the ambulance, and help me inside next him. At the hospital, I hear words like code blue, emergency room, surgery, but no one has the time to explain anything to me at the moment. I am beside myself, and I feel so alone. At the hospital, a very sweet and patient nurse asks me questions about insurance, Zack's identity, allergies, and things like that. I absentmindedly hand her his wallet, and searching through it she finds some of what she needs. Later, I find out that I should have left the crime scene as I found it, but at the moment none of that concerns me. I sit in a quiet waiting room alone in the clothes that share his blood, and I can't stop my fear or my tears. I talk to police, and try to ask them as many questions as they are asking me. When they leave, I pace back and forth for what seems like hours and in truth, it is about three hours before the doctor comes to tell me that Zack is in a coma, that he has lost a lot of blood, but they have been able to stop the bleeding, stitch up his wounds, and stabilize him. His ribs are bruised, and he tells me that Zack was stabbed in the shoulder area, and fortunately, the knife did not enter far and did not touch anything vital. He says that I can sit with him, but he has no idea, at this point, when or if he will come out of the coma. He adds that they are giving him medicines to decrease the swelling in his brain, and that the next 24 hours are critical.

With that news looming over me, I have another mission before I go to see Zack; I do what I think is essential first. I make my way to the hospital chapel to pray. The atmosphere is serene and the lighted candles comfort me. I sit in a front pew, quietly at first, and then, after some moments of stillness, I talk to my God.

Lord, it's me . . . again . . . I come into Your presence right now thanking You for Your grace, Your mercy, and Your goodness knowing that this is what guides You and what saves us. I'm weak right now, but I know that You will make me strong. I'm fearful right now, but I know that You will give me the courage that I need as You remind me of Your Holy Word: 'I will never leave you or forsake you.' Lord, I'm leaning on You right now, and I'm depending on You to light my way.

My friend, Zackary, is laying a few feet away from me, close to death's door, but I'm here praying for him. Right now, I call on You, Jehovah Rapha, the Physician, the Healer to seal up his wounds and mend the broken places. I call on You, Jehovah–Nissi, to spread your Wings of love and protection around his bed and guard him against further danger. I call on You, Jehovah Jireh, The Provider, to send the right doctors, the right nurses, the right medicines, and all that he needs to get up from his bed and be whole again. And then Lord, I call on You, Jehovah-Shalom, Our God of Perfect Peace, to come with holy angels and surround his bed with Your loving kindness so that he might open his eyes with a sense of serenity completely opposite of what he felt and witnessed when last he closed them. Father, he doesn't know you, but I know that you know him, and you have known him since before his birth, and I know that you love him. Watch over him right now, Lord, and give him the miracle and experiences that he needs to come back and learn of You. In the matchless name of Jesus, I pray. Amen, My Lord, Amen.

When I get up, my face is soaked with tears, but I feel a sense of strength and peace that only comes from God. I light a candle, look around this place of quietness and move out into the hallway, and back into the hustle and bustle of hospital life, but with me now, I carry a greater sense of peace, a greater sense of faith and hope that will sustain me through this tragedy. I feel the angels watching over us. I push the door open to the ICU unit, and I hear the drip of fluids, the hum of several machines, and Zack's labored breathing through the oxygen mask. I see the bruises on his face, the bandages covering his cut shoulder, his head, and his split lips. What I can't see are the bruised ribs, the stab wound, and the punctures to his side. I can simply read them on the documents at the foot of his bed. I sit beside him, and I want so badly to touch him. Finally, I find one place, one small place, and I jump at the opportunity it offers me. On top of his covers, he has his hand across his stomach, and I wrap my fingers around his and hold them. I absentmindedly caress his hand from time to time as I talk to him and reassure him.

At some point, when morning breaks, I call his office and inform his secretary. I call Derek in Virginia just to let him know. I break down when I tell him how close I think our friend is to death, but I end assuring him that Zack is strong, and he will pull through all of this and be better than ever. I can tell from Derek's voice that I don't convince him, and he tells me that he's on his way. I try to discourage him since I know that Arianna is pregnant, but he will not hear of it. I am also vaguely aware that there is a brother, but I don't know his name or where he lives. I take out the wallet from my jean pocket, that I'm sure should be with the police, and fortunately, I find a name, an address, a cell number, and the cost of rent. I think I have found the mystery brother. I only know about him because Zack muttered something about him once, but would never repeat or explain what he really said. I called the number asking for Chad Belford.

"It's me, Sweetheart. What can I do for you?"

"Chad, my name is Jazmin Grant, and I'm a friend of Zackary's. Is he your brother?"

"That depends, Sweetheart. What has he done now?"

"Nothing, that I know of, but he is hurt very badly and he is at St. Jude's Hospital. I think you need to come and see him as quickly as you can. He's hurt very badly."

There is a silence at the other end. It's that kind of silence that comes from surprise and fear, a fear that you can sense even at a great distance. Finally, Chad responds.

"What happened?" His voice is serious, confused, and fearful.

"I don't know." Then, I say the words that I can't believe need to be said and that they are coming from me. "All I do know is that if you want to see him alive you might want to come now. Chad, he is very bad. He's in ICU on the fourth floor. He has lost a lot of blood. Tell them you are his brother."

The phone goes dead, and I turn my own phone off and pick up Zack's fingers again. He is so still except for his slight breathing, and every now and then I see his eyelids twitch. At some point, sleep takes over my body, and I don't wake until I see Chad standing over us.

"What's your name again, girl?" *He's gruff.*

"Who are you?" I ask looking up from my seat still half asleep.

"I'm Chad, Zack oldest brother."

"I'm Jazmin. I'm a close friend."

"How close?"

"Enough."

"Hmm. I see. Who did this to him? I want to know."

"I don't know. He left my house, and he was supposed to call me when he got home, but he never did. He had promised that he would so I got frightened that something had happened, and I came looking for him. That's when I found him on the cement floor of the parking garage collapsed in a ball."

"This boy never could really fight. I tried to teach him, but he was always reading a book."

He mutters those words almost to himself, and shakes his head like he's disgusted, and then he does something that frightens me. He starts to shake Zack with his big hands and yell at him.

"Zack, Man you better wake up. Wake up, Man. It's me, Chad. Wake up."

"No Chad. Don't shake him. He's really hurt. He's in a coma! He has stitches, broken ribs, and he was stabbed. You can't shake him!" I'm almost screaming now and pushing Chad away from the bed. The commotion causes the nurse to rush in and tell us both to leave the room. When I look back, I see her checking the fluids and readjusting his covers, but what I don't see is what disturbs me the most. In all of that shaking, shouting, and turmoil, Zack still does not move an inch.

—☳—

Outside, in the hallway, with Zack's brother, I really break down. The tears are unstoppable. All of this is so foreign to me, and it surprises me that Chad, this man who was so gruff and rough just a few minutes ago, wraps his arms around me and tries to comfort me.

"Look Jazmin, Zack can't fight a bit, but he's tough. He'll be all right. I'll kill him if he doesn't wake up soon. ...making a pretty girl like you cry like this. When I get back in there, I'll make him wake up. He's scared of me. He'll wake up. Watch and see."

I push out of his arms, and think to myself that this man is crazy. No wonder Zack keeps him a secret.

"Look little lady, since we got put out for the moment, do you need a ride someplace. Don't you want to clean up and change your clothes?"

For the first time in over five or six hours, I'm aware of my blood-stained clothes. My jeans are colored brown from dried blood. They are stained on one side where I lay next to Zack on the cement floor; my shirt is stained, and my arms are a mess.

"Yes," I manage. "Could you give me a ride back to his parking garage. I left my car there."

"Sure, but maybe you shouldn't drive right now. You're kind of upset. Let me drive you home, and I'll bring you back here if that's what you want."

I hesitate and for the first time I really look at this strange man who is Zack's brother, and I see Zack's same face in his. I see the same honey colored skin, the same big brown eyes, and the same little dimple that shows up when they press their lips together. The difference is Chad is at least an inch taller, a little more muscular and has

144

long brown very neat dreadlocks pulled together and hanging down his back. He is very handsome, just like Zack.

"Come on, Jazmin. Let me take you home to get cleaned up. You know how fanatical Zack is about being clean. He wouldn't want you touching him or his bed looking like you look right now. When he wakes up, you need to be together, girl. That boy is crazy when it comes to a little dirt."

"All right. I guess I should shower and put on something clean."

Chad is the perfect gentleman. He helps me into his beautiful black BMW, and I direct him to my condo. Inside, he takes a seat in my living room, and I take a shower, change into a pair of black slacks, a white silk tank, and a short black jacket. He stands up the minute I enter the living room.

"You feel better now, don't you?"

"Yes, but I'm still so worried. I want to get back to the hospital right away."

"When was the last time you ate something?"

"Last night when Zack came over, we had some snacks."

"Let me pick up something for you on the way or maybe you want to get something at the hospital, but I hear hospital food is gross. I don't know that for a fact 'cause I've never been in a hospital, but I think you need to eat something. When I wake that fool up, you need to be able to help him."

"I'll get something at the hospital."

"OK. Suit yourself."

The drive back is fairly quiet except for the rap music on the radio and the occasional questions Chad asks about our relationship. I'm not in the mood for talking especially to a stranger so he doesn't get too much information, and he seems all right with that. At the hospital, Chad goes to find me a sandwich, and I head straight for Zack's unit. When I push the door open, I see that he still has not moved. I stand at his side and whisper another silent pray when I touch him. I find my seat next to him, and pray. I feel the tears stinging my eyes, but all of that is interrupted when I hear shouting in the hallway, and I know it's Chad. When I open the door, I see him with my sandwich, a soda, and a salad.

"They want to give me all of these orders...what I can do in there and what I can't. That's *my* brother," he shouts. "I don't take a lot of orders, Jazmin."

"Chad, Zack is very sick," I say quietly moving closer to him. I put my hand on his shoulder. "He's close to death so we both have to make a few sacrifices for him."

"You're right," he admits calmly and with a sense of resignation. "Look, I'm going to make a few calls and see what the police know, and if he doesn't wake up soon, I'll have to call our other brothers. They would want to know." He hands me my food, and at that point, I swear, I think I see the glistening of tears, but he turns quickly and leaves.

I know that I should be hungry, but I'm not. I'm just sad and worried. But still, I push the salad around in its plastic container and take a bite or two of the sandwich which feels like cardboard in my mouth. Somewhere between telling Chad goodbye, eating a little, and whispering my constant prayers, I sit in the uncomfortable chair next to Zack's bed and lay my head down on the edge of the bed as close to him as I can get. Somehow, in the midst of ticking and dripping machines, nurses moving in and out checking this and that... in the midst of the sounds of squeaky rubber soles, and the smell of antiseptics, sleep takes over my exhausted body.

Seconds, minutes, and hours tick pass in my sleep, and somewhere in the steady rhythm of time passing, I am nudged awake by the soft touch of a hand playing in my hair. With my eyes still closed in a dream-like awareness, I move my hand to the top of my head, and there is a meeting of the soft, manicured fingers of a friend. When I lift my eyes, I see him quietly looking at me, and without any other motion, a very slight smile crawls, like the steps of an old tortoise, across his swollen lips.

11

LOVE REVISITED

Love comes in different shapes, sizes, colors, and sometimes, shades of doubt and fear.

The rest of the day is a blur to me. Zack being awake and recognizing me is all a blessing. To me, it's a sign that my prayers are being answered. He has so much he wants to say but can't. I can read the desperation in his eyes, but I'm able to calm him, get the nurse and from there, the day is filled with more tests, more police questions, and lots of calls and visitors in the waiting room.

"Jazmin, I've talked with the police, and I think we all will know something very soon."

"That's all good, Derek, but I just want to know that Zack is going to be all right."

"He will be. He's young, he's strong, and he's in very good shape. You know how well he takes care of that body of his. He'll be fine."

The doctor approaches us, and the news is good. He tells me that while Zack was in a coma, he reacted well to the medication and the swelling in his brain is down. For the moment, he has some problems with his memory, and he has some deep bruising to his body. "He will be very sore for quite a while," the doctor tells us, "but he is a very lucky man." He lets us know that even with this news, his visitors should be few at the moment and their time with him should be short. Zack still needs rest. I know that Derek is extremely anxious to see his friend so I go in with him first.

When Zack sees Derek, I see the surprise in his eyes.

"I let you out of my sight for two minutes, and look at you, man. Am I going to have to take care of you all of my life?" Derek grins. How did this happen to a guy with a bunch of bodyguards?"

He takes Zack's hand in his. and they look into each other's eyes, and immediately I can detect years of bonding and the silent unspoken knitting together that comes with years of secret joys and sorrows. They are as close as any brothers. I see the admiration in Zack's eyes, and I see that smile again crawl across his bruised lips. Then I see that he is determined to speak, but I also see how hard it is for him.

"You...tol...told...me to get ..." I see Zack swallow and take a breath.

"Don't try to talk now, Bro. I know I told you to get rid of them, but I didn't think you'd do it," he laughs.

"I"... He closes his eyes, and I can see how tired he is. "I did," he whispers. "You told me to."

"Look, stop talking now. You're going to be fine, and you can count on me to do whatever I can on the legal end. These guys have to serve some time for this."

I see Zack shake his head, and I touch Derek's hand to indicate that we need to let Zack get some rest. I move over close to the bed, straighten the covers, and kiss Zack on his cheek.

"Get some rest, Baby. We'll be right outside the door, and I'll be in to check on you soon. Most of your co-workers are in the waiting room wanting to see you, but you need to sleep now. I'll be back." I turn to go, but I feel him catch my hand, and I look back in his eyes and he mouths the words, "thank you" and he closes his eyes in sleep.

Out in the waiting room, I give them the news and help them understand that they need to come back in a day or two when Zack is stronger. I tell them what I know, and they all seem to understand. Some insist on staying until he wakes, and I understand that. Derek spends his nervous energy talking with the police. I try to make small talk with Zack's office staff, but I find it hard to keep my mind focused on their conversation; I'm really glad when I see Derek at the door, and he beckons for me to come outside.

"I've got some good news, but I can't talk about a lot of it so I'll just tell you this: Where Zack lives, they pride themselves on their state -of- the- art monitoring system. It seems that there were two guys that mugged Zack and both of them are clearly visible on the surveillance tapes placed right outside the elevator door. Allegedly, they thought they had knocked out all of the cameras in the area, but they missed three that are strategically placed in obscure areas, but capture a lot of the garage. They have their full faces and the entire attack is on the tape."

"So they have arrested them?"

"Yes, but let's not talk anymore about that other than to say that I've already gotten one of my New York friends to be Zack's lawyer if he should need one. Look, I have a hotel room not far from here, so I'm going to go and get some rest. You should do the same."

"No, I'm not leaving. I have to know that nothing else bad is happening to him."

"Jazmin, this is an excellent hospital, and they will keep a very close eye on him. You can go and get some rest. You've been through a lot in the last few days. You need to rest."

"No. I have to stay."

When Derek leaves, I look out of the window at the starry night sky and wonder how so many bad things can happen under the umbrella of such a beautiful gift from God. I feel tears burning my eyes, and I turn, push the door open, and take my seat at the side of the man that I know I am falling madly in love with by the hour. I take his hand in mine. I don't want to wake him, but I want to touch him, feel his life, and know from the warmth of his touch that life is still coursing through his body. When he stirs, I'm glad, and I wait to see his eyes open on me again. There is that smile immediately when he sees me, and I know he wants to tell me something or ask me something. I see it in his eyes as he forces the words out that are so hard for him right now.

"Did you..." He takes a breath. "find me?"

"Yes, but stop trying to talk. I found you because you promised me that you would call, and I knew you would never break that promise on purpose, so I came looking for you when you didn't call."

"You... you trusted me?"

"Yes, I trusted what you had said to me, and I knew something had happened for you not to call. Zack, do you remember what happened?"

"Yes. ...most of it, but I don't remember your being with me." I stand up, and look directly into his eyes and kiss his fingers. "Jaz... you...you look tired. Go get rest."

"No. I won't leave you. You close your eyes and get some rest so you can get better soon." I see him nod his head, close his eyes, and sleep takes him in a matter of seconds.

I sleep fitfully through the night waking each time I hear any kind of sound from Zack. I check on him almost as many times as the nurses on duty. Occasionally, they make a few comments to me when they know that I'm awake. They ask me how I'm doing... if I need another pillow. They tell me that Zack is doing well, that his blood pressure and his pulse are good. They are very encouraging, but until he is out of ICU, I cannot be satisfied.

In the morning, they bring in food for him, which I'll admit we share because he's not hungry, but I am and, I don't want to leave him. The doctors come in and deliver the GREAT news. They are moving him to another room because he is so much better. The morning is busy with more tests, and the move. He no longer needs the oxygen, and all of the tubes and dripping machines are gone. He looks a lot better, and he says he feels better. During this time, I run home to my condo, take a quick shower, grab a bite to eat, go to Zack's place, retrieve my car, and drive back to the hospital. I find him in a private room sitting up, and my heart leaps with a secret joy.

"Hey girl. I was wondering where you disappeared to."

I want to leap on the bed and give him a big kiss, but I know that is not wise so instead, I smile and move slowly over to his side.

"Oh, you woke up long enough to miss me, huh?" I tease.

He takes my hand. "Yes, I missed you. I saw you asleep last night... when I woke up once, ...but I didn't touch you ...because you needed to rest."

Before I can answer him, we both hear loud voices outside his door, and we both know that it's Chad. The door swings open wide, and a grinning Chad bursts through it like some wild tornado.

"Hey, Man. ...You looking better...sitting up and everything. I'm glad to see the baby browns. How you feeling?"

I see Zack take a deep breath. "I'm fine. I'm fine, Chad," he answers quietly.

"Hey Jazmin. You stay all night again?"

Zack looks puzzled. "You know Jazmin?"

"Yeah. I took her home to get her out of them bloody clothes. Man, she was a mess. You wouldn't have been able to take it. I told her she had to clean up before you woke up cause you can't take no dirt," he laughs. Look, I don't have much time, but I got a big surprise for you. Close your eyes."

"Chad, stop playing games. I hear I had my eyes...closed for almost three days. That's long enough."

"Well, that's true. Turn your head then. I got a big surprise."

"Man, stop playing. I'm not turning my head. It hurts, so stop talking so loudly."

"OK, whatever. I got a huge surprise."

I can tell that Chad is happier than he has been in a long time, and he is happy that he can do something good for Zack. He was very worried about him too, even if he didn't want to admit it. I got a quick glimpse of his tears the first day, so seeing Zack sitting up this morning is a special treat for him. Zack, on the other hand, seems testy, impatient, and not too happy to see his surprise.

"You ready?" That got a very slight smile from Zack.

"Yes Fool, I'm ready."

"See, you won't be calling me bad names when you see my surprise."

"Well, as long as you're taking ...to show me...I might be in another ...coma before I see it."

"Nope, no more comas. Ready?" This time Zack just looks at me, rolls his eyes, and slightly smiles.

"OK. Here is comes."

He rushes to the door, stands there for a brief moment with a big grin on his face and finally pushes the door open. Zack sees his surprise, and, for a moment, he's speechless.

"I don't ... I don't believe this." He is shaking his head in disbelief.

I'm looking from Zack to them and from them to Zack as they move close to the bed. Everybody is grinning from ear to ear.

"I got all your brothers here to see you, Zack."

"So glad you're better, Man. Chad scared us to death."

Later, I learn that is Andrew or "Drew" with the big smile and drawing a bigger smile from Zack as they have an awkward hug. I can tell that Drew is afraid he might hurt him if he touches him in the wrong place.

The next to do the awkward hug is Louis and then Colin. I see tears in Zack's eyes, and I see tears in theirs.

"It's good to see you guys. It's... been a minute," Zack grins.

"See, I told you you'd like my surprise."

"I love your surprise, Chad," Zack admits.

I look at these three handsome men who all share Chad and Zack's face with just a few differences. I can tell that Colin is the youngest of the three and the closest to Zack because they hug a little longer and, though careful, I can see that they linger with each other. I see Zack wink at him.

"You look good, Colin. You taking care of yourself?"

"Yeah, obviously better than you," he grins. "I'm a doctor now, Zack. I'm a fourth- year resident in LA, but I keep up with you still."

"I know. I keep up with you, too. I might be able to use you since... you're a head doctor," he chuckles.

"I'm going to be a Neurosurgeon, but you don't need me. I checked already. You're going to be fine. The two brothers release each other, and then I see Louis move in to shake Zack's hand again.

"You... still working on cars, Lou?"

Yeah, I'm still a mechanic, Man, but I had to go back to school with all this technology."

"That's good," he nods. "School is always good."

"And Drew, I know you're teaching Biology at a high school in Chicago. I guess collecting all those bugs you used to show us paid off for you," he laughs.

"Well, it took me a minute, but I made it. I was lost for a while... getting in minor scrapes, you know...but...I'm sure you also know being lost doesn't buy bread and the truth of the matter is it disappointed too many people I loved...people who were trying to help me, so I had to get it together. I kept thinking about something you used to say to us all the time before the family split up."

"What? I was so much younger, and no one listened to me. You listened... to something I said?" he chuckles.

"Yeah, actually, I tell it to my high school kids now. 'If it is to be, it's up to me.'"

"That's right, Brother." Zack winks and tries to reach up and pat Drew's face, but the move is too painful, and he settles for touching his arm. Zack looks around at all of his brothers together again, and I see a single tear travel down his cheek. He beckons me over to him and takes my hand. "Look guys, I want you to meet Jazmin...Jazmin Grant. She found me, and saved...my life."

They all smile and tell me how grateful they are, and while I hear all of the accolades and appreciate their gratitude, the thing I notice most ...the thing that stings a bit ...the thing that I resent...and what makes me feel so much like an outsider at this reunion is that Zack does not even say that we're friends...just that I found him and saved his life. I think to myself, there is a lot missing from that statement, and there is a lot packed in that statement. I try to ignore it and enjoy the laughter, jokes, and reminiscence about old times. While they are laughing and remembering, at some point, I see Zack drop off to sleep, and it's at this point that the brothers decide to let him rest while they all go out to get something to eat. In my sadness, I decide to go home, but before I exit the room, I look back at this man sleeping peacefully, this man I think I love, and I wonder to myself what I'm doing and why I'm doing it.

At home, I shower, do a little cleaning, and decide to go to the studio to check on things; however, keeping busy doesn't do what I want it to do. It doesn't keep my thoughts from Zack, and it doesn't keep me from thinking about his insensitive omission. At this point, I'm wondering what I really mean to him, how he really feels about me, and if there is any future for us. My heart is hurting. Maybe I expect more than he is willing to give, even more than the capacity he has to give, but one of our last conversations before the mugging made me think we were moving closer to something important. His kisses feel real, his embraces are convincing, and his words speak of a growing love, but introducing me as the person who found him and saved his life sounds like a stranger that just happened by. Did I just happen by his life, and is Derek right? He says Zack can hurt me at a moment's notice and never look back. In my heart and even in my mind, I feel differently. I hear Zack's voice, and I can't believe that he wants to hurt me, but what I don't know is essential: Does he have the capacity to help himself? I want desperately to believe the words he speaks: *You're different. You have something the others never had. You make me*

feel it, and I've never felt it before. Why does he say these things if he doesn't mean them?

I wheel my car into my parking space, get out, and look up into the navy- blue star filled sky. I choose one and wish on it, then shake my head and smile to myself at my own foolishness.

Inside, I throw my purse on the love seat, move into my bedroom and plop on my bed. I kick off my shoes and fall back on my pillows that are still in the middle of the bed where I left them when I went to find Zack. I close my eyes, and I see him. I open them, and his smile is staring me in the face.

Good grief, girl, you've got it bad. You need to get a grip. You don't even really know this man. I get off the bed and snap on the television and surf the channels when my phone buzzes.

"Hello?"

"Hey Jazmin. I thought I'd see you at the hospital, but I guess you had to get some sleep," Derek says in his lawyer voice. By his tone, I know he's after information as usual, but he will get none from me. I don't need an *"I told you so"* moment right now.

"Not really. I had to check on my studio today. I hadn't been by there is three days so I needed to see if it was still standing," I giggle.

"Ahh...I see. Well, our guy is a lot better, and the police have made some great progress. They questioned Zack this afternoon about what he remembers, and he did great. He even identified both guys from some mug shots even though the police had their images on tape. He spent the rest of the time with his brothers, and even though he's in a lot of pain, he seems pretty happy right now. I gather they haven't seen each other in a very long time. It seems that they have been split up for quite a while living in different parts of the country. Chad took care of Zack for most of his childhood, but after their grandmother died, the others went to people on their mother's side. I know they all have had a pretty hard life before the family had to break up, and go separate ways."

"Zack doesn't talk much about his past, so I don't know a lot about what he experienced. I guess he'll tell me when he's ready."

"Yeah, I guess you're right."

"So, what was Zack doing when you left the hospital?" *I couldn't help myself from asking.*

"... inquiring about you. He wanted to know who had seen you. He asked where you were, but we didn't know. Honestly, Jazmin, is everything all right?"

I take a deep breath. I don't want to sound petty, and I don't want Derek to have too much information that he can use to hammer me over my head, like I know he will do if he gets half a chance. Like Arianna says, "*The lawyer will be home.*"

"I hear the deep breathing, Jazmin. You may as well tell me. I know something is wrong. What has he done? No one has been able to tear you away from his side since you got him to the hospital, and now you're hiding out, and you haven't checked on him since this morning. Clearly, you're running away again. What is it?"

"Derek, stop being a lawyer and be a friend," I snap.

"I'm trying. I keep asking questions because you aren't giving me any answers. I'm about to leave in an hour and I don't want to leave you in despair. I'm being a friend whether you realize it or not. I told you to be careful with Zack. I told you to be careful with your heart because he won't be."

I'm silent because what he's saying is irritating me to no end.

"Jazmin, you have to protect yourself, but you are a grown woman, and you can make your own choices. When it comes to Zack, you'd better make the right ones, or you'll be very hurt. He'll walk away unscathed, Jazmin. I'm trying to tell you."

"You're like a brother to him, but you're so hard on him. Why?"

" It's because I know a lot more about him than you do, Jazmin, and I have been deeply hurt by him, but I can't just leave him to destroy himself. I'm always trying to help him no matter what. Everybody needs somebody, and I guess I'm his somebody. You do what you want as I know you will. I just want you to be careful. I don't want to see you hurt. Whether you realize it or not, I still am very careful when it comes to Zack because I know he can't seem to help himself, but I don't want to ever again be on the receiving end of his dysfunction."

"I'll be as careful as I can, Derek. I promise," I say softly and sincerely.

I hear him sigh loudly, and he tells me that he's leaving for Virginia. He has to "get back to Ari." We say our goodbyes, and he makes one more attempt to find out what happened in the last few hours with Zack and me, but I refuse to say anything before I talk with Zack. I think I owe him that much.

When the phone goes dead, I glance at the time, and see that it's after nine. I wonder if Zack is asleep by now, if he has thought about me before he drifted off or if he just went to sleep with an "out of sight out of mind" kind of attitude. I undress and decide to go to bed early when my phone buzzes, and I see Zack's face.

"Hi."

"Hi yourself. Where have you been all day? I'm missing you."

"Really?" I ask sarcastically.

"Yeah, really. Are you coming back tonight?"

"No."

"OK. Do I dare ask why not?"

"Zack, I'm tired."

"I see.... Ok, now tell me the truth. What's wrong?"

"Nothing. I'm tired," I snap. There is a long silence.

"Jaz, from what I understand, before today, you hadn't left my side more than an hour since all of this happened...I understand that you lay down beside me in my blood and willed me to live when life was slipping away. I hear that you've talked to my doctors, entertained my friends, kept watch over me moment by moment, and now you're telling me that you left me today because you're tired. I don't buy that. Tell me. What's wrong? Did somebody say something to hurt your feelings or something?"

"...or something."

"Am I supposed to guess... or are we going to be adults and you tell me?"

"Adults, huh? Do adults forget, so quickly, how much they're been kissing on each other or the words they're spoken of love and just introduce that person as the person who found them and saved their life?" I snap.

"What are you talking about?" I hear puzzlement, irritation, and impatience in his voice.

"I'm talking about the way you introduced me to your brothers. You said I was the one who found you and saved your life. That could be any stranger who just happened by, Zack. Not somebody who purposefully went looking for you, somebody you kissed over and over, held in your arms and said that this feeling you have is something different...something you're never felt before. I told you that you were going to hurt me...that everybody is telling me you're going to hurt me...to be careful of you."

"Hmm...and you keep looking for it, right? You keep expecting it? I can't just be myself with you, right? I have to be forever on guard that I'm not falling into some trap that I don't even know exists, right? You can't take my word. Nooo, you have to keep waiting and expecting some hammer to fall and then you're ready to run... like you did today. I told you, I don't want to hurt you. I feel something different with you, Jazmin, and *that* is the truth, but you can't hear that for hearing the noise from everybody else, especially Derek. Listen, Derek is never going to tell you to love me. Ok? As much as he loves me, he is never going to take a chance telling you to do the same, and I deserve that from him. I have to deal with my own past sins, but that has nothing to do with how I feel about you. Look, I can't do this tonight. If I could, I'd come over and try to straighten this out, but you know that's impossible for me right now. I have to go. This is starting my headache all over again. I got to go."

Without letting me say a word, I hear the phone go dead, and I feel the tears forming and spilling over as I fall back on the bed in exasperation. I glance at the clock on the wall, jump up, get dressed and drive back to the hospital. When I get there, the hall lights are dimmed, it's quiet, and I know they have now switched over to the night shift. I glance at my phone and see that it's after eleven o'clock. When I push Zack's door open, he's sitting up in a very dimly lit room staring into space. It's quiet, and I stand in the half- opened door, and we stare at each other for a moment.

"How's your headache?" I ask quietly.

"Better... now that I see you." He holds out his arms to me, and I almost run into them, but I'm careful. I don't want to hurt him, and I know his body is very sore.

"I want to hug you so tightly, babe, but I don't want to hurt you."

"You already did, on the phone. That hurt far more than these little bruises. I'm sorry if I hurt you. I really didn't mean to at all. Jaz, I'm not going to let you stay angry with me, and I'm not going to let you believe what other people say about me, especially Derek. I need you in my life, but more than that, I want you in my life. You mean everything to me."

"Then why did you introduce me as just the person who found you and saved your life? You didn't add anything else."

"Baby, I just came out of a coma. I have had one of the most horrible things to happen to me. I guess I just wasn't thinking at the time."

"Hmm...I don't buy that. The way you say you feel about me should be the first thing you think of when you talk about me, but it isn't."

"Well, you weren't here the rest of the time when I couldn't stop talking about you all day. I told my brothers what you mean to me, and I don't really share a lot about my personal life with anyone other than Derek. He's about the only one who really knows who I am, and why I am the way I am. He's cautious of me, but he has very good reason. It baffles me every day, how he can still be my best friend, but he is. He just doesn't want me to hurt you, and I won't. You're my angel. Come here, baby. Lie here with me tonight, and let me just hold you as best I can. Please."

I know I'm not going to get inside the bed with him, but I do move over on top of the bed, and pull a blanket over me. Zack and I hold each other as best we can through the night. Every now and then I feel him kiss the top of my head, I hear him sleep, I feel him move in his pain and suck in his breath when the pain is unexpected and unbearable. ...but me? I feel a sense of peacefulness in his arms...a sense that I have finally found where I actually belong, and in my prayers, I have a feeling of serenity that for some reason, my God has put me here "for such a time as this."

~ Zack ~

12

SHATTERED PIECES

Old habits and distant memories make their appearance at will.

Most of my days in the hospital are a huge blur, but there are four things that are crystal clear: Jaz's devotion to me and my appreciation for it, the sheer joy I experienced seeing my brothers for the first time in years, and the unbearable pain coursing through my body. Jaz has no idea how comforting her presence has been for me, and Chad has no idea how grateful I am for the gift he gave.

After some painful days, too many tests, and just the longing to be in the comfort of my own place, I'm thrilled to be going home in the morning. Jaz and Chad have already selected and brought me clothes to wear home, and I am impatient for the sun to rise.

I feel Jaz near me on the bed and I am so grateful for her presence. I try not to toss and turn because of both the pain and my desire not to wake this woman who has been everything to me through this horrible ordeal. I close my eyes and think about my visits with my brothers...getting reacquainted with them again...for some, even a first time really seeing who they are. I was so young when they all left home and traveled to places unknown. Only Chad stayed to take care of me. At the beginning of his junior year of college, he quit school, gave up his dream of becoming an architect and his full ride to Columbia U, got a job working at a clothing store, and made sure that his hours fit my schedule. Because he didn't trust the neighborhood, he saw me get on the school bus in the morning and was there to pick me up most days in the afternoon. He helped me with my homework, went to PTA meetings, was my father on Father/Son Day, and generally became my very strict parent who insisted on straight A's at all cost or there was hell to pay.

Those were hard days for me, but seeing Colin in my mind's eye now makes me smile and remember the few good times we used to have together walking the tracks, fishing in what we called "the polluted hole," climbing trees and doing whatever we could to escape the reality of the life we were living.

"Colin, a doctor—amazing," I whisper and smile in the darkness. It was not until yesterday that I learned that Colin had gone to live with my mother's sister in Florida, an aunt we had never met. She is married to a doctor and Colin was raised well in an affluent family, going to all of the best schools and living the lifestyle of the rich.

He and I had been close pals because we were the youngest— only two years apart. He was nine on The Day of Horrors, and of course, I was seven. He never blamed me for what happened, so we had our own pact and shared our secrets with each other until Grandma got sick and died. Colin left me when I was twelve and he was fourteen. The departure was gut wrenching, and when he was gone, I felt a loneliness that was unbelievable—a loneliness from which I have never been able to recover. So many nights I cried for him, and there was no one to comfort me...no one to talk with about it...no one who seemed to care that my best friend in all the world was gone, and I didn't know where.

Grandma was gone, too, and on the Day of Horrors, Mommy had left me far too soon. She was lying in a pool of her own blood pleading...begging Chad to take care of me—making him promise that I would be successful in life. When I cannot avoid a trip back to that place of anger, of hate, of helplessness on that day, I see my Mommy clutching desperately to Chad's shirt, him crying, her whispering and choking out her words, and in that final moment, him hiding my eyes and screaming for me to hide. Lying here, in the quietness of my hospital room, I try to shake these thoughts away, scare the demons back to their pit, and bury the sights and sounds in the deep place where they usually reside, but in the attempt to push them into their secret hole, I wonder to myself, *after Mommy left,* what would have really happened to me if it had not been for Chad, my grandma, and Mr. Garrison, my teacher.

Lying here, with sleep avoiding me, my thoughts fly back to the day Colin left. In the dark stillness of this room, the sounds and colors of that day parade before my eyes and ears as if the events are current. It is a very sunny Saturday. We get up early and because there will be no breakfast, lunch, or dinner today, we decide to walk down by the railroad tracks to forget our hunger or steal a loaf of bread and some fruit from Gracen's Market. I remember Chad calling us back just as we get to the edge of the yard. I remember how sad his voice sounds, and I remember what Colin whispers to me.

"Oh man, what now? Be cool, so we can still go."

I remember us standing still for a moment, and Chad losing his tempter as usual.

"Y'all deaf or something. I said come here." At that point we both run to him because we understand well what might happen if he has to call us a third time. He tells Colin to wash up because he's going to take a little trip, and I remember asking if I can go, but Chad just looks at me and says nothing. In about an hour, a shiny black car drives up and a man in a suit and a dressed- up lady in high heels get out. They talk quietly with Chad for a minute, and Chad talks quietly with Colin. I see him hug Colin and hand him an old suitcase. All of it is very strange. Colin is crying. Chad is crying too, and the lady gently takes Colin's hand and puts him in the backseat of the car. The three of them drive off with me running behind the car shouting, "I wanna go," but the car speeds away with Colin looking through the back window waving at me. I never see him again until he's thirty years old walking through the door of my hospital room.

Somewhere between my last thoughts of Colin and the breaking of dawn, I sleep. I wake to sounds of water running and Jaz singing a soft song behind the bathroom door. When she comes out, she looks refreshed and beautiful.

"Well, sleepy head, today is your big day."

"Yeah, and I can't wait."

"I'll wait outside while you clean up and dress. Your nurse and Chad are going to help you." She stops and smiles from the door.

When the nurse comes in, I find out that Colin has been invited to look at my last x-rays with my doctors and Chad, as my next of kin, is also in on the reveal. I'm told that they all will be in to talk with me soon. When my nurse leaves, Jaz returns and finds me sitting in one of the hospital chairs waiting impatiently for my release. She's prattling about something that does not really get my attention when I remember something very important to me and panic hits me like a ton of bricks.

Jaz, where are my clothes?" I ask cutting into the middle of whatever she's saying. She hesitates a moment trying, I'm sure, to understand what I'm asking her since I'm already dressed in the clothes she brought to me.

"Jaz, where are my clothes?" I ask again with more anxiety. I see her speechless hesitation again, and I realize that she notices the extreme change in my demeanor, and I can tell that it's frightening her.

"Zack, you...you just put on your clothes. What's wrong with you?"

"No, not these clothes. The clothes I wore here. Where are they?" I ask in the same desperate voice.

"Oh, I see. I'm going to bring them, Babe, when we get ready to leave. I don't think you need to see them. The police brought them back to the hospital in a plastic bag, and they are really no good now. They can't be cleaned especially good enough for you," she laughs trying to lighten the mood.

"Jaz, I want them."

"Zack, you..."

"Now, Jazmin. I want them, now!" I shout, uncontrollably, but at the moment there is nothing even I can do to quiet my fear. I see her hesitate again, but turn and go to the closet and retrieve the plastic bag and slowly bring it to me. My hands are trembling as I take it from her. I look at her and see her distress, and I know that she can feel mine. I rip off the ID tag, and riffle through the bag. I see the bloody shirt. I see the T-shirt and the belt. I grab the slacks that are stiff with my blood. I search the pockets, both those on the sides and the ones in the back—nothing. I turn the side pockets inside out—nothing. I pull out the inside of the back pockets—nothing. I throw them on the floor and frantically empty the remaining contents of the bag on the floor and try to bend over to search more thoroughly, but the pain in my rib cage is unbearable, and I cry out in unexpected agony and distress. Jaz quietly helps me straighten up to a sitting position.

"Zack, what is it? You're going to hurt yourself and end up back in that bed if you don't stop. What is it? Tell me so I can help you."

I look at her, and as bewildered as I am, and as helpless as she looks, I don't want to tell her because I know intellectually how silly it will sound to her; however, for me, at this moment, I'm desperately seeking one thing, and one thing only—the rock that I know was in my pocket because I carry it with me all of the time. I never leave it anywhere. Because I have to know for sure if it's gone, I slowly let the words slip pass my still swollen lips.

"There was a rock in my pocket...I had it in my right-side pocket. It's not here."

She moves over close to me now and puts her hand on my face and gently lifts my head to see her eyes.

"Baby it's not here because I have it. I knew when I saw it that it was extremely important to you, so I kept it for you."

I feel my shoulders fall. I hear the deep sigh from my inner being, and I sense the tension melting away as I listen to her words...words that reveal another chapter and verse of the days that I have lost...time that has ticked pass my awareness.

"When the police returned your things, I saw that they had put it in a small plastic bag and I put it in my purse."

I watch her move over to the small chest of drawers, take her purse from it, come back to me, and kneel down at eye level in front of me. She opens her purse and pulls from it the plastic bag, and takes out my prize possession; she takes my hand and places the rock in the center of my palm, and closes my hand into a fist. She covers my hand with hers, and lets her long eyelashes flutter away her tears.

I don't try bending again, but I take her hand in mine, kiss it, stand up and pull her gingerly to me.

"Baby, how can I ever thank you for everything you're done for me? How can I thank you for knowing what I need and when I need it?"

"Maybe one day, you'll let me explain why you no longer need to carry your rock...that there is a Rock higher...maybe, you'll do that for me."

"The One my Grandma talked about, right?"

"Right."

"Well, it's getting to a point when I'll do almost anything for you," I smile.

"Almost?"

"Yeah, I have to save a little something." I pull her as close to me as I can without pain, kiss her, and we slightly hug.

"I've got to work on those pitiful lips of yours when we get home," she giggles.

"What's wrong with my lips?" I ask teasingly. "You still want them, bruised and swollen."

"Let's put it this way: You still want me to want them," she giggles. "I'm going to see if the nurse can give me something to help them heal faster. Ok?" She moves out of my arms and at the door turns and copies me. She winks and smiles while I slowly try to sit back down without screaming again.

After about five minutes of sitting alone, I start to feel the anxiety creeping back. I hope they aren't finding something that will make me have to stay here longer. I really want to go home. I see the door push open slightly, but no one comes in and then I see it close. About ten seconds pass, and I see the door push open again, but still, no one comes inside.

"Jaz?"

"No, it's me. ...sorry to disappoint...." I see only her face playfully pop inside the slightly opened door.

"Summer," I say quietly with a certain allure to my voice.

"Hi, baby. Jazmin told me I could come in to see you," she lies sashaying in knowing how sexy she looks in her tight jeans, long hair falling over her pea green cutoff top, her sassy short coat and those very high heels.

"Really? That was kind of her."

"Well, we did have words in the hall, but it's all right. She's not bothered by it. She's so sure of herself."

"What did you say to her, Summer?"

"I told her not to get too comfortable with you, Baby. That she's just a detour in the road. You know you want me, Zack."

"You know, Summer, you make a detour when you have to make a detour, not because you want to. What I have with Jaz...Jazmin is not a detour. I don't have to make changes if I don't want to do so."

Summer puts her hands on me trying her old tricks, but first of all, I'm in no shape to respond and secondly, I've learned a few more life lessons since I saw her last.

I move her hands from my face. "Summer, have you forgotten our agreement: Friends with benefits and no commitment?"

"Yeah, but that was then and this is now."

"No, that was then and that is now."

"Do you have the same agreement with Jazmin?"

"Well, it's none of your business what I have with her, but I'll tell you. No, we don't have that agreement. Jaz and I have never made love. She believes in marriage first then lovemaking, something you wouldn't know anything about."

"And I'm sure for many days and nights, you're glad I didn't. Right, baby? but great. That's great news for me. That just means she will never have you. Excellent, baby! I like that. You really know how to play both games don't you. You know you'll never marry that little girl." She's laughing now and trying to touch me in places that she knows are hot spots for me, but again I push her away.

"Summer, you need to leave."

"Why? So that little girl can have you all to herself? She told me in the hallway, 'you have no idea who the man is in that room.'" She bats her eyes and changes her voice to try to sound and look like my Jaz, but she is not even close.

"I think I know you very well. I know every inch of your body, baby."

"Hmm, in case you don't know, sex is one thing, but love is another. Jaz has never had my body, but take my word for it, she knows me far better than you do. You see, there is a big difference between knowing someone's body and knowing their heart."

"I don't think you've been calling me to take a look at your... heart."

Baby, you come every time I call, and you know why I'm calling. You're a beautiful woman, but you sell yourself too short."

"Just for you."

"It doesn't matter if it's just for me or one thousand like me. It all shakes out the same way. You don't demand any respect, and you don't get any. So, that's a problem for you. You're not the girl that men take home to Mama.

She leans over close to my face, with both of her hands on my knees, and looks directly in my eyes. "Well, since you're not the marrying type, and you don't have a Mama, who cares? I wouldn't have that option anyway."

The reference to Mommy stings and makes me angry too so I push back.

"Look, thanks for coming, but I need some time alone before these doctors come in again."

"Ok, baby. You call me when you feel better. You're a lot better than the first few days I came and they wouldn't let me see you. At least you're awake even if you are talking nonsense. You take care." She leans over to kiss me, but I lower my head.

"Ok...be that way, but you'll call me, and I'm patient."

"Summer, don't count on it."

She leans over with both of her hands on my knees, again close to my face. "Hey," she touches my chin and giggles. ...little girl ain't giving up nothing...you'll call," she smirks looking directly in my eyes. "I know you, Baby...every... inch of you."

She moves over to the door, looks back at me and winks. "You'll call. When you're feeling better...more like yourself, Zack, don't hesitate because I already hear the phone ringing." The door opens, and she slips back into the hallway. I take a deep breath, exhale loudly feeling what she stirs inside of me, and as much as I don't want her to be, I wonder if she's right.

13

HOME AGAIN

Sometimes only playfulness can revitalize life.

When the door opens, again I see Jaz, Chad, Colin, and my two doctors. Chad rushes over to stand beside me, and Jaz stands on the other side holding my hand. At first, I feel nervous wondering if they are about to tell me something that I don't want to hear, but Chad helps to erase that quickly.

"Well, little Bro, you ready to go home?"

"Yeah, I am." I look at the doctors standing in front of me. The surgeon, Dr. Mason, speaks first. "Well, everything is looking good. You'll be very sore for a while and we'll have to watch how you heal, but we're going to release you today as long as you promise to take it very easy for a while."

"I can do that."

"You're a very blessed young man. You're strong and you take good care of your body and that has helped you a lot. You have to keep taking care of yourself. We'll give you some specific instructions and if, when you get home you have some questions, don't hesitate to call us. We're here to take good care of you. All right?"

"Yes, Sir. Thank you all for everything."

I stand and shake my two doctors' hands and they leave. Colin tells me a few more things about taking care of myself, and I let them all know that I'd rather talk at home. I'm ready to go. They bring in a wheel chair. I try not to get in it, but they insist and when I see the long distance from my room to the car, I secretly admit to myself how glad I am that they didn't listen to me.

At the first sight of my apartment building, I see the horrible scene in my mind, and I try to shake it away. Even though I know the two guys who attacked me are safely locked away, that they were caught on camera, they have admitted the crime, and my things have been returned to me, I still have a sense of uneasiness looking at the place where I almost lost my life.

At my door, I think I hear noises and it frightens me, but I don't want anyone to know how shaky I am so I say nothing. Chad opens the door, I walk in, and people are everywhere shouting, SURPRISE!" I see a big banner on the wall reading, "WELCOME HOME, ZACK!" Balloons of every color are everywhere, and the scene looks like something out of a crazy movie. I feel weak and silly. I have no idea what to say. All of my aplomb is gone, and I'm standing in the doorway speechless with, what I think is a very silly grin on my face.

My boss comes over first and slaps me on the back at which point I stifle the scream from the instant pain.

"Welcome home, son. It's so good to see you on your feet again."

"Thank you, Sir. It's good to be home."

I move into the room and it's impossible to miss the fact that Summer is here standing in front of me. I don't miss her wink or her smile, but also, at the moment, I don't care about either which I quietly communicate to her by rolling my eyes. Others come to greet me, shake my hand and tell me how glad they are to see me, how good I look, how lucky I am to be alive, and how much they are missing me. They ask when I think I'll be back to work and back to my old self. Someone puts a drink in my hand, and I feel it shaking there. I take a little sip and since I'm not much of a drinker, it doesn't go down very well. And then Jaz comes to my rescue. She excuses me from the group.

"I have something I want to show you, Babe."

She walks me down the hall, away from the crowd, away from the noise and into the quietness of my bedroom. As the door closes, I close my eyes, lean up against the door, and take a deep breath.

"Open your eyes, Babe and look over your bed."

I open my eyes on the beautiful painting that I had left in my car. There it is, hanging over my bed with a little light that showers down a soft ray over the beauty of the watercolors that create an important image from my past.

"Jaz, it's so beautiful and, more than that, it's so very comforting to me."

"I'm glad you love it. I had the studio hang it yesterday, and I think they did a wonderful job."

"Yes, they did," I say taking her in my arms and holding her there for a long peaceful moment.

"Whose idea was it to have all of these people in my house when I got home?"

"You have to ask that?"

"Not really. Chad means well, but they are a bit overwhelming for me right now. I'm so tired, Baby. I just want to lie down."

"And that is what you're going to do," she says and immediately begins moving the pillows from the bed and pulling back the covers.

"I'll get Colin or Chad to come in and help you get in bed, okay?"

"Thank you so much, Jaz. Please let everyone know how much I appreciate their coming over and their well wishes. I really do appreciate it. I'm just exhausted."

At the door, Jaz, blows me a kiss, and I smile and pretend to catch it.

"Thanks, Babe. Will you be here when I wake up?"

"Yes. I'll be here."

In a moment, Chad comes in, selects some pj's for me, and helps me get ready for bed.

"I hope this little surprise wasn't too much for you, Zack. There were just so many people who waited around the hospital wanting to see you, so I thought this would be a good way for them to wish you well."

"It's fine, Chad. I'm just very tired now."

"Well, you get your rest, little Bro, so I can get you back to work to make me some more money. I'm almost broke again."

"Huh, so that's what your help is all about—getting me back to work to make money for you?"

"It was just a joke, Man. Don't be so serious all the time."

"You know they say that 'things that are said in jest are often meant in just.'"

"What?"

"Never mind." I wave him off with my hand.

"Oh, I see...that's some more of your high-end Harvard talk, huh? Too heavy for your unintelligent brother to understand, right? Useless to repeat it, right? You're so arrogant, and that's what I hate about you."

"Chad, can you just help me get in bed, and let me get some rest. I'm not up for your nonsense right now."

"Hold on to my back so you don't fall, fool, and step into these pants so I can get you into this bed before I deck your butt."

"You'd hit me now, right?" I ask stepping into my pajama pants.

"Get in the bed, fool, before I lose my temper."

He pulls the covers back, and I finally get inside the comfort of my own bed. I take a deep relaxing breath smelling the clean, cool sheets, and Chad pulls the covers over me.

"Wanna a little kiss goodnight, little Bro?" he asks as if he's talking to some infant.

I roll my eyes at him, turn toward the wall, and I think I'm asleep before he can open the door and join the noisy celebration outside.

—ɯ—

When I wake, I see through the blinds that the sun is moving quickly toward the westward sky, and Jaz has been staring at me while I slept.

"Hey," I mummer waking and stretching as best I can. "Were you watching me sleep?"

"Yes, I was," she grins. "Asleep, you look so beautiful, peaceful, and harmless."

"What's that supposed to mean?"

"It means that you can be a bit dangerous awake sometimes," she giggles.

"Really?"

"Yes, really. All I have to do is remember our football date to know that."

"I don't want to talk about that. Where is everybody?"

Well, all of your guests have gone, and Chad asked if I could *handle* you by myself, and I assured him that I could so he left with Colin. I think I heard him say he was going to go back to LA with Colin when he leaves."

"I'm sure. Since for once, I really need his butt here, he's going to LA. Great!"

"Look, don't worry about that. Are you hungry?"

"Yes, but I don't feel like going out or cooking."

"You don't have to do either, Baby. I fixed dinner for both of us."

"Thank you, Babe," I say taking her hand in mine, and smiling up at her. "Let me get up and clean up a bit and I'll be right out. I have a very bad taste in my mouth."

"That's the medicine I put on your lips while you were asleep," she laughs.

"You sure are concerned about the care of my lips for some reason. You want them to get back to kissable fast, don't you?"

"Just go and clean up and meet me in the kitchen."

"I will, and you can bet I won't have this mess on my lips when I get out there, and they'll operate just fine. Take my word."

"You're not kissing me with those chapped things. I'll wait till later—much later," she laughs. "You have a little more of the healing process before I'll come near those things."

"We'll see about that."

"Yes, we will," she smirks making her exit.

Dinner is delicious, and I had no idea I was that hungry or that Jaz could cook that well. I did notice, however, that my stovetop had splatters, dishes were in the sink, and there were a few spills on the floor. I was wondering to myself if I would be able to leave the mess, but I had my doubts. As I cram the last few morsels in my mouth, I look over at this beautiful woman and the spills and dirty dishes vanish from my mind.

"Jaz, I have something important I want to ask you."

"OK. You look serious."

"I am—very. I've been thinking."

"Well, THAT could be dangerous," she laughs.

"No, I'm serious, Babe. I want to get out of here for a while. I think I need a break from New York." I take her hands in mine and we face each other on the bar stools. For a moment I hesitate. "I . . .I was wondering if you'd consider coming with me."

"Where?"

"I don't really know—out of New York for a minute and definitely not to Virginia. I don't need Derek's lectures. I want to go someplace where I don't know anyone—someplace where I can heal without looking weak and helpless. Someplace where no one is paying any attention to me except you." I stand up and pull her closer to me.

"I need you to go with me, and I've thought about your work, but this will give you a chance to take pictures and paint in a lot of different places. We can drive from place to place and stop whenever we want and rest. If we like a place, we can stay for as long as we like before we hit the road again. What do you think?"

"I think you're crazy. Zack, you just got out of the hospital today; you almost lost your life, and you want to take a trip to God knows where. You're not strong enough for that right now. You can barely bend over. How do you think you're going to manage all of that?"

"Baby, I need this. I need this badly. I had a lot of time to think about my life while lying in that hospital bed. I've never done anything spontaneous in my life. Everything has been planned out for me ever since I was seven years old. Everything I've done has been because someone told me I had to do it. I've never had a choice or been able to make up my own mind about my life. But something has changed since I met you, and even more in the last few days. I almost lost my life, Baby, and I thought about the fact that I have never even seen more than five or six states in this country. I've... I've never done anything that was just... fun—not even when I was a kid. I don't know anything about toys or cartoons or playing on monkey bars—none of that stuff. All of that was forbidden to me. Everything for me has been about work and success. I'm young, Jaz, and I don't know anything but work. This is the moment I want to live in. I can't do anything about yesterday and based on what just happened to me, I know that tomorrow isn't promised. I'm young and alive now. I want to live now."

"Are you thinking about doing this tomorrow?"

"No, not tomorrow. I know I have to get a little stronger, but I think I could leave next week. I know that I won't be close to completely healing, but I can do that while I have some fun. I remember that Derek took the summer off before he started his career, and at the time, I thought that it was silly, but now I understand why he needed the time. I need time off now too, Jaz, but I don't want to spend it looking at this apartment, and I definitely don't want people coming over just to hang out because they think I need company. I want to see something different, do something different, and I want you to be with me."

I can tell that she is speechless for the moment so I pull her closer to me and hold her. I feel so comfortable with her in my arms, and I kiss the top of her head. She makes me happy. In her arms is home to me.

"I want you with me, Babe. Please..."

"Zack, if I do this, what else do you expect?"

"Just to have fun with me, Jaz. Be with me and experience things with me that I've never had a chance to experience. There are so many things that I've never done because, like I said, work was always a priority for me."

"But what do you mean *be* with you? I told you, I'm not doing the sex thing."

"Okay—here we go," I release her from my arms. "Jaz, have I pressured you one time to have sex with me—one time, any one time?"

"No, but if we're together all the time, every day, you might then, and I'm not ready for that. I need a husband first. I told you that, and I mean it," she states emphatically.

I take a deep exasperated breath. "Jaz, I'm not going to ask you for sex. Can we just get that out of the way now?"

"You're not?"

"No, I'm not. We will have adjoining rooms when that's possible, but if you don't like that idea, we can have separate hotels," I chuckle.

"You're never going to even ask me?"

"No. Never."

"You don't think I'm sexy?"

"Baby, you're very sexy. You drive me crazy."

"But you're never going to even ask me? You think Summer is sexy, and you ask her."

"Jazmin, I don't have to ask Summer, and this has absolutely nothing to do with her."

"Sometimes you need her. Don't you think you'll ever need me?"

I slightly lower my head and do everything I can to stifle my laughter and even my smile because I know that won't go over well right now. I try to look as seriously as I possibly can with this beautiful woman standing in front of me—this angel of mine—this woman that still has a lot of little girl in her, and that is the innocence that I love every time I touch her, every time I hold her close to me, every time I look into those beautiful eyes shaded by those long, alluring eyelashes. When I am as composed as I can be, I raise my head and cup her chin with my index finger and look directly into her eyes.

"Jaz, I need you right now. I need you like flowers need rain, like the sun needs fire, like the stars need light, like cookies need milk, Baby. I need you far more than I will ever need Summer Carlton." She pushes me away.

"Just not sexually, right? And that stars need light and flowers need rain sounds like some old overworked outdated line of yours. And if you made that up, you're a very bad poet," she pouts.

"Well, it's not an old line, and yes, I may be a very bad poet, but let me put it this way: You are my angel, and I know that means something far different from anything I have ever had or will ever have with Summer."

"But does that mean I'm not sensual to you?" She emphasizes the word sensual and flirts close to my lips.

"Hmm. You know what? We can clear all of this up right now, Baby," I lean over whispering in her ear. I can show you right now how I feel about you sexually, and you won't have to worry about that anymore. Is that what you want, Baby?" I ask lifting her chin and coming close to her lips.

"No, silly, I don't want that," she says taking her hand and pushing my mouth away from hers, "but I also don't want you telling me that you're never going to even act like you want me. That's embarrassing," she pouts turning away from me again.

"Look, Jazmin," I say grabbing her arm and pulling her to me. "I'm going to follow your lead, whatever that is, Okay? But let me say this: If or when I get the opportunity to show you how I feel about you, it will not be having sex." I take her face in both of my hands and look deeply into her eyes. "It will be making beautiful, romantic love. There is a huge difference, baby, between the two; however, until that time, will you just considerate my proposition and go with me?" I kiss both of her eyelids. I feel her respond and pull her closer to me. I feel her move her hands up and down my back as she puts her head on my shoulder. *Did I say I'd never ask?*

"I like the idea, and you're right, I can take photos and paint anywhere. I'll get things straight at my studios and I'll go. It'll be fun," she smiles.

"Wow! I wish I could pick you up right now and swing you around. I'm so happy. I bend down to kiss her, and she shoves me away.

"Those lips are not even close to being ready yet. Go put some more of that medicine on."

"Not a chance—not even for one of your kisses. That stuff is nasty and makes my breath stink," I laugh. I grab her, and through the pain, I swing her tiny frame around, and we fall onto the sofa laughing while I playfully poke out my bruised lips and try to get a kiss while she covers her mouth with both of her hands.

"I see right now that whenever we get to the lovemaking part of this relationship, if my lips are not healed properly, it's going to be a bit difficult," I chuckle.

For the moment all of my pains cease even through the playful tickling, the hard laughter, and the little shoves I keep getting as I continue to try for a quick teasing kiss. Pain, however, returns when I see Jaz pick up her things preparing to leave my dirty kitchen. She calls down for security to walk her to her car, and blows me a kiss from the door as she makes her exit for the night. She didn't offer to wash one dish. She knows me. She knows I can't sleep with the kitchen left like this.

When she leaves, I look around at the mess, exhale loudly, and start to make my kitchen look like my kitchen. When the last thing has been wiped up and the dishes put away, I grab the phone and call Jaz.

"Babe, you in bed yet?"

"Yes, I am. I thought you'd never call."

"Somebody left a mess in my kitchen, and it took me a while to clean it all up."

"Oh, what a shame. You've got to get better friends."

"My friends are just fine. Jaz, I'm so glad you're going with me. Thank you."

"If you went without me, I wouldn't get a thing done because I'd be worried to death."

"Really? I would be fine, but I wouldn't have a good time. Goodnight, Babe."

"Goodnight, get some rest."

"I will."

Getting ready for bed by myself is quite a challenge, but I manage better than expected. Chad calls to check on me, and then I click off the light, and I'm out before the room dims.

14

NEW LIFE

Life reveals beautiful surprises when we seek them.

The week passes slowly, especially the two days when Jaz is in Virginia. She almost misses her plane because our goodbye is so long. We stay on the phone a lot, but I can't wait for her to get back to New York. In Virginia, she gets things settled with Arianna and her manager, and makes sure that everything will run smoothly in her absence. Early Saturday morning, she rings my bell, and stands at my door with a huge grin on her face. Her suitcases are packed and she's as ready as I am to go on our little adventure.

By nine, we are on our way, and I'm so excited because I have never done anything like this before. I feel so free—almost giddy. I have had a chance to put together a few great surprises for my lady, and I can't wait for her to see all of them. We have a great trip laughing and talking about silly things and sometimes the conversation

195

drifts into something more serious, but I change it quickly because I don't want to talk about anything that brings me down.

Our first destination is right outside of Raleigh, North Carolina and I'm hoping that I can find the place where I've planned for us to stay. I've done most of the driving and I'm beginning to feel it in my back. I take the exit and begin the winding private road to my first surprise. It is as easy as Ryan predicted. We drive up to this beautiful lakeside cabin—a secluded romantic place that my friend designed and built. Even the lake is man-made.

"Where are we, Zack? This is absolutely beautiful."

Ryan told me that he would have everything prepared for me, but I had no idea it would be this spectacular. The front of the cabin has a lighted path up to the porch where I see a swing, several rocking chairs and beautiful yellow pansies that are still blooming. We get a few of our things out of the car, and I open the door to a gorgeous living room with high ceilings and a back wall that shows us a pier and the lighted lake outside. In the living room, the fireplace is already burning, and the décor is done in white and turquoise. The rug in front of the fireplace looks like the material is twelve inches deep although I know that can't be true. Candles light the room and create a very romantic coziness. As tired as we thought we were, I think we both feel our bodies relax as we take in this incredible place. Music is playing throughout the cabin and since Ryan knows how much I love Jazz, the sounds of Najee seem to take over the atmosphere.

We put our things down at the door, and I take Jaz in my arms.

"I did this for you. I hope you love it."

"What's not to love? Where are we?"

"We're not far from Raleigh at a place that my friend, Ryan Daniels, dreamed of, and with some of his millions, he designed it and had it built. He, his wife, and two children spend their vacations here, and I hear that when his wife is angry with him, she comes here until she cools off," I chuckle. I don't believe that, but that's what he tells me. Since he's always laughing when he says stuff like that, I think it's a joke. He's a real family man."

"I see. Maybe you'll copy him one day. Who did all of this to greet us?"

"He has caretakers who get things ready when he's coming. We don't even have to cook. He prepared that too."

"Wow! You have friends with planes that can fly you all over the world at a moment's notice and now a friend with an enchanting cottage in the woods by a lake. You have some very special friends."

"Yes, I do, but I work hard and help them make a lot of money, and I make a lot of money so these are just some of the trappings that I've never allowed myself to enjoy. I never even thought of buying someplace like this. Jaz, you know, this is what's so different about me now, so different even I don't really understand it. This is what you've changed. I've never thought of buying anything to make me happy other than maybe clothes, jewelry, and cars. I've never thought about going anyplace that would make me happy. You make me want more—a lot more—something more substantial: like a home with a cozy fireplace, somebody to share my life and honestly love. So, maybe I'm copying Ryan a little already."

"Hmm."

"Well, let's get comfortable and enjoy all of this while we have the chance."

We look around and find three bedrooms. Of course, one is a master bedroom with a master bath, and I don't have to tell you who gets that. I take a room that is not quite as large but it, too, is beautiful. After cleaning up and changing into something more comfortable, we meet again in the living room in front of the fire.

Jaz, in a bright yellow caftan, joins me on the exquisite white rug in front of the fire. I get Jaz to share a very expensive wine with me, and we relax letting the sounds of jazz float over us, embrace us, and take us to its splendid place of peace where we both surrender to its magic. We don't talk; we don't even look at each other. We just close our eyes, shut out the world, and hold each other close.

"Are you happy, babe?" Her voice is mellow, soft, sexy, and it breaks our precious silence.

"I can't even express how much," I answer quietly. I don't have to think about work, or Chad doing something stupid to me, or anything but how beautiful you are lying here next to me."

I open my eyes, touch her chin, and smile. "Do you have any idea how beautiful you are?"

"I never really thought about it until I met you."

"Really?"

"No, it wasn't my focus, but now I want to look good for you."

I stand up and pull her to me. In sync, we move to Kenny G's smooth jazz "You Are So Beautiful," and the sound and the feelings in my heart fill time and space. I kiss her neck, her shoulder, her eyelids and I feel her move her arms up and around my neck and slightly pull me closer to her as we keep the rhythm, and mentally review the power of the words, *"you're everything I hope for and everything I need. You are so beautiful to me."* The saxophone envelops us in a sound so intoxicating that before we know it, there is the kiss. It's the kind of sensual, slow kiss I've wanted to give her for a long time, the kind with depth and meaning, and she responds to me perfectly. When the kiss is spent, I slightly push her from me and look into her eyes. I touch her cheek and I know what I think I want to say. Do I dare? Is it what I really feel? Do I take this moment to venture out into the deep? Her eyes tell me yes.

"Jaz, Jazmin…"

"Yes," she answers playfully letting those long eyelashes flutter and put a knot in my throat.

"I… I need to tell you something." My smile keeps alarm from her face.

"Yes."

"Hmm. Do you know how much your eyes talk to me?"

"No. I don't think I do. So, what are they saying right now?" she asks slipping her arms tighter around my neck.

"That I love you…that I've never felt like this before about anyone."

"Really? My eyes are telling you that you love me? Zack, do you even know what you're saying to me?"

"Yes, I do—very much so. I let your eyes talk to me all the time, and they never fail to offer truth."

"Well, if that's true, what is *your heart* telling you? I pull her closer to me and smother my face in her neck. "My heart tells me that I love you so much."

"Well, I hope you listen to my eyes and hear your heart," Jaz whispers in my ear.

"Now I need to ask you a personal question.

Ok."

"At this point, do you love me enough to ignore the warnings about me? To trust me? To give me a chance?"

"I think so. The warnings just come so frequently, Zack, and sometimes, I get scared. I don't think I'd be so scared if the warnings didn't also come from you." She releases me and walks a pace or two away. I turn her back around to me and look into her eyes again.

"Don't take this from me, Jaz. Let me love you the way I feel right now. Let me have this beautiful feeling without worry—without feeling that there's someone right around the corner ready to steal this from me like they've taken every other thing in my life that I've loved. I'm scared too because I never seem to get to hold on to what I happen to love. As if that's not enough, sometimes, I don't trust me, but I want to. I just have this confounding history of giving up on the people I love first before that can give up on me. I can only pray that I break that pattern with you. I want you so much, and I've never wanted anything more in my life."

She comes back to my arms, lifts her lips to mine, and we make an attempt to seal secret personal deals with the power of the kiss.

At some point we move into the kitchen where a delicious meal is still in the warmer, and it's quite a feast. We enjoy the food, talk, and laugh about silly things, and just act like carefree kids. When we check the time, we see that it's almost 3:00 AM. It's been a long day, but despite that, I can't believe that without any kind of fight, I'm letting this beautiful woman, here, alone, in this romantic place help me clean the kitchen, give me a brief hug and kiss and politely excuse herself to the master bedroom *alone*. It irritates me that she can leave to her own private space, and it makes me mad with myself that I don't demand more from her. I push the stools under the bar in the kitchen, turn out the lights, blow out the candles and find my way down a long hallway to a lonely place at the rear of the cottage. I shouldn't tell this, I know, but it is what it is: as I make my way to the back of this house, my thoughts find Summer who would never send me to a back room alone, and her words ring in my ears. *"You'll call."* I dig my phone out of my pocket, sit on the side of the bed and scroll to her name. I move to her last text and read it. *"I'm waiting."* I smile to myself and decide that I love Jaz enough to beat the odds this time. I close off the text and get ready for bed and some sleep that I desperately need.

The smell of coffee nudges me awake, and the sun coming through the windows tells me that the day is well on its way. I lay still for a moment thinking of Jaz and the fact that I actually verbalized my love for her and that I didn't give in to Summer's urgings. I feel so rested and relaxed. I think this is a first for me. I can't remember a time when I have been this happy or this mellow.

The quietness seems to interrupt my thoughts and something draws me to the window. I throw the covers back and peek through the binds, and I see one of the most beautiful sights I have ever seen in my life. Surrounded by towering trees, green grass, and a placid lake meeting a blue sky, stands my Jazmin before her easel and paints. She is dressed in jeans and a red leather jacket. Her short hair is blowing in a soft breeze, and I click my mental camera and snap an eternal picture of her that I stamp indelibly on my mind. I stand at the window and watch for quite some time, smiling to myself wondering if this is a gift from my Mommy. She always wanted to make me happy, and when she would embrace me, and plant one of her wet playful kisses on my check, I felt her love. Standing here, I feel that love, not a romantic one—something greater than that. My life is changing so rapidly, and the changes are awesome.

I slip into the master bedroom shower and the water is refreshing and feels like a soft rain on my still sore body. I linger enjoying its warmth, but mostly relishing the thought that there is no need to rush, no need to think about what has to be done in this day, no need to make money at some ridiculous pace, no thought of having to please anyone but Jaz. I dress in my black slacks and a red turtleneck sweater, black leather jacket, my gold chain, and some soft black shoes. I move outside in the cold winter air. Despite the coldness, I sit with a warm cup of coffee comfortably and quietly on the porch, just watching, enjoying the view, taking in the beauty of my Jaz's loveliness. I can smell her perfume drifting on the wind and the intensity of her attention to the details of nature is alluring. I sit for over an hour observing how she looks, how she moves, and then I walk quietly up behind her and without touching any other part of her, I kiss her neck.

"I knew you were there," she giggles, never stopping her strokes. "I just wanted to see what you would do."

"How did you know? I was very quiet."

"You were quiet, but your cologne was not. I've smelled it for over a half hour. I could never mistake that smell," she says turning to me lowering her eyes, giving me that shy look that draws me to her and makes me want her in my bed.

"I see. Do you like it?" I plant a kiss on her forehead.

"I love it. It's so sexy, so masculine."

"Well, it's not working in those area on you, or if it is, I see no evidence," I say nuzzling her neck again.

She throws her left hand out in front of her and spreads her fingers.

"And I see no evidence of a ring on the fourth finger of my left hand."

"You know what, Jaz?"

"What?"

"You really know how to spoil a moment."

"And you really know how to keep me out of your bed."

~ Jazmin ~

15

A WORLD OF FREEDOM

Freedom is never free.

We have an exciting time traveling a short distance to PNC Arena in Raleigh to a Wolfpack basketball game. Zack meets some friends there who are members of the Ledge Lounge so we go through the VIP entrance and meet them there. Everything for the day is planned perfectly just like Zack likes. He rarely likes surprises when it comes to business, and his friends know that about him. The game is great, the food delicious, and I make sure I never leave Zack's side. I sure do not want a repeat of the events at the Giant's game. After a Wolfpack win, we return to the cabin and spend another night in front of the fireplace playing chess, talking about the day, laughing and teasing each other and just having fun together. In the morning, I get what I think is a great idea. We are finishing up breakfast and I'm looking forward to another lazy day when I ask the question on my mind.

"Zack, have you ever been to Florida?"

"Florida? No. Why?"

"Could we spend Christmas there?"

"We can do anything we want. Is that what you want to do?"

"Yeah, I think we could have a fantastic time."

"OK. You want to set it up or do you want me to go ahead with my now spoiled surprise?" He grins at me.

"Oh, did I spoil something?"

"Well, not completely. We are going to Florida; I've made plans, and our plane leaves in about two hours."

"We're going to Florida! We're going to Florida? I ask in disbelief, jumping around with more excitement than I've been able to express in a while.

"Yes, we are," he says pulling me around to face him.

"But two hours? Zack, you have to learn that a girl needs time to prepare for trips. If we only have two hours we should already be at the airport."

"Not if I have my own plane, and my own pilot, and my own chauffeur."

"You bought a plane, Zack?"

He chuckles. "No. I borrowed a plane; I'll buy one for you later," he jokes. Maybe I'll make that your wedding gift from me, but, right now, we're going to Disney World," he shouts laughing with his arms outspread waiting for me. I let him fold me into his arms, and he plants a big kiss on my cheek. "I love you. You even think like I do. Right?" he chuckles.

"Lord, forbid," I giggle.

Landing in Florida is so exciting. Zack's eyes are darting here and there, just taking in everything as we ride down the Florida streets. He's pointing out trees that he has only seen in pictures. He stops the car, gets out, and touches the bark of a palm tree. He looks up and down the street and remarks how the cars are going so slowly that we actually have a chance to see them—that we can actually stop on the side of a street without getting a ticket or getting hit. In December, we see people walking on sidewalks in short sleeve shirts and shorts. The day is sunny and beautiful, and there just seems to be a special glow on everything.

Finally, we find our way to our elegant housing and have a great time exploring the grounds, playing, running through and around trees, dodging each other, and later eating fantastic food in this unbelievable restaurant. At night, we take a swim in the lighted pool, and Zack finds out quickly that he still is not completely healed. When the pain hits him, he frowns and we end up sitting on the lounge chairs just talking about our little adventure and how much fun we arc already having.

Early the next morning, we go to one of the theme parks, and Zack's first roller coaster ride is priceless. Just moving along in the line, his face is filled with childhood glee. As we spin, dip, drop, and climb to incredible heights in this monster of a ride, he squeals like a teenage girl. I can't stop laughing at his face and his noises. I see his playful fear, excitement, thrill, and the joy of just experiencing something so very new and different to him. It's almost like he's a totally different person. Gone is the serious look or the sensual come-on allure. He's a little boy doing something that he had no idea even existed. Off of the second ride, I think maybe we should sit for a while, but those are not his thoughts.

"Let's do it again. Let's ride it again. Come on, come on, Jaz," he pleads pulling me from my seat.

"I can't ride it again right now, Baby. I have to put my stomach back in place. I'll wait right here for you if you want to ride again."

"Okay. Wait right here. I have to do it again, Jaz. That was so much fun even though my shoulder hurts."

He jumps around as he talks, and he can barely get the words out before he's walking backward waving to me like I'm his Mom and he's ten years old. The whole thing makes me smile and feel a sense of satisfaction that Zack, for once, is really happy—actually beside himself with joy.

"Watch me up there, Jaz. Watch me." He dashes away and even when he's gone, standing in the line, I can see his anticipation standing on one foot and then the other. On the roller coaster, I see him wave, then grab the bar, and scream as his car takes a fast drop, a dip, and another rapid spin all in a matter of seconds.

After his third roller coaster and his seventh ride, he drags me to every souvenir booth in sight and buys so much junk I wonder if we'll be able to get out of the park without a truck. We lick huge swirl lollipops, eat cotton candy, candy apples, peanuts, popcorn, hotdogs, ice cream cones, and drink more soda than I think I've ever had in my life. We play all kinds of games and Zack wins me a huge pink teddy bear to add to all the rest of our loot. We wear our Mickey Mouse watches, our Minnie Mouse scarfs, and blinking light necklaces. We dance at some magical place and when he takes me in his arms there, the mood changes for a second, then he smiles down at me and we both burst out laughing together for some reason. I guess because that mood is totally out of sync with every other thing we've done in this day.

At nightfall, we both are exhausted, but Zack is on some energy high and doesn't want to leave, so we go to a show for me to rest. The music is beautiful and the dancing is outstanding, but more importantly, I get a chance to stop and sit. The colors that swirl around us from the set, the costumes, the theater are all fascinating, and we hold hands, kiss a few times, and I see something in Zack's eyes that I have never seen before. I even would venture to say, that look has not existed until this day. It's a look of awesome wonder. It's like a two- year old's first Christmas, or a five- year- old at a birthday party with more gifts than he can handle. It's an amazing look, and I feel so blessed to be experiencing this with him.

Finally, I get him to agree to leave, and we go back to the hotel. We cart in some of the stuff we bought and Zack throws it all on the bed in his room. We start plowing through it, and he takes each thing up in his hand and really exams it thoroughly. He turns is around, upside down and tries to discover exactly what he is supposed to do with most of it. He tries to write with the huge pencil with a tassel and asks where would he use that. He finds the Mickey Mouse back scratcher immediately useful after I tell him what it is. He puts on his Mickey Mouse ears and tries to get me to wear mine. He chases me around the room trying to put them on me.

"Come here, girl, and put these ears on so you look like me," he laughs.

"No. Don't mess up my hair," I say covering my head and dodging out of his grasp. He grabs me and pulls me to him. At first, we are laughing hard, but then he puts on his serious look, and I know that he is about to kiss me. The kiss is lovely. It simply says I love you, nothing more.

"Thank you, baby, for sharing this with me. Thank you so much. I have never in my life had so much fun. I'm ashamed to tell you that I didn't even know this much fun actually existed. Derek and I have been to the casinos together, and I thought that was fun, but that was adult fun. Today was kid fun—something I've never experienced."

I sit down on the sofa in the living room part of the suite. Zack follows me, and positions himself comfortably with his head in my lap. I look down at his beautiful brown eyes, his tender healed lips, and his hands folded over his stomach, and, in this moment of stillness, I want desperately to kiss him and make love to this man that has claimed my heart. I bend down to him. He meets me half way, and the kiss is long and sensual, full of the very thing I am desperately trying to keep at bay. Sex. I want this man so badly, but I think, *"I have promises to keep, and miles to go before I sleep."*

"What a day," he murmurs almost to himself breaking into my secret thoughts of him. "Do you know, Jaz, that today is the first time I have ever been on a roller coaster?" he muses. "The first time I've ever had Mickey Mouse ears, or his watch, cotton candy, candy apples, or just been to a place like this where fun is everywhere. This is the first time. I was never even allowed to watch cartoons." His voice trails off, and I know he is reviewing memories, childhood wishes, and things that, for years, he has locked behind some secret door of his mind. At this moment, in our quietness, there is nothing between him but time and space. No words can adequately convey his history, so in this moment, I realize that he finds silence to be his friend.

I see his eyes closed, but I know he's not asleep. I see a sudden sadness take over his face, and in his voice when he speaks.

"Jaz, today was unbelievable for me. You have no idea—no idea how different today was for me than every other day that I've lived on this earth. Nobody ever allowed me to know this feeling existed, not even a glimpse into this kind of freedom or that this kind of world was even possible. I feel like I've been shut up in a locked room, and today, somehow, I found the key and opened the door to a whole new world. Even at Harvard, I obsessed over my work, and I never seemed to have the time to look up from my books and out at the world. I was so determined to be what Chad demanded me to be—a success. That's what he always said I had to be—a success. This is the first time I've ever allowed myself this kind of freedom. I work all of the time, and I'm noticing now that I don't even allow myself an opportunity to enjoy the money that I make, and I have more money and investments now than I'll ever be able to use in a lifetime."

"Why did this happen to you, Baby? Better yet, how did this happen? I know that you don't like to talk about your parents or your past, but maybe you should tell me the story."

"No...no, I don't want to talk about it. It's too horrific," he mutters shaking his head.

I pick up his hand and bring his fingers to my lips and kiss them.

"You can trust me, Zack. You can trust me with your secrets," I say bending to kiss his trembling lips and wipe the single tear that escapes from his still closed eyes.

I know that his thoughts are taking him back to those places that he hides from, places where he denies light to cast even its reflection—those places that are denied an entrance to reality, never allowed out of their pseudo fantasy world where he tries to pretend the events never took place. However, they are the places that will not allow him to deny them always, and at certain times they loom up out of their darkness into their own reality and the light of them smacks him in the face and startles him into their devastating realness.

Today, despite his joy, they are pushing forward and demanding light, and he battles trying to push them back into their abyss, into their secret black hole, but because of today and his new knowledge of what real happiness is—happiness he has been denied for a lifetime, he wants so desperately to set his demons free in order to free himself.

Today, the warrior is weak because of me, because I am here with him promising a new and different life: holding him, loving him, soothing him and refusing to let them remain secret. Zack loses the battle this time. I ask the questions. I pray the prayers, and the weary warrior is dethroned.

My voice is quiet. "Zack, why was today your first time at Disney World? Your first time on a roller coaster? Your first- time buying souvenirs, or watching a Disney show? Why didn't your parents bring you here?" My questions pour out of me, but before I can steady myself to hear him, the answer pushes out into the light.

"Because... when I was seven... I saw. I saw."

He tightens his lips together as if to try to seal them shut, but more words are determined to push forward.

"Jazmin, I saw my father kill my mother."

The pain of the words spilling out into the light for the first time is almost too much for him to bear. I see him squeeze his eyes tightly shut, and then I see him slowly open them and look up at me as if to ask if what he has said is all right—if I'm all right to hear more. I wipe away the tears that are escaping, and he blurts out more of his once hidden story.

"He stabbed her seven times—once for every year that I was born." He looks up at me. "That's how much he hated me...that's how much he never wanted me...how much he blamed me for our poverty. When my mother got pregnant with me, I am told that I was the straw that broke the camel's back. Can you believe that?"

The tears crawl from his flickering eyelids and spill down the side of his face.

"I came home late that day because I wanted to finish my homework. I liked to finish it at school and leave it there so it wouldn't get dirty or no one at the house could get it and tear it up, laugh at me, and make me get a zero; so, I was late—just thirty minutes late. He was waiting for me with that huge black belt that always tore my skin. I remember he grabbed me as soon as I came through the door. He was yelling about what he had told me to do: get home on time. He was yelling, 'You think you're smarter than me, don't you? Don't you?' He struck my face and hit my eye and blood was dripping from it. When Mommy saw it, she rushed to grab me—to save me, but she couldn't save herself. He said because she wanted to help me so much, she could take my punishment. She snatched a knife from the counter to keep him away. I was crying. Chad was yelling for him to stop, but he got the knife from her and then … and then …" I hear him take a very deep breath. "…and then… seven hard stabs and it was over. He knocked me into the wall and yelled, 'See what you made me do! See what you made me do,' and then he ran from the kitchen. Jaz, blood was everywhere. It was everywhere in that filthy place. Chad was kneeling in her blood, and she was trying to talk. Chad yelled at me to run and hide in case he came back, but I was frozen in that spot. Jaz, I remember her last words. At night, when I try to sleep, I still hear them in my head. I still see her. She was puffing and pulling Chad close to her; she had him by his shirt. Her voice was so weak… hoarse. *'Chad, please take care of my baby. Please. Make sure he does good in school. Make sure he makes something of himself…something good… something important. Make sure he's successful. He's smart. He can… do it. Chad, promise me you'll take care of my little Zack…my baby…You make sure he's successful…a proud man. Promise me."*

"And he did. He promised her, and when he did, she slowly closed her eyes. I saw her slowly let go of Chad, and I heard her head hit the floor with a thud. I still hear it. Jaz, I still hear it." He chokes on the words.

That's when he really breaks, and his cry is harsh, agonizing, aching, and deep. I hold him in my arms and rock him like a baby until he falls asleep from exhaustion. When he is fast asleep, I take a blanket from the bed, cover him, go to my room, and cry myself to sleep.

~ Zack ~

16

INNER STRUGGLES

Reaching for new relationships while holding on to past lovers is a sign of one's undeniable insanity.

Some time, late in the night, I wake and tiredness seems to weigh me down with an unbelievable heaviness. Perspiration beads my forehead, and I'm exhausted from my revelations, my admissions, my secrets finding their way into the light—into a reality that I have denied until tonight. However, there is this incredibly strange dichotomy. There is a lightness in my heart, a freedom that did not exist until tonight—until I found, in a theme park, an unknown happiness, unchartered waters that allowed my captives to take flight. I toss on the uncomfortable sofa trying to find the energy to get into my bed when I hear the buzz of my cell. I dig it out of my pocket and look into Summer's face staring back at me. I can't resist looking at the clock reading 3:00AM before I slide the button to allow her access to me.

"Summer," I sigh. "What? What is it? I ask sleepily"

"I'm missing you, Babe. I need you. Where are you anyway?" I hear the exasperation in her voice. "I've been by your penthouse and to your job at least five times. I've called you at least twenty times. Where are you, and why won't you pick up? You know I worry."

"Summer, you need to stop calling me, and there is no need to worry. I'm fine." I slowly sit up on the sofa and wince from the sharp pains in my shoulder, my back, and chest. The roller coaster rides are making themselves known in a different way. "I haven't answered you because I have nothing else to say to you. As far as I'm concerned our arrangement is over."

"Because of Little Miss Perfect? Right? Where is she anyway? I'm positive she's not in your bed."

"No, she's not in my bed, but I know you would be."

"You got that right, Baby; there's no denying that. I want to be there, and somewhere inside your thick stubborn head you want me to be there, too. I wouldn't treat you like she does—the little tease. I come through for you every time you need me—every time you call, Baby."

I'm silent because I'm not going to try to defend Jaz to Summer; there's no use, and I don't want to talk about my angel to her at all. I wish she wouldn't let my Baby's name touch her lips.

"Look, it's late, I'm tired, so good night."

"Wait! When are you coming home?"

"Summer, I have no idea, but you need to know that there is nothing left between us and you need to move on."

"Move on to what, Zack?" I hear her anger. "Where do you want me to move? If I do move on, there won't be any way you can keep calling me no matter how much you need me, and you know you would try. Look, I'll see you when you get home because you're talking nonsense. You let that little girl wrap you around her finger, but I know, very well, how to untie that knot. By the time you come home you'll be begging me to come over, and I'll decide then if I want to or not. In the meantime, have a Merry Christmas and a Happy New Year. By the way, our deal is off 'cause somewhere along the way, you made me fall in love with you." She snaps the phone off without allowing me to respond.

The call ends with my knowing one thing for sure: Summer can never do what Jaz is doing for me. I could never trust Summer not to move on with someone else or even be true to me while she is with me. I know even now that there are others. Summer will always be just a convenience to men because that is what she allows herself to be, and that is all that she will ever be to me. She knows less about love than I do. Jaz, on the other hand, is mending the broken places and teaching me how to love someone for the first time in my life.

I struggle from the sofa in all of my pain, undress, and climb into bed. I try to think about the happiness I found during the past days and the joy of having Jazmin in my life, but, instead, I lie awake for hours in the darkness remembering the last time I saw my Mommy. I am remembering my little ship smashed to smithereens, and remembering the first, of many times, that my heart is broken and my life lay before me in shattered pieces.

~ Jazmin ~

17

HAPPY NEW YEAR OR NOT!

*Carefully examine both the inside and outside of "picture perfect"
lest there be some unseen flaw at its core.*

In the morning, when I hear the knock on our adjoining door, I
hesitate to open it immediately. I'm still trying to process all that
happened, and at the same time trying to decide how to act now that
I know so much more. Should I be loving, funny, or sad. I decide to
take my clue from Zack.

"...You decent?"

"Yes, I am," I answer snatching the door open.

"Ah shucks! Just my luck," he jokes moving into the room.

"You're silly."

At first he just looks at me, and then he moves over closer to me
and takes me in his arms.

"Thank you," he almost whispers. "Thank you so much."

"I really didn't do anything."

"You have no idea what you did for me, and I don't expect you to know or to really understand. I have never allowed those truths to slip from my lips, but you helped me do that, and I will forever be grateful because now my spirit feels so free."

During the day, we have a great time. It's Christmas Eve and the day is so different from any Christmas I have ever seen. This is definitely not a New York Christmas. There is no snow, no coldness, absolutely no hint of winter. In short sleeves, we go from place to place enjoying all that Disney has to offer. We experience Disney Christmas, the parks, real food, junk food, playful time together, and I see Zack reveling in his sense of freedom again. He's the kid that has been missing for twenty-seven years. The Christmas lights seem to mesmerize him, and he is in this magical place and breathing in every second of it.

At night, in the hotel, we experience a private moment that is unbelievable to me. Sometime during the day, Zack has managed to have a Christmas tree not only delivered to my room, but decorated in beautiful white lights and multicolored balls and silver garland. Under the tree is a beautifully wrapped package in foil red and green. A soft Jazz envelops the room, and in the cozy light, this man I know I love takes me in his arms and moves with me to the music. I feel him playing in my short hair and teasing my neck with his kisses.

"Jaz, I love you. I know that we belong together. Derek used to tell me that I would know the one when she came along, and I have to say that he was right. You feel so right in my arms and in my mind," he says leaning back looking in my eyes.

"Do you love me, Jaz?"

"Yes, more than you know."

"I want to make you happy and do things for you that make you smile. Merry Christmas, Baby.

"And Merry Christmas to you. I had no idea that you were doing anything like this for me, but I did something for you too."

"You did? What?"

I move over to the closet and pull out my big tote bag and empty it of five boxes, wrapped in Christmas paper. I place each of the gifts under the tree, and turn back to see Zack with a look that clearly says that he can't believe what is happening.

"Close your mouth, Zack," I giggle. "You're not the only one who can keep secrets."

"I see that. When did you do all of this?"

I come to him and circle his waist with my arms and look up into his eyes. Both of us are grinning now, and he is playing in my hair.

"I shopped in Virginia because I figured that we would be together at Christmas, and I wanted you to have the best Christmas of your little life. Ho, Ho, Ho!! Merry Christmas," I giggle.

"Well, you are definitely the prettiest Santa I've ever seen, and I've only had one Christmas gift in my life and that was two years ago from Derek and Arianna. So, this is definitely an improvement with you here in my arms."

He leans down to me and kisses me thoroughly, and I enjoy it thoroughly. We break our embrace and sit cross- legged in front of the tree to open our gifts.

"Are all of these for me?" he asks with disbelief in his voice.

"No," I answer emphatically and to his surprise. "Only one is for you."

"You bought four gifts for yourself?"

"Yep, I sure did," I joke. "No, silly. Of course, they're for you. I bought them all for you," I say touching his face and looking into his beautiful eyes.

"Wow! This has never happened to me. What should I open first?"

"This one," I say reaching over and handing him a medium size box. He starts to open his gift as only Zack opens a gift...with some strange incredibly meticulous attention to detail.

"No. Let me teach you how to open a Christmas gift. We'll be here all night if you get to do it your way," I say snatching the gift from his hands and ripping the paper off in two quick moves. When the box is bare, I hand it back to him sitting with his mouth open again.

"That's how you open a Christmas gift, Zack. Now, close your mouth and look in the box."

"Gee, you ruined my paper."

"You'll survive it. I promise. Now, look in the box."

He shakes the top off, moves the tissue paper aside, reaches in, and pulls out his first gift.

"Wow! This is fantastic. Notice I said FAN-tastic," He grins holding the NFL Giant jersey up to his chest. This is awesome. Thank you, Babe. You know I love this, and it has the quarterback's number. I love it!"

His eyes are sparkling and he folds it better than it was at first and places it carefully back in the box. I slide the top underneath so that the shirt is still visible.

"What next?"

I reach for the second box and he rips the paper before I can get the box out of my hand into his, and he bursts out laughing like he has just discovered something else new and different and fun. He tears into the box and lifts out an NFL Giant's hoodie and matching sweat pants.

"Babe, this is awesome and in my right size too."

"Yep, that took a little spying to get that. I had to sneak around in your closet."

"I thought I noticed some of my things moved aside and out of place."

"No, you didn't."

"Yes, I did. My clothes weren't spaced right, but I fixed them back."

"I bet you did. Zack, that's pitiful," I giggle.

When all of his gifts are open, he has added a watch and a MP3 set for runners. He is happy beyond words when he reaches over and hands me my gift from him.

"This is for you, Baby and you can open it anyway you want," he smiles. I pretend that I'm going to rip it open quickly, but then I change and open it more slowly.

I take the paper off somewhat carefully, but near the end I rip it off, and slip off the cover. I pull out a beautiful music box. Zack takes it from my hand and finds a key underneath and winds it up. The music begins to play *"You are So Beautiful"* and I smile at him. He is lying down on his side now just watching my every move. It is as if he's taking these mental pictures of every moment in this span of time.

"Open it," he prompts.

I follow his direction, and inside everything sparkles. The lights from the tree reflect on my gifts and what I see is unbelievable.

"Now it's my turn, Jaz. Close our mouth."

"I can't. Zack these are beautiful and they cost a fortune."

"Yep, a small fortune, but nothing is too much for you, Babe."

I lift out the diamond necklace and matching dangling earrings. All I can say for the next fifteen minutes is Wow!

Christmas and New Years are both like some mystical time for the two of us. We spend New Years' Eve in our secret little cottage watching the New York Ball drop on television. Our moment is special because we know somehow that this is the first of many New Years to come that we will clink our glasses and walk into a new time together—or at least that is what we think at the time.

At the end of our stay, we pack our things and Zack does what I thought was impossible: he makes the cottage cleaner and more organized than it was when we arrived. I have to pull him out of the door before he fluffs one more pillow, arranges one more chair, wipes one more counter or spruces up one more area. Our ride to Virginia is rather cool because I break the news to him at the last minute that I want him to drop me off at my beach condo in Virginia, and he will have to make the rest of the trip to New York alone. That is a very hard pill for him to swallow, and he tries to change my mind a hundred times. He gives up when we see the blue sign with the red Cardinal reading "Welcome to Virginia." When he drops me off, he doesn't even come in and barely kisses me good-bye. He does tell me that he's going to Derek's to visit and spend the night and asks me one more time to come with him, but I have things I have to do that have gone lacking for almost a month so I stand firm in my decision to stay in Virginia for at least two weeks.

When Zack drives away, I feel my heart sink. I feel a loss, and it takes everything in me not to call and tell him to come back and pick me up, but I don't. I know how needy he is, but I have to be my own person and do things that are best for me sometimes. His leaving in anger or hurt and his coolness definitely bother me. It troubles me so much that I begin to rush through things so I can get to New York in at least a week. I'll surprise him even though he claims he doesn't like surprises. Somewhere in the back of my mind, red flags wave ferociously, and I'm hoping against hope that I'm not the one who gets the surprise.

~ Zack ~

18

BREATHE AGAIN

Love and Selfishness cannot reside in the same home.

Pulling away from Jaz's condo, I feel the steam of my anger, and I allow the wheels to spin a bit and the engine to roar a little too loudly. I can't help but look back at her in my rearview mirror seeing her standing there with her bags at her feet. I know I should be grateful for all that she has already done for me: for the time she's spent, the experiences we've had, and mostly for the gift of release that she has provided. But why does she always get her way? Why do we always have to do things the way she wants them? There's no compromise with this girl. I think sometimes she's turning me into a wimp, and I'm nobody's wimp.

When I pull up to Derek's and Ari's cottage, I sit for a moment so I can pull myself together: put on my mask and my fake smile because I'm really not feeling the laughter right now, but I'd never let Derek know that. It would just put a perfect sparkle in his eyes and that smug, lawyer "I told you so" look that I can't stand. When I think I'm ready to act like my old self, I get out of the car, slam the door to release a little more of my anger, and grab my overnight from the back seat. Derek hears me and is already at the door with that big fake grin on his face. Well, maybe it's not fake, but mine is.

"What's up, Bro?"

"It's on you, D. It's been a minute," I say grabbing his outstretched hand and leaning in for that old familiar Harvard hug of ours.

"You look good. Jazmin must be doing something right with you," he says slapping me on the back and ushering me into the cottage.

Arianna waddles towards me in very stylist red and white maternity wear and I can't believe my eyes. It's so hard to realize that she has grown so much in what seems like just a short time since I last saw her.

"Hey, Zack. I guess I look a bit different," she grins as she wraps her arms around me for a quick hug.

"You look beautiful. When is the little prince making his entrance?"

"We've got about a month and a half to wait now," Derek chimes in, "and we are two impatient parents," he beams wrapping his arms around his wife.

I watch her look up at Derek with a look that has so much love in it that it melts my anger and makes me realize how important it is to find that right person to love. Their eyes sparkle into each other, and there is just a feeling of warmth that's virtually impossible to express in words. Suddenly, I see Ari grab her stomach and giggle.

"There he goes again—back on his little in house trampoline," she teases.

Derek puts his hands on his wife's stomach to feel the baby inside. "Man, I can't tell you how unbelievable this is. Ari and I still can't get use to feeling this little guy jumping and sliding around."

"Want to feel the baby kick," Ari asks excitedly, grinning at me.

"Is it ok, D?"

"Yeah, hurry up before the little Olympian stops."

I move over to the two of them, and at first, I just put my hand near without actually touching Ari, but she grabs my hand and presses it slightly again her tummy, and I don't believe what I feel. I know the grin on my face is almost as wide as D's.

"Wow! Look at that. You guys do have a little football player in the making. Wow! He kicked me," I laughed. "This is wild." I take my hand away, but I don't want to. I want to keep playing with him like Derek is. He keeps trying to catch the baby's hand or foot as he seems to move it across Ari's swollen belly. I watch Ari's clothes move around and I can't get enough. I can't resist putting my hand back on her stomach, and when I do I feel a *thump, thump, thump* and we all fall out laughing at this little guy putting on his own private show for two proud parents and an astonished soon to be "Uncle."

At the end of this beautiful moment together, one that makes me completely forget my anger, Ari has dinner ready and when we sit down to eat, I can feel the love in this room: a beautiful spirit, the joy of anticipation, and trust that two parents had to earn a few years before. We spend the night playing cards, laughing, joking, and catching up on what Jazmin and I have been doing. Derek tells me more about what happened with the two guys who attacked me, and even finds it in his heart to wish Jaz and me well. I leave early in the morning, and I do take a moment to call Jaz to let her know that I'm on my way home. The conversation is short and cool, but at least we talk.

Back in New York, I feel loneliness envelop my days like an unwanted cocoon, so I spend a lot of time putting all of my things away, creating and organizing new spaces to put things, wiping away dust that has settled on a few pieces of furniture, and then I try to relax in front of my television, surfing channels until I give up and take me and my sour mood to bed. By Saturday afternoon, I have had enough of the silence so I call Chad in LA.

"Hey."

"Hey. What's up?"

"When are you coming home?"

"I can't believe you want me anywhere near you. I thought I'd give you a little break—you being sore and all. I don't think you could take my punches right now," he chuckles.

"It's boring here, man. This is the first time I've taken a vacation, and I don't have any idea what to do with myself."

"Where's the lovely Jazmin? I can't believe you've let her out of your sight."

"She's in Virginia doing something. I don't know, Man. When are you coming back?"

"Not for a while, Zack. Believe it or not, Colin has me in school, and I love it. I'm finally getting to do what I wanted to do years ago."

"School? What kind of school?"

"I'm back studying Architectural Design. Man, it's so fascinating. It's almost like I'm finding myself out here. I don't really have to worry about you anymore. You're rich, intelligent, handsome, and making more money than you know what to do with. I did what Ma wanted so Colin says it's my time now. So, I'm staying. You'll be fine. Right?"

"So, you're leaving me too, huh?"

"Man, grow up. Get married. Have some kids to climb all over you and be happy. I think I did my part. Like I continue to remind you, if it hadn't been for you, Ma would be alive, Dad wouldn't have committed suicide in prison, and I would have been a rich Architect by now."

"Yeah, it's always all on me. Right? I always have to take the blame for everything, right? It's always going to be my fault, right? Your baby brother's fault. But we all know there were a lot of people to blame for what happened that day, and you know it. I was only seven years old, man. I was just a kid. What blame do you put on Pop? What blame do you put on yourself? At least you were fourteen. It looks like you could have done something."

He doesn't answer me. "Well, you enjoy."

"I intend to do just that."

I hang up the phone, and decide it's time for me to have a party.

I look around, and my luxurious high rise is perfect, just like I like it: smooth jazz sounds melting over me, lights set on cozy and a look out of my glass wall unveiling the moonlit night and a gorgeous New York skyline. Wow! Life is great. A few speed dials just three hours ago, and look what I created. Cassie, tall and slim, is standing in a corner of the room, drink in hand, looking my way, in her white sexy jumpsuit with a very low neckline, her jewelry sparkling a bright gold, glassy high heels, and dark brown hair almost to her waist just waiting for me to play. I saunter over, and we flirt a bit, but she's definitely not my pick for tonight. I smile, touch her chin, and Cassie is already forgotten. I let my eye canvas the room. Asia, Carmen, and Tiana are perched on my yellow leather couch chatting about me I guess, but I move over to my choice for the night—Taylor. I feel Summer's eyes burning into me, following me around the room, but I ignore her. She's lucky I invited her. I don't need any more drama. I just want my kind of fun: free, careless, and hot.

Walking over to Taylor, I realize that if it were not for my Jaz, she would probably be the one. She's quiet, smart, and absolutely a dark chocolate beauty.

"Hey Baby. What's up?" I lean over and whisper in her ear.

"I'd say you. You called, I came so from here on out, it's on you, Baby."

I pull her into my arms and lean back taking in all of her beauty. Her gorgeous brown eyes find mine, and I scan her look from head to toe. Her skinny jeans are skin tight, her low cut lacy white top, hitting just below her waist, is dainty just like the small white genuine pearl around her neck. It drops perfectly, near her breasts, from its silver chain. Her long brown braid over her shoulder is just waiting for me to take it loose and have some fun. I let my hand run down the lengthy braid and slowly move up to her teardrop pearl earring. I give it a slight tug as I find her lips. Standing in the middle of this floor, I know that all eyes are on us, and Taylor is the envy of the room.

"You in for the night?" I smile circling her waist.

"If you want me to be," she whispers looking around the room at the other ladies.

"I do."

"Then I'm here for the night," she says touching my lips with hers. I hear the doorbell, but I don't really pay it any attention. I know someone will get it so I keep my eyes on Taylor until I hear a high-pitched laugh that I know is coming from Summer. Still holding Taylor in my arms, I turn my head, and see the one thing in this entire world that I never would have wanted to see—the one thing that will change my life in an instant. I see Jazmin, standing in the light of the hallway with her white top glittering and even from where I stand, I see her eyes glistening with tears. She seems, like me, unable to move for a moment, and then I feel myself release Taylor from my arms, and I feel my bare feet walking slowly toward the door. I don't know if it is as silent in this room as I think it is or if I'm moving in some kind of daze. Everything seems to be in slow motion. When I reach the door, I take her hand and try to pull her into the room, but she resists. I turn to my guests and ask them all to leave. I hear a resistant mumbling, but I see them gathering their things and each files pass me without a word, except Summer.

"Call me when she leaves," she says raising up close to my ear, but keeping her eyes directly on Jazmin.

Some of the ladies take the elevator near my door, and some walk down the hall to the one at the other end; I barely hear their chatter as they leave. All I'm aware of in this moment is my beautiful angel standing in the doorway in front of me disappointed in me again.

241

I see her shifting her weight from side to side, her hands on her waist then folded in front of her, then unfolded and back on her waist again. She stares at me. Her mouth is balled and tears begin to fill her eyes.

"How could you? How could you Zack?" She punches her finger into my chest aggressively then quickly wipes away a stray tear. No others follow as her eyes blink rapidly. She looks at me as if she can burn a hole right through me. "After all we've been through together? ...after all I've done for you. After all the sacrifices I've made, this is what you do?" She pauses and begins speaking before I can respond. "I thought I meant more to you than this, Zachary!" She looks quickly around the room then back at me.

"Say something Zack, and give me your lame excuses. I've never been more disappointed in a person than I am in you right now. We need to talk."

"We can talk if that's what you want."

"That is what I want, Zack."

"Then you got it, Baby," I say trying to find my "I'm so cool" voice. I've known for quite a while that Jaz is tired of playing my games; I'm tired of playing my games, but I just don't seem to be able to get it all right. After our vacation together, I know something changed in me. I think I love her, but when I get lonely, despondent, or angry I get careless, and do stupid things like fill my house up with beautiful women to make me feel special. Jaz and I have this beautiful connection, and I guess that's why she keeps hinting about a ring, a wedding, and kids; personally, however, I think she can look around and see that idea is rather far from my reality.

We move into the kitchen area, and I fix us both a fruity drink that I know Jaz loves. She is completely quiet through the process. The music is still playing, and it does help to slow the pounding of my heartbeat. I have no idea what Jaz is going to do. She is far too calm now. She is sitting at the kitchen bar sipping her drink, and I try to kiss her neck, but she dodges that without a word. I sit beside her.

"Well, Zack," she says quietly, "after all we're been through together, after all the things we've experienced together—life and death things, I hate to say that I'm still wondering where I stand with you. What do I really mean to you? Am I just a convenience? More importantly, I'm wondering if I even care anymore. I keep asking myself what's the point. You can't be trusted two seconds out of my sight."

There is an undeniable seriousness in her eyes that I can't help but detect—one that I've never seen there before: a kind of resigned look with all of the anger gone, and that scares me, but I mask my fear.

"Huh. You know me, baby. I do stupid things sometimes, but despite the craziness around me, you're always my number one."

"So, this is the prize for your number one: a few eye-popping gifts and then slammed with disappointment after disappointment? Who's your number two, Zack and for how long am I going to be your number one?"

"Wait, let me look into my crystal ball," I remark playfully. "Come on, Jaz, you know that you're my forever."

"You're not serious about anything, Zack, and I need you to be. I need you to be serious and honest now. It's important. Stop playing and grow up."

I take a deep breath, sigh, pick up her hand, and look into her eyes.

"Ok, you want honest? You want serious? Here it is. You mean everything to me, and I don't want you to leave me. I told you, every time I love someone, that person leaves me for some reason or other. You left me last week to spend time in Virginia instead of coming home to New York with me, knowing how much I need you now. I didn't like that. After all that we had done, things I'd told you that had never come to light, I shared with you. ...and after all the things we've been through recently, it was hard for me to accept taking second place again or to believe that you would even consider not staying with me. Another thing: I just found out tonight that Chad's not coming back from Cali. Everybody leaves so sometimes I leave before I can be left. That's honest. And then, Jaz, you want to play house, and husband/wife stuff. I don't know that game. I love you a lot. I need you, and I want you to stay with me, but I'm just not ready to do the husband thing so you have to take that or leave it."

"Well, at least you're honest now; I respect that, and I'm going to be equally as honest. I think I'm going to have to leave it, Zack, because I really don't want to play house. I want a real life with a man that loves me and eventually wants a family to love, and it looks like that's not you. As much as I want you to, it seems like you don't want that at all. I want you to love me more than need me and respect the fact that I, too, have a business that is important to me. If I have to pay some attention to it, it doesn't mean that you're taking second place. It simply means that I have a life of my own where you can fit if that's what you want. However, I see now that's not what you want—not really."

I rub her arm and move my hand up to tilt her chin for a kiss, but she moves off the bar stool and looks into my eyes.

"You can't solve everything with a kiss or sex. I hope one day you don't find yourself regretting your choices, Zack. Our vacation together was so beautiful with so many wonderful moments. Why can't that be our life together?"

"It can be—just not married. We had it then, and we weren't married. Jaz, I felt D and Ari's baby kicking inside of her a week ago. I'm not ready for that. As wonderful as that feeling was with them, I don't think I can do this now."

"So let me get this straight. You want to just have me live with you and keep being free to call your girlfriends over for sex whenever you want? I know one of them was going to stay here tonight if I hadn't come home. You can't keep hurting me and expect me to still be happy. You take so much from me and refuse to give even a little. I know I could love you if you really let me inside, but after all of these months of playing this game with you, I have to give this up. It's beginning to seem hopeless, and wear on me terribly. I have already given too much. I'm losing myself in all of this madness. You keep inviting all of these women over giving them hope that you might pick them one night instead of me. And the thing that hurts the worst is the fact that you keep toying with my heart. You make me love you one minute—every inch of you, but then the minute you don't like something that I do, you find a way to hurt me to my core. You make me believe you when you don't actually believe anything that you're doing or saying to me. You think I don't hear you running around the house making secret phone calls ten minutes after you're kissed me good night? After months of this, I have to face reality. I don't have a choice now."

"Jaz, what do you want from me? I'm a man. I have needs."

"I just told you. I want love from you—real love."

"Or what?" I ask with a lot of irritation peppered in my voice.

"Or it's over, Zack." Her irritation surpasses mine.

At the mention of my name, I see the tears spill from her eyes, and I take her in my arms and feel her body shaking against me, but even with all of that I can't tell her what she wants to hear—that she can be my wife. Somewhere inside of me, I want to tell her that I love her, and I want to marry her, but the words don't form on my lips, the idea does not permeate my mind, and the feeling does not take control of my heart. I know in this moment that whatever love we have is at risk, and it is again my fault. Jaz looks up at me, and her eyes seem to plead for me to change my mind, but I'm not in control at all—the old anger is, ancient guilt is, distant hurt is. The fear of being rejected reigns supreme, and the horrible memories of my past still rule; I push the secrets down into my inner being as far as I can, but still, like Chad says, I know it's my fault, and I lose again.

We stand in each other's arms, and I kiss her cheek. "Don't go, Jaz. Give me a little more time."

"I can't, Zack. I'm exhausted. I think time, for us, has run out. We've been through this too many times, and you don't change. No matter what I say about how I feel, you don't hear me. I've asked you a million times how you think it makes me feel when I know that Summer is always waiting in the wings ready to do whatever you want, whenever you want it? I've asked you over and over how you think I feel? Why can't you end that once and for all?"

"But, baby, I always choose you. It's your clothes in my closets, and you stay whenever you want and as long as you want. I don't pressure you to be intimate with me. I've accepted your promises, your faith, your wishes to wait until marriage. I've told you that you can move here with me anytime you want. You're the one who decided to keep your apartment and live there."

She sighs. I feel her shoulders drop in despair, and I know what that means. My answer is wrong again. I feel her push away from me; I see her search my eyes for something—anything that speaks of love for her, and then I see her move away into the guest bedroom. I sit at the bar, while I hear her gathering things: things that have been in the closet for months, and things in the drawers. Then I hear her pull the storage baskets from under the bed, and I know she means to leave. I don't move; I can't move. Someone else is leaving me again, and, like always, I don't know how to stop it. I hear the door open and close several times, and I know she is making trips to her car. I'm still almost immobile at the bar. I want to love her the way she wants to be loved—the way she deserves to be loved. I want to tell her that I am hers alone, but because I know that's not close to being true, I sit in my stillness and watch her return, with keys in hand, and come over to me, possibly for the last time in my life. She puts the keys to the penthouse on the counter, and somehow, I don't know how, I find the energy to stand up, and we look at each other letting the hours, days, weeks, and months that we're spent together flash in front of us. I reach for her hand.

"Are you sure about this?" I ask looking directly into her watery eyes.

She smiles a sad smile, cocks her head, looks up at me and asks, "Are *you* sure about this?" I pull her to me, and we kiss a warm friendly kiss. I feel her leave my arms. I watch her walk to the door, open it, walk through it, and pull it shut. She's gone, and I am alone again.

In the middle of the night, I finally decide that I can move, that I have to, that I can fight to save whatever it is that we have left—that Jaz means too much to me to just let her go. I throw on some clothes and find my way down to my car. Inside, I try to decide what to say, but then I just turn the ignition to start the car and let it find its way to my angel. At her door, I knock quietly and call out her name, and I hear her moving to the door. When she opens it, her eyes are puffy from crying.

"Jaz, I'm sorry."

"Zack, just let it go. Just let it go. Go home. Leave me alone. I can't do this. I can't do this with you anymore. You don't love me. You love the idea of me."

I push the door open enough to force my way inside, and I see the surprise on her face.

"Zack, GO HOME!

"No, Jaz. I won't go home because there is no home without you in it. You're home to me. We need to talk this out."

"We did that already, and I want you to just leave me alone, and let me get on with my life."

"That's not what you want."

"Obviously, based on what was said this afternoon, you don't have a clue what I want. You come in here, disturbing me in the middle of the night so your fake self can tell me again how sorry you are when you're not sorry at all. If I allow it, you'll do the exact same thing to me tomorrow or even tonight if you have the opportunity. Zack just get your phony self out of my face, and don't try to talk to me, soothe me, calm me 'cause it means NOTHING anymore. NOTHING! You're as fake as press on nails, man. Where are you, Zack? Where are YOU!! Where is the REAL YOU?"

Jaz yells at me through her tears and clenched teeth, and pokes her finger in my chest.

"Somewhere inside of this chest of yours is the real you, but you keep refusing to let him out for more than a few minutes. You keep hiding him behind those gorgeous abs and this evil, heartless, hurtful clown keeps showing up instead. Where are you, Zack?" She seems to be shaking her head almost without control, and the question is a whisper as if she's too tired, too exhausted to yell more words at me. She turns away and walks to the window.

"Get out, Zack. You're drowning, and I can't save you. I keep holding my hand out trying, but if I keep reaching for you, I know what's going to happen. I've been duly warned." She turns her head and looks at me. "You're going to grab my hand one day and pull me under with you. I can't go, Zack—I can't go. I have too much to live for and there is someone who will appreciate me for who I am, and not just a little angel placed on a shelf waiting for your attention." Her voice is still, quiet, and exhausted. "Please, just go."

"Will you at least let me say something?"

She turns around now and faces me, looks me in my eyes so that I can really feel her. "Zackary... Tyler... Belford, do you honestly think that people crave hearing lies? That they want to be fooled and hurt repeatedly? That they can't get enough of the tortured life you personify? Well, let me enlighten you, Sweetheart. We can get enough; we're not addicted to the lies; we don't crave them, and we can finally look past your good looks and see the twisted ugly person you can be. No, you can't say anything else to me. I'm done. When I closed your door today, I was done. I closed the door on anything that we could have had. I closed the door on all the memories I thought we were building. I closed the door on your promises, your looks in my eyes that seemed so real. Zack, I closed the door on everything I thought was ours."

She moves a little closer to me, and I reach for her hand. She snatches away and hastily holds up an outward palm in a gesture that clearly says, "stop."

"Zack, I'm . . . I'm not even asking for the crown jewels, the knight in shining armor, or the prince to steal me away to happily ever after. I'm not asking for any of that because it's not real. I want REAL, Babe. I'm not perfect, and I'm not looking for perfection or even close to it. I simply want the husband who struggles with me through our problems and helps find a solution; a man who comes home at night to his family dead tired with an ache in his back that I can rub and make the pain go away; the guy who can't quite get everything just right, but is close enough that we can work together to make it happen; the guy that loves me enough to just hold me close to him when he knows I'm hurting, when he knows I need him; the guy who can make love to me and mean it. "

She takes a very deep breath. "But you keep bringing me phony, so now I'm just asking you to do the one thoughtful thing that you can do for me right now, and get the hell out of my life so I can breathe again.

~ Zack ~

19

CLOSING DOORS

Often the largest gift comes in the smallest package.

The winter months have been long, hard, and cold in so many different ways. Saying goodbye to Jazmin hasn't been easy at all, and our big blow up depressed me beyond anything I would have imagined. Every now and then, when she allows me a very few minutes of her time, I've spent them on the phone pleading a case that she has obviously closed. When we talk, she gives absolutely no indication that there is any chance for reconciliation. Her quietness is most disturbing to me because it shuts me out of her thoughts, out of her life in such a conspicuous way. It has left me hopeless. I miss her terribly, and I'm hoping that this quick trip to see Angel, Derek, and Arianna will help ease that pain, and I can move on. I've drowned myself in work, and driving down to Virginia for the weekend in the early summer breeze has been a bit freeing, but when I pull up in Angel's driveway, I feel exhausted.

"Let's bounce, baby," I say aloud in the darkness trying to give myself a mental boost that seems elusive. I swing the door open, get out, and straighten my clothes, but before I can ring the bell, I hear voices and music coming from out back, and I decide to go around and check it out. The backyard is lit with colorful lanterns, and I immediately see Angel. There are quite a few of her friends, getting food from the grill, swimming and playing in the pool, or dancing to the driving beats of hip-hop blasting from strategically placed amps. Then there are others just sitting or standing around chatting. She spots me right away.

"Hey Zack. Come on in and join the party," she yells over the music and greets me with a friendly hug.

"You got here faster than I thought."

"Is that all I get, girl? Just a hug from my favorite lady? Come on, now."

"Maybe you'll get a little more when I'm your *only* lady," she winks, laughs, and gives me another little hug. "Grab yourself something to eat, and come back and tell me what's going on in your busy, and I'm sure, adventurous life." She laughs again and pats my shoulder.

I'm hungry so I fix me a rather healthy plate, sit at a nearby bar to enjoy this delicious food, and Angel joins me.

"I don't want you getting lonesome over here all by yourself. Something's wrong. You don't look like King Casanova tonight. You're not mingling with the singles." She leans over looking directly at me. "I see sadness behind those eyes of yours. You know you can't fool me, Zack. I've known you too long. What's up? Talk to me."

"It's just life, baby. You know some days you win and some days you lose. This is a time when I lost," I mutter with a mouth full of food.

"I see. So, what did you lose?"

"Quite simply, a very good friend," I muse."

"And I know whose fault that was. I've been there and done that with you."

"My fault, huh? You sure?" I ask scooping up a mouth full of potato salad.

"I'm as sure as I'm sitting in this seat next to you, and that's pretty sure don't you think?"

"Hmm." I sigh loudly and take a big bite of fried chicken.

"Was it serious for her? I keep chewing, and I don't answer.

"Zack, was it serious for *her*?" She waits a moment, and when I don't answer a second time, she moves off of the bar stool and runs toward the pool and dives in. I see her throwing a big beach ball around to her friends, laughing, and racing them back and forth from end to end. I sit alone watching, and I realize that for the first time in my life, I'm not trying to woo some stranger with my charm. For the first time in my life, I feel out of place at a party, and there is no laughter in my spirit, no game in my talk, and no play in my step. I suddenly realize how sad I really am and how much I want to see my sweet Jazmin—my angel. I have retired my mask, and this is simply me in the flesh.

I finish my food, empty my trash, and let myself into the house. Inside, I turn on the TV and begin flipping channels, and nothing interests me. I hear the door slide open, and Angel is suddenly standing in front of me wrapped in a gorgeous swim cover. Even with her hair flat and dripping wet, she is as beautiful as ever—a true model. My mind flashes back to a time when she could have been mine, but I screwed that up too. My memory sees her standing in my living room with Summer in nothing but my shirt. That was a really bad scene. I think about our breakup, and it registers with me that Angel said some of the same things that Jazmin said to me when we last really talked.

"You are a mess tonight. All those single women outside, and you're in here alone. This is downright serious, Zack baby," she laughs. "All right, you've had your moment of silence, so talk to me. What did you do?" she asks slinging her wet hair to one side and coming to sit next to me.

Why is it that everyone always thinks that I'm to blame for things that happen?"

"Well, I guess because you generally are. Honestly, I can't think of a time when you weren't to blame."

"Huh."

"Ok Zack, no kidding, tell me what's going on with you. There won't be any I told you so voices tonight. I put them away some time ago when we decided to be just friends. Okay? So, tell me what's going on with you?"

"Well..." I start very slowly because I actually don't know what to say. "I'm in a relationship sort of, and she left me."

"*You're* in a relationship? Okay, let me see if I can picture this," she laughs. "I'm sorry, Baby. I don't mean to laugh at you, but I don't even think you know what that means. You don't know what a relationship is let alone be in one," she laughs slapping her knee.

"That's why I didn't say anything at first cause I knew you'd just laugh at me and blame me for everything." I drop my head because I really don't want to see her laugh at me when I feel so sad. There is nothing that I see to joke about, and I can't even play this one off.

"When you say, you're in a relationship, Zack, does that mean that you think you're in love?"

"See, Angel, you keep playing. This is serious, and I don't know. What does that mean? Does that mean I want to get married?" 'Cause if it does then, no, I'm not in love."

"Is she in love with you?" With this question, I detect seriousness in Angel's voice—a different tone: a tone of sad remembrance when *she* had fallen in love with me; a time when I played with her heart, and she was hurt to her core; a time when she had to make the hard decision to walk away. However, at this point, I think she's also realizing that this moment is different because this time it is serious for me.

"I think so. I think she is in love with me. She wants to get married. She wants me to give up the life I know, but you know me Angel. I can't do the husband thing, and when I told her that, she left."

"So, you said no, and she just up and left, just like that?"

"Not really. I had some friends over. When she saw them there, something seemed different this time. She was more direct, more serious, more decisive."

"Yeah, your friends will do that to a lady in love. I know that for sure. Has she asked you to marry her before?"

"No, not asked me directly—more like hinted, strong hints, like showing me rings that she likes in magazines and talking about wedding dresses and stuff."

"Are you seeing a lot of other women too?"

"Not really. Like I said—just friends."

"Is Summer still around?"

"Yeah, but she's just a friend."

"But see, Zack, the lady in love is just a friend, too, or I'm strongly guessing that's what she thinks. Knowing you, you haven't given her any reason to think that she's any more important to you than the others, especially Summer."

"I think I have. I was waiting for her."

"What do you mean, waiting for her?"

"You know...waiting."

"So... you all weren't intimate?"

"No, because she wants to wait until she's married, and I was cool with that." I raise my head up and look at Angel. "Can you believe that?" I chuckle a little. "I don't know," I say getting up from the sofa. I walk over to a nearby table just to get away, stand up, and do something. "This is all just so confusing to me. Even the way I feel is confusing. I never felt like this before. I'm a love 'em and leave 'em kind of guy. You know that."

"Or you're a love 'em and GET LEFT kind of guy," she laughs remembering that she left me begging her to come back to me.

Angel walks over and stands in front of me. "Somebody finally really got in there," she says poking my chest. I look down to see her finger resting where I feel my heart beating. "And don't give yourself any prizes for just respecting her wishes. She knows you're not faithful so she is very smart to make you wait until there is some kind of commitment."

"I know." I take her hand in mine. "Is it all right if I stay here with you tonight?" I ask, not sure what I want to do with myself.

"Not in my bed, Zack, but sure you can stay here."

"You're funny. You haven't let me in your bed since you walked away from me, but thanks. I just don't want to be alone right now. I need a friend, and you are a very good friend, however, without benefits, but, what can I say?" I smile for the first time.

"Why do you think you're so sad, Zack?"

"I miss her, Angel. I really miss her."

"Yep, that ought to tell you something, but I'm sure it doesn't. Well, I'm going back outside, and you're perfectly welcome to join us if you like."

"No, not tonight. I'm tired, so I'm going to hit the sack. I'll see you in the morning."

"Suit yourself. If you change your mind, we'll be out here for quite a while." Angel walks to the door, turns, and smiles without saying anything.

The door slides open, and I hear her already yelling to her friends. I go out to the driveway, get my overnight and garment bag out of the car, and walk down the hall to the room Angel has allowed me to use a few other times. I hang up my suit, take out a few things from my overnight bag, and sit on the bed. Impulsively, I dig my cell phone out of my pocket, and speed dial Jaz. It has been three months since I even heard her voice—since she yelled, "Don't call me again!" Three months since last I tried to beg my way back into her life. I hear the dial tone, and feel my heartbeat pick up speed, but then the message that comes back at me leaves me stunned, speechless, and completely confused.

"The number you are calling is no longer in service."

The sunlight filters through the blinds and nudges me awake. With eyes still closed, I stretch and feel the tiredness of my bones still aching from the stress that seems to live with me now. Slowly, my consciousness brings me back to reality, and I open my eyes on one of Angel's beautiful guest bedrooms. Any other time the light tan walls would soothe me, the luxury of the blue silk sheets would comfort me, the extravagance of amenities placed so neatly throughout the room would exhilarate me, but none of it, this morning, can stir me from the sadness that envelopes me. I turn my head slowly to see my cell—the cell that still rests on the nightstand where I placed it after calling the same number over six times; the cell that gives me a message that still defies reality for me. *The number you are calling is no longer in service.*

—⟊—

In some kind of daze, I find my way to Derek's and Arianna's beach cottage just before noon. The Saturday sun is high in the sky, and I see the glitter of its natural diamonds sparkle on the surface of the water. The breeze off of the ocean is mild and feels refreshing, but I have taken a deeper dive in my spirit, and I expect nothing to brighten my mood at the moment. I've called Jaz five or six more times thinking the message must be a mistake, that the number must somehow be wrong, but the same hollow voice comes back and crushes me every time.

I ring the bell and Ari greets me at the door with an unbelievable surprise that makes me smile and forget myself.

"Hey, Zack. Come in and meet our little bundle of joy."

"Oh, my goodness. Look at what you have," I gush moving inside and glimpsing Derek rushing from the back of the house.

"Hey, man. See what we have."

"I see." I touch little Chase's cheek for the first time in his life— for the first time in my life.

"You want to hold him?" Arianna asks.

I hesitate momentarily, and Ari moves closer and hands her precious three- month- old son me. I'm awkward taking him, but I manage. In my arms, he feels warm, and soft, and so very comforting. Looking down at him, my mind immediately recalls my first encounter with him as I touched Ari's stomach and felt his thumping kicks inside the safety of her womb. Spreading across my face is the smile that I thought I had lost. I move away from the parents and with my back turned to them, I feather touch the baby's face to make sure this moment is real. I feel tears sting my eyes. My thoughts shout at me that maybe I will never have this for myself; maybe I have lost this forever. I hush the voices in my head with a song. It is as if only the two of us are in the room, and the words my Mommy used to sing to me pour out of me in a softness and a sincerity that I didn't know I possessed.

"Hush little baby don't say a word, Mama's gonna buy you a mocking-bird...if that mockingbird don't sing, Mama's gonna buy you a diamond ring...If that diamond ring won't shine...." I hum to him and rock him, and at some point, I turn to see Derek and Ari locked in each other's arms smiling at a Zack they have never seen before—a Zack that even I didn't know existed.

Throughout my two-day visit, I monopolized little Chase. I can't put him down, and Derek keeps teasing me that I will have to stay and hush his spoiled cries if I don't put him in his crib. I hold him through dinner. I hold him while we play cards. I hold him while he sleeps. I hold him while Ari tells me how Jaz quit her job, sold her studios, and became lost to us all. I hold him while we dance around the rooms, and I hold him when the four of us are just quiet in our friendship that needs no words. Chase and I bond for sure when I change his diapers, and I surprise myself at my devotion to this little person with tiny hands and feet, a pinched-up nose and beautiful hazel eyes like his mom. When I leave their home, I feel like I'm leaving an old friend, and I have a longing for something in my life that is permanent, meaningful, and full of life; somehow, I don't know how, I have to have it no matter the cost to me.

20

MAN TO MAN

Sometimes being a father has absolutely nothing to do with biology.

Back in New York, I make a decision: I have to find Jazmin. My heart tells me emphatically that I have no choice. I have to have at least one more time to talk with her; one more time to look into her eyes and search them for any hint of love for me that still might linger, one more time to watch the length of her gorgeous eyelashes slowly flutter their way to my heart. After a workday where I can't say I added a whole lot to our progress, I drive down to the waterfront. I take off my shoes and socks and let the sand ooze its way between my toes. I walk down the water's edge and let the calm waves lap at my feet as I ponder my plan—a plan that is stubborn and refuses to show up. Do I just drive up to her parent's house and ring the bell? I'm pretty sure she has to be there. Where else would she go to seek solace?

I stand quietly drawing imaginary pictures with my feet in the wet sand. I watch kids build sand castles, get buried beneath the cool grains, fill pails with water, dig in the sand, run toward the little waves and dash back to the safety of a parent's arms. I hear their giggle when they are picked up and swung around, and here on this beach, I experience another first. In the faces of the mothers, I see Mommy—my mommy when she would let me race to her and swing me around with my legs dangling in the air. I can hear my giggle and see her bury her face in mine and smother me with her sweet kisses or blow on my cheeks making silly noises. I feel her presence so strongly here. I find a quiet rocky place of solitude and sit watching an orange-red sun kiss the water goodnight and fade westward. I know she is here, and for the first time in a long while, I close my eyes and let her talk with me.

"You're here, aren't you, Mommy? I feel you. Tell me if you can...what should I do? what can I do? I feel so alone. You left me far too soon, and I have no idea how to stop this ache in my heart. I'm losing myself in this sorrow. I'm drowning. If you're with God...a God that I admit I don't know, ask Him to help me anyway. They tell me that He's a loving God... that He cares. I know He sent Jazmin to me, but I think I messed that up. Ask Him to do what Derek says He will always do...direct my path. I need His direction, Mommy. I need His help. Ask Him for me."

I feel the tears wash down on my face, and I wipe them away, but they are replaced with more. When I open my eyes, the scene before me blurs into blues, and greens, and reds, and yellows, and as darkness descends on the light of day, I hear my Mommy's persistent voice tell me to go, and "He will direct my path."

I let my vehicle steer itself toward the open highway, and ready myself for the hour drive to Jazmin's family home. I switch on the radio and hear the smooth sounds of jazz that remind me of the North

Carolina cottage where we danced. My mind rewinds a memory film of us running through the house playing a cat and mouse game. I watch my angel at her easel in the backyard as I sit and admire the view. I feel her arms around my neck and my heart responds to the kisses that we shared. With memory raging, the car snakes its way around the New York hills and finally comes to a stop at a beautiful lighted home on a hill where my Jazmin lived during her teen years. She brought me here once to pick up a few things, and I had a chance to spend a little pleasant time with her lovely parents. It was then, however, that I could see their "tight rein" on her—their desire for a kind of perfection in her life, but since that was nothing as harsh as what I had experienced in my youth, I thought nothing of her rant on the way down the hill about how their expectations were unbearable. I simply smiled to myself and listened.

At the door, I take a deep breath, still wondering what my first words to Jazmin will be. The door is a decorative glass, and I visualize her slender fingers hesitating to unlatch the knobs that will admit my entrance. That is the vision in my head, but after I ring the bell, it isn't Jazmin at the door. It is her father who stands in front of me, who pushes open the door, who speaks first.

"Zackary, come in."

"Good evening, sir."

"How are you, Son?" His voice is deadpan.

I take a deep breath. "I'm fine, but I think I'll be better when I see your daughter, Sir."

"No doubt, but I'm afraid that's not possible. Because of you, she's not here."

"Well, can you tell me where I can find her?"

"Yes, I could, but the problem for you, Son, is I won't. Come have a seat. We need to talk."

My heart drops because now I realize that this is going to be even more difficult than I thought. I follow David Grant into a cozy den area, speak to Mrs. Grant, and try to exchange pleasantries. She is a bit cold to me, so my flattery, and my attempt at casual jokes fall on deaf ears.

"Well, I'll let the two of you talk. You take care of yourself, Zackary."

"I will."

Sitting here in front of Mr. Grant, I'm extremely nervous, and I really don't know what to say, but then that isn't a problem because he does most of the talking.

"Son, Jazmin has quit her job, sold her studios, and left this area to get over you. She's trying to start over. I don't think you should try to see her again. She's been hurt enough, lied to enough, played with enough. You've done enough."

"I understand what you think, but I know something now that I didn't know then. I love her, Sir. I don't think I can live without her."

He sighs deeply and loudly, and I see his brow furrow. "Huh! Well, try. I think you can. I know you can. She's doing the work now to live without you so you will have to do the work to live without her. Zackary, you've done a lot of damage, and I don't think you can fix it."

I feel my head drop, and I look up at this man who is responsible for the life of the woman that now I know I love—a life that I want to be a part of so desperately. For some reason, I see little Chase flash in my mind's eye, and my eyes water.

"I see your tears, Son, and they make me wonder."

"Wonder what, Sir?" I murmur glancing up at him.

"Well, I wonder what got you to this place—this place where you are now—willing to come here and beg me to tell you where my daughter is...a child I love with every fiber of my being—my only child—my child that you've hurt so deeply that she's vanished from everything familiar to her. You did this, Zackary. I won't tell you where she is. You don't deserve her."

"You're right, Sir. I don't deserve her, but I want to try to change all of that."

"Son, you have no idea what a daughter means to a REAL father. You... have... no... idea. Those daughters are the light in our eyes, the breath we breathe. When we trust another man with our daughter, we trust that he'll honor her, adore her, treat her with dignity, and by all means do whatever he can to avoid hurting her. She is our precious little girl all grown up." He stops and seems to see something in his mind's eye that I can't see, and when he speaks again, his voice is soft at first, and he speaks slowly.

"Zackary, she's the one we first met in her mommy's womb when she moved for the first time. She's the beautiful little pink bundle we brought home from the hospital. She's the little one we allowed to paint our fingernails a rosy color, or put wigs on our head to be invited to the tea party. Huh! Son, you have no idea who you just messed with." I hear such passion in his voice that it actually frightens me. Now, I see tears in his eyes, and I watch them trail down his cheeks.

"She's the one in my memory, Zackary, cutting out little paper dolls on the floor at my feet while I read the daily news. She's the one bubbling with delight riding horsey on my young shoulders. She's the one squealing with joy in front of her presents at Christmastime, blowing out candle after candle as the birthdays tick up. She's the one we give a high ride to on a swing in the backyard and listen to her giggles as she tries to touch the sky. She's my baby on a family vacation with wide-eyed wonder at everything new she's experiencing. She's the one in high school cap and gown. Zackary, that girl's heart that you're playing with is the one I watched for years in adoration grow into a beautiful and talented young woman. Man, you took something so dear to me, and almost destroyed it. When she left here, she was crushed: shoulders sagging, no smiles, lifeless, just a body of shattered pieces staring back at me, and you think I'd tell you where she is? Huh! Never, Son. Never...Never!" I hear his passionate voice and see more of his tears fall.

"People change, Sir. I've changed." I know he can barely hear my voice.

David Grant leans forward resting his elbows on his thighs, steeples his fingers at his lips, and looks deeply into my eyes. Somewhere at Harvard, I'd learned that this is a power stance. Whether Mr. Grant intends it or not, it is how I perceive it, and it makes me nervous. His stare is not an angry one; it is more on the inquisitive side of things.

"That's talk, Son. You say that you've changed. That's just talk, and I hear you're very good at that." He sits back in the leather recliner still staring in my eyes. "What are you actually *doing* to demonstrate your change, Zack? What are you *doing* to prove your words?"

"I don't know a *particular* thing. I just feel the change."

"Well, that's not good enough, Son. You talk to me when you do something *PAR-TIC-U-LAR!*" He over enunciates the word, and I certainly get his point.

"Like what? I want her back. I'll do whatever it takes."

"You'll do whatever it takes. Huh! Well, you're an intelligent guy. I'm sure Harvard prepared you for a lot of different situations in life. Figure that out, but I will tell you that you will have to do a lot. I'm not ignorant of your past Zackary. Jazmin shared a lot with us about things that you've had to endure, but that's all in the past, and you can't take that kind of baggage into a relationship and think it's going to work."

"Should I get counseling?"

"It won't hurt."

"Would you go with me? Help me?"

Mr. Grant says nothing at first, and I see the wheels in his mind turning. After a few moments of silence, he looks up at me, and I see him shake his head yes.

"Yes, I'll go with you, Son, and I'll help you, but let me tell you why. A very long time ago, I needed some help from someone who I thought would never reach out to me, but he did, and he saved my life. I would say that he's responsible for the adult life I've lived, and I am still most grateful. I, too, was a mess just like you, for different reasons—different circumstances, but a mess all the same. So, I'm going to pay it forward, and try to help you save your life, but Zackary, let me tell you this as emphatically as I can: Don't ask me where Jazmin is ever again—not as long as you live and breathe on this earth. Don't ask me because I will never be the one to tell you—not ever."

"Yes, Sir."

—⁓—

At this stage in my life, there is very little that I find definitive, but I know this one thing for sure: Time, like the symmetry of a single flake of snow is ever fleeting. Seconds move secretly into minutes, and minutes slip quietly into hours. Hours crash into days, days melt into weeks, weeks run into months, and the months quickly, almost unnoticed, build a tower of years. This, one thing, is my undeniable FEAR that keeps me awake at night, haunts my daydreams, and stumbles its way into too many of my waking thoughts. I fear that this inevitable ticking clock that will not cease, this clock that refuses to return one single moment will ensnare my Jaz—my Jazmin—my angel and steal her away from me forever. So, it is this FEAR that propels me, drives me and demands from me a call to a very old friend who never fails to help me, no matter what.

I dial the number that I know will reach him in a distant land, and as it rings, I wait impatiently until I hear his familiar voice.

"Bonjour."

"Frank?"

"Oui."

"Frank, this is Zack. What's wrong with you? Did you forget how to speak English?"

"Zack, my Man. What's up. No, I haven't forgotten English. I just don't get much chance to speak it very much anymore. Where are you?"

"I'm in New York. Where are you?"

"I never left Paris, man. I'm still here. I love it here."

"You mean you're still on that mission I sent you on years ago? You're still watching Jean Paul?" I chuckle.

"Naw, Man. That guy left right after he saw that Arianna was married. He's harassing another woman from Spain now. He moved there thinking I couldn't catch up with him there. I still know every move he makes," he laughs. "But my life is very different now, Zack. I fell in love, married a wonderful French girl, and we have some beautiful twins bouncing around on my knee now. I decided it was time for me to grow up and quit the faux cop business," he chuckles.

"I see. Well, I'm happy for you but I desperately need your help. I need you to find someone for me, but I guess you don't do that anymore, huh? But I *really* need you, Frank."

"No problem, Zack. You know I'll do whatever you need as long as it's legal. I have to stay legal. I have too much to lose, Man."

"I understand that."

"What's up? Talk to me."

"My lady disappeared on me, and I have to find her. I have no idea where she is. I can't give you any direction. She could be anywhere."

"You know me, Zack. I can find anybody, anywhere, anytime. I'm straight now. I have my own business, and I'm quite successful. No more New York street mess, faux cops and junk. The money you paid me in the Jean Paul situation with Arianna helped me get my life on track, and meeting my wife was the best thing that has ever happened to me. You're talking to Private Eye, Frank Gillman. Fax me a picture and any other information you have. I'll find her."

We talk a long time just to catch up, and of course, a lot of the talk is about Jaz: her profession, her habits, things she likes to do, places she likes to visit, but we also talked about Frank's new life, and for the first time in my life, I realize the real sting of jealousy. As messed up as Frank's life has been, even he can move on, find love, and grab it.

During the next few months, my life also changes quite a bit. Papa G, as I affectionately call him now, keeps a very close eye on me and threatens to pull his support from me for the slightest infractions. He rules with an iron fist, and because I need him so much, I have to listen even when it irritates me to no end. We go to regular counseling sessions, and I have to admit that they help tremendously. I'm finally convinced that none of the things that happened in that House of Horrors is my fault. I also have to admit that I love having Papa G around. He is the closest thing I have ever felt to having a real father. I just wish he would trust me, but he says that has to come in time. The biggest change in my life is my relationship with God. I can feel it growing every time I go to church, every moment in my Bible study class, every time I talk with Papa G, every time I start to feel down. There is this urging, this whisper, this feeling of things being all right, with or without my Jaz. I just want it to be *with* her. I rarely think about *without* her.

I have even begun to put down some roots. I bought a beautiful house on a hill that is far too big for one person, but I plan to fill it one day with a wife, children and laughter, but Papa G says that will come in time when my head is ready and he keeps reminding me: "Son, you have to be ready, and that's not now.

21

BURYING THE PAST

Brutal criticism of others, camouflages the fault that lies within.

Papa G and I wind our way around the streets of New York and finally find the quiet countryside where we have been heading for the last forty minutes. We finally see grass and trees and even a few fall flowers as we move closer to our destination.

"You sure you don't want me to drive the rest of the way, Son?"

"No, I got this. I'm fine."

"No, you're not fine, and I don't want to find myself wrapped around one of these beautiful trees so you need to let me drive the rest of the way."

"No, I told you. I'm fine."

"Son, your eyes are darting here and there, you keep braking for no reason, you're constantly tapping your fingers on the steering wheel, and perspiration is beading your forehead. Let me drive. You don't have to be strong about everything. Some things are unnerving, and this is one of those things for you. Pull over."

I pull the car over and stop in front of a no park sign.

"Now, hurry up and change seats with me before a policeman sees us in this illegal situation you put us in."

I move as fast as I can, but I have to admit it's not very fast, but it's the best I can do in my emotional state. Papa G takes the wheel and we find our way and drive through the tall gates and around the curvy professional landscape. When he brings the car to a stop, I feel the perspiration drip from my face. I notice my sweaty palms, and I feel the tears burning my eyes, but I will myself to pull the latch on the door, get out, and walk up to my latest *PARTICULAR* thing that I'm doing.

The headstones are close, and the marble is smooth and beautiful. It is the best that I could find, the best that I could buy. Each is a different color, but each is equally exquisite. I move over to the center one first, and I read what I asked the stonecutters to inscribe:

To the Dearest Mom in the world:
May God's grace
Wrap you in His loving care.
Until we meet again....

I slowly run my hand over the words, touching each precious letter, each profound word. I finger the outspread wings of the Dove that hovers over the words and view the cross and crown resting on top the structure. I see my mother's smile and feel her comfort, but my body still begins to tremble in some deep emotion that I have kept at bay for years. Words won't come, but the agony of my loss is without control now. The burdens that I have born for years, in my own hell of secrecy, need and find their total release, and I burst at the seams. Only one word escapes my tortured soul, and I feel the screams that seem to come from someone else and in another time and space. Mama! Mama! Mama! My voice is breaking, choking, grasping for air when I feel Papa G's arms wrap around me and pull me strongly to him. Our tears mingle as he tries to comfort me. His strength is what I need at the moment.

"Let it go, Son. Let it go. Get it all out. Don't hold back a thing. I've got you. Let it go."

I hear more of my ache breathlessly finding its way to the surface of my pain, and I yield to it. I feel the words that have followed me all of my life pushing violently out through my lips to find their freedom, and I look up to the heavens and scream them at Him: "Why God? Why? Did you forget about me? I was just a little boy. Why did you take her from me?" The ache is so deep, the pain so fierce, the agony so indescribable. I sit on the ground and feel the coolness of the manicured lawn around me. Through the blur of my tears, I see the blueness of the sky, a rainbow of natural colors surrounding me and, from somewhere, in this parting moment in time, I feel a sense of here and now...a sense of the absolute presence: no past and no future, just right now. In that special moment, I sense a profound peacefulness that I have never felt before—a feeling that my Mama is all right and that I will be all right. In that solid moment, my ache is silenced, and I am shaken, but quiet.

Papa G pulls me up from the ground now, still holding me at my waist, and I proceed to finish the task. I move to my right, and touch the only thing that I can touch of my grandmother. I read her inscription:

"To my Grandmother:
FINALLY,
"On Christ, the solid Rock, I stand.
All other ground is sinking sand."

I touch the raised engraved ROCK done in a lighter shade of her granite, and I see the perfection of the stonecutter's work. It is done exactly as I asked. My tears fall, but the shaking has stopped, my heart has slowed its beat, and again I feel a sense of peace fall on me.

"Ok Son, it's almost done, but this may be the hardest of all."

I move over to the left of my mother's headstone, but I back away. I feel my lips tighten into a straight line as I bite down on them trying to will myself to move ahead—to finish this.

"You can do this, Son. You can do it. Go ahead."

"Papa G., I can't."

"Yes, you can, Son. Go ahead and finish this. You're almost there. Go ahead, I'm right here with you. Your Mama is here, and your grandmother is right here with you. Now, go ahead and finish this."

I take a small step forward, and I look, but I don't touch the words. I see them, I know I wrote them, but at the moment, for some reason, touching them is far too hard. Touching, somehow, makes them far too real, so I simple read them to myself.

"To my father: I forgive you."

I feel my hand move forward, reaching, but still not touching, and then I break down in agonizing tears. I feel my body shaking again uncontrollably, and I feel arms embrace me.

"Come sit with me, Son. This is hard. I know it's hard. Let's sit here on this bench you put here to talk to your Mom, and you and I will talk for a minute. I need to remind you of something. We've had a lot of lessons over the past few months and I need to remind you of them."

"Huh! This dude killed my Mama. You don't need to remind me of a thing! He took her away from me when I was just seven years old, Papa G. He stabbed her seven times for every year that I was born, and told me so." My voice cracks in my sorrow. "How do you expect me to forgive that? This dude... killed... my... mama!" I almost scream the words that wrench from my throat.

Despite my anguish and despite my hesitancy, we move over to the seat, and I can feel Papa G almost holding me up. He lets me sit for a moment before he speaks, and I try to calm myself.

"Son, I want you to remember something beyond whatever else you end up doing in this situation." He pauses. The pause is powerful because it allows his words to pass through my ears and reach my mind. "All of your life, you've been able to use your head and win, Zack. You can think through almost any situation and come out the winner. You've learned well, and I'm sure early in your life, how to deal, manipulate, connive, hoodwink, and many times just honestly outthink everybody around you to get what you want. You're in a different ballgame here, Son. This is a *very different* ballgame. This is nothing about the head. This is all about the heart—your heart. This thing called forgiveness is simply for you, not anyone else. You need to remember that above all else. This forgiveness is so that *you* can come out from under that shadow that shades *you*, so that *you* can shake off that heaviness that keeps *your* shoulders slightly bent, so that *you* can finally acknowledge that all of us have flaws and that does not exempt your father. This forgiveness is for *you*, Son. Your father is deceased. He lived his life the way he chose to live it, so your forgiveness means nothing to him now. He's not even here to receive it. This God-given moment is for you so that you can find the love that you so desperately are seeking. You can't love in the midst of hate and confusion. That's a major reveal that you need to remember now. Let it go, Son, so you can move on to a better life—a more rewarding life where you can treat people the way they deserve to be treated, so you can see women in a different light, and you can stop killing their spirit like your father killed their body."

His words hit me like a ton of bricks. Sto*p killing their spirit like your father killed their body.* My mind rapid-fires through imaginary black book pages flipping like cartoon characters move when you flip through the pages as fast as you can. Summer dances before my eyes. Carmen strikes a pose. Taylor moves to me seductively and in a nano-second a hundred other victims flicker through my mind, and then finally, my eyes rest. Standing tall and angelic is my Jazmin. What have I done? I feel my head turn and look deeply into this man's eyes, and in them, I see nothing but love, a softness, a fatherly desire for a son. He puts his arms around me and pulls me to him. "Allow yourself to find love, Son. Let the hate go 'cause love and hate can't live in the same house."

I look up to the sky. I see its vastness, and I whisper a scripture I'd recently learned and for the first time, I feel its meaning: "...and the peace of God, which surpasses all understanding, will guard your hearts and minds through Christ Jesus." I get up and I feel a lightness to my body like I've slammed some two- hundred- pound weight to the floor. I move with conviction to the headstone, touch the words and let my fingers linger at the word "forgive." This is for me. I look up at Papa G who tightens his grip at my waist and he wraps his arms around me again and hugs me tightly. I smile to myself and in his ear, I whisper two words that have a far deeper meaning than I can express at this meeting. I will have to express these words with action.

"Thank you. Thank you."

Together we walk slowly back to the car, and in an instant, I begin to feel every bit of my exhaustion. My thoughts fire through the last three months that have brought us to this culmination. I think of these tasks: having each body exhumed and moved from three different cemeteries, finding this beautiful spot on a hill overlooking this tranquil sparkling lake. I think of meticulously selecting the different granite, writing the inscriptions, and bringing the three of them to their final resting place together . . . not for them, but now I know it's all for me. My mind flashes to the lessons in my Bible study class that helped to bring me to the serenity of forgiveness, the late-night talks between Papa G and me that helped me understand that without forgiveness, I would forever be stuck in my own bitterness—a bitterness that would continue to impact every facet of my life and eventually consume me. I think about talks that helped me have a new understanding of what it really means to be a man. In this moment, with a true and lasting friend by my side, I feel a sense of peace, freedom, and gratitude that I have never felt before. He opens the passenger door for me, takes out my car keys from his pocket and, more than ever before, there is this unspoken togetherness that we both sense as he drives us back to his home.

On the way, I think it's the perfect time to hint . . . to joke . . .to see where his head is now about my Jaz and me. I've done some *particular* things. I take a deep breath.

With some trepidation, I look over at Papa G. "May I ask you a simple question about Jazmin without your getting all upset with me?"

"No. What did I tell you, Boy? Today doesn't change that."

"Pop, I want to talk to her before she leaves me."

"Huh! You're worst off than I thought, Boy. I guess you haven't noticed: She already left you, Son. You need to move on. That's what today is about—moving on."

Without another word to him, I slip down in my seat and let sleep take me to a secret dream world where the universe allows Jaz and me to find each other again.

~ Jazmin ~

22

SILENT TEARS

*The pain of a broken heart will not be denied,
no matter the ferocity of battle.*

Rushing has never been my favorite thing, but here I am again running to another photo shoot—late. This past year has been one frustrating thing after another. My paintings have been less than ideal, my photography uninteresting, and my work in general lacking that uniqueness—that thing that makes it sing—the spark that makes it a work to be recognized, applauded, and most importantly, the thing that makes it me. I've lost too much weight, feel homesick even though my parents call often, and I find myself generally to be one complete mess. Sometimes I don't recognize myself. I want desperately to get my life back on track, but it just doesn't seem to be happening for me right now, but still, I'm trying to be patient with me.

The streets are crowded and I still haven't gotten used to driving on what I call the wrong side. However, there is something about

England, even in my exasperation that has provided a sort of quietness for me. Living in St Albans with its beautiful medieval architecture, the lush greenness surrounding me, intriguing market places, and delicious food at the finest restaurants have all been new and fascinating, but it has failed miserably to do the one thing that I most wanted it to do: find hidden in the shadows, untainted by other females, an amazing mystery man for me to love. I search for one who would allow me to forget Zack completely, make him stop haunting my dreams, make him stop appearing at every corner and turn in my life, and allow me finally the peace that permits me to sleep on a dry pillow every night.

I wheel into a space near the gazebo and spot Brooklyn immediately even though the park is a bit crowded. She stands out from the crowd, and I rush to take what I need from my car. I see her walking toward me with her usual smile that lights her big brown eyes and creates her unique beauty. She has a face that any artist would love to paint, any photographer would give a million to snap, and any song-writer would love to immortalize in verse. Simply put, she is a beautiful young woman who demands attention the minute she appears in all of her deep chocolate magnificence.

"What took you so long? I was beginning to think the American was lost again," she giggles in her thick British accent.

"No, the American was not lost—just late again."

She gives me a quick welcoming hug and we walk together to the gazebo that I already see will be the perfect backdrop. The sun is high in the sky and provides a perfect light, and Brooklyn is an exquisite model that knows how to move just right to make her shots unbelievable. We spend more than an hour completely immersed in the task of making her magazine shots breathtaking, and without looking at any finished product, we both know that we have touched perfection.

"Do you have time to get a bite to eat?"

"Yeah, I do. I don't have a lot planned for today. I am a bit anxious to review what we have here, but it can wait. Where do you want to go?"

Well, I thought we'd drive out to London. There's a place there I'd like for you to see. Just in case you and Zack get back together, it'll be a great place for you to take him."

"Brooklyn, please don't start with Zack today. We are not getting back together. I haven't even talked with him in almost a year. I'm sure he's moved on by now. I keep telling you that he is not a one-woman man, and that is what I need. That is what I have to have in my life, so please don't start with me today about getting back with Zack. I told you a hundred times that he does not want me."

"And I keep telling you all you need to do is dial his number and find out what he's doing. You should never have changed your number. I bet he'd call everyday if he knew your number." The beauty of her British accent almost makes me believe her words, but I resist.

"No, he wouldn't call every day. You are living in that fantasy he had me living in for a while. You saw his picture, and you're doing what I did. You fell for the looks, but I've learned the hard way that things are far deeper, and you have to look deeper than that face of his," I say throwing my things in the backseat while I watch Brooklyn get in on the passenger side.

"Where's your car?" I ask with exasperation.

"Oh, I got a ride here. I figured that you would take me home." We drive into London and Brooklyn directs me to a beautiful waterfront restaurant where the seafood is fresh and the atmosphere is outstanding. We are seated on the waterside, and the artist in me can't stop looking around at the design of the building, the décor, and the general look of the entire place. This would be a very romantic place if one happened to be here with Mr. Right.

"This place is absolutely beautiful. Do you come here often with Shawn?"

"Not too often, but on special occasions."

"So why did you want to bring me here?" *I know exactly why she's bringing me here. She's not one bit subtle. She's never going to give up this matchmaking idea. Zack has her in his grasp, and she's never even met him.* I can't help but laugh to myself at his power.

"This is the place where you're going to bring Zack when you forgive him," she giggles.

"I see this is going to be a very long afternoon," I snap feigning anger at this woman who has become my very best friend.

"It doesn't have to be. Just call him and see what he's doing right now," she laughs ignoring my attempt at anger.

"Do you think that I would have moved all the way to England— another country, if I wanted to talk with Zack?"

"Well, you've had some time to think about it—some time to cool off. Based on what you've told me about the things you two have done together, the places you've been, and the miracles you have seen, you two belong together. I just believe that you two have something special, and I'm going to keep nagging you until you see it. That special one generally only comes along once in a lifetime, and I don't want to see you throw your soul mate away just because he made a few mistakes and you can't get over it."

I can feel me steeling myself before I speak because I know that Brooklyn has no idea the depth of my hurt, but I also know that the minute my words are out, they will be even more real to me, but I have to say them for Brooklyn and most of all for me. For almost a year now, I have secretly hoped against hope that Zack would come for me. I've played the mind game: today will definitely be the day that he comes and sweeps me away with him, but it never was that day. I know he has that ability, but he would have to want to come for me. He has not, and I know that I haven't hidden myself that well. If he wanted me, he would find me. That's Zack!

I fold my arms across my breasts, and look out at the water. I think about the lake that Zack and I shared, and in a flash, a multiplicity of thoughts fly in a wide stream of consciousness through my mind. I think of our nights in the cabin; I see the hide and go seek games we played on the Disney lawn, the Mickey Mouse hats, my big pink teddy bear, the bundles of Christmas gifts we shared. My mind crashes into the moments I held him somewhere between life and death, the prayers I prayed for him to know the God I know, the words we whispered in the hospital, the laughter that made our bodies shake, the movies, the popcorn snacks, the swim after the release from cancer fears, the reveal of his deep dark secrets, the tears that escape to freedom—so much we shared, so much that had to be real for both of us, but despite my thoughts of authentic love, I take a deep breath, and still, looking out at the water, I slowly murmur the words.

"A friend once warned me to guard my heart from Zack. He told me that I'd get hurt and Zack would walk away unscathed, but I didn't listen, and that is exactly what happened, Brooklyn."

"I doubt that he walked away unscathed. You just didn't stick around long enough to see his pain. You have this uncanny gift of having a great impact on people without even trying, and you don't even realize it—you don't even know. I bet he told you a thousand times that you were different from any other girl he'd ever met. Am I right?"

"Yes, as a matter of fact he did tell me that quite a few times."

"Jazmin, you love Zack, and I believe, from what I have heard about him, he loves you. Why don't you fight for him? Isn't he worth that?

"Why doesn't he fight for me?"

"Somewhere in his world, I think that he is fighting for you. It's just that he has so much more to fight through than you do. It will take him a while to punch through all of the trash and flying debris."

"Why are you, my friend, taking his side?"

"I'm not. I'm taking your side. You have been here for almost a year and you are no better than you were when you first came. No, I don't see the swollen eyes everyday now; you don't sit silently looking out at space as often, and you can say his name now without blowing up like some exploding volcano spilling over with hot lava, but in reality, you are no better. You just hide better. I think you need to clear this thing up. You need to talk to him, and if you find him no better, then you will know and you can heal. But this thing that you're doing:

this running and hiding is not working. Jaz, go home, face him, and see what happens. Stop wasting away here in England."

"Look, I'm going to drop you off at home and I'm going home— St Albans, not New York."

We pay the bill and quietly walk to my car. At some point she grabs my hand and squeezes it, but not a word is spoken until I reach her door.

"Look, Brooklyn, you have been a life saver for me. There is no doubt about it. You have no idea how much you're helped me, but on this, I can't take your advice right now. It still hurts far too much, and I can't see him right now. I have to get stronger, and I have no idea how long that will take."

She looks at me without a comment, opens the car door and blows me a kiss as she leaves. Me? What do I do? I drive home in a blur of tears hearing a cacophony of Derek's screaming warnings mixed with Brooklyn's persistent pleas for second chances. Through all of the noises in my head, I miraculously manage to find this quiet spot inside of me where I simply wonder if what Brooklyn advises is the only thing that will satisfy and save me.

~ Zack ~

23

IN THE MIDST
OF THE STORM

*God is always in the midst of the storm, and in it,
there is Salvation.*

My house is unique, big, beautiful, immaculate, quiet, and empty. I climb the spiral marble stairs, walk down the upstairs hall, and look at the white closed door that I pray one day will be a nursery. I open it and visualize the beauty of baby furniture, a Mom rocking her baby to sleep, and me checking through the night to make sure all is well. I think about Chase and how soft and sweet he is, and I picture my own son or daughter cradled in my arms. Just the thought makes my heart leap.

I close the door to this empty room, turn my back, lean up against the door, and slide to the floor. I sit in the quietness—alone and tremendously lonely. I know I can make some calls and in a matter of a few short minutes, this house would be full of people, but what I know now is that it would still be empty—so, I make no calls. Instead, I whisper a prayer. In the middle of my plea to this God that I am still getting to know, I feel my phone vibrate. I pull it from my pocket, and Frank's face is staring up at me. I look at his smiling picture, and hold it in my hand afraid to answer—afraid not to answer. Slowly I slide it on and put the phone to my ear.

"Hello?" I almost whisper.

"Bonjour mon cher ami," booms the voice on the other end.

"Hey, Frank. How are you?" My voice is still quiet.

"I'm great and so will you be, my friend. I found her."

"You found Jazmin Grant?" I sit up straight.

"Oui."

I take a deep breath and sigh loudly. I feel the tears burning my eyes, my heart racing, and a weakness in my knees. I brace myself, stand up, and ask again.

"You found my Jazmin?"

"Yes, Zack. Did you have doubts that I would? You know me, Man. I can find anybody, and she was very easy."

My legs give way in their sudden weakness and I slide to the floor again, and I try to stop the tears, but I can't. I hear my voice crack as I attempt my next question.

"Where is she, Frank?"

"She's in a quaint little place just outside of London called St. Albans. It's very nice: quiet, religious. It's the site of the shrine of St.

Albans, Britain's first saint. I learned that little trivia while I was there. She is a praying Mademoiselle, and she visits her church regularly."

"You saw her?"

"Of course—quite a few times."

"And you went there?"

"Of course. Did you think I wouldn't go? That's the way I operate. You know that."

"I do know, but I thought with your family and all, it would be different this time."

"No. No different. I'm still quite thorough."

"How is she, Frank?"

"Mademoiselle looks sad, but she keeps busy. Man, she's very thin—like she needs a good meal," he chuckles. Maybe you can see to that when you go to her."

"Did she see you follow her?"

"Zack, come on, Man. Don't ask me that. I'm no amateur. You know that."

"I do know that." I sigh. "Thank you, Frank. I don't know how I will ever repay you."

"When you marry this beautiful girl, bring her to France. I'd love to see you two together. I know you can make her smile again. Despite how much I love it here and love my family, I still miss you guys a lot. I'd love to see you, Zack. I'm glad that I could help you. I'll fax her information and my bill to you tonight. Now go get your girl and be happy."

"I'm going to do my best, and I'll pay you whatever you ask. I just hope I'm not too late to get her back."

"Well, she's not seeing anyone else or I didn't see her with anyone else, other than a model named Brooklyn. They are good friends and work together. I watched her house a lot. Only Brooklyn came to her. Go be happy, Man. Au Revoir."

"Thank you, Frank. I'll be in touch."

The fax, with Jaz's address, comes through in a matter of minutes, and I begin to pack before it arrives. I call to get my new plane, *JazAir*, ready for takeoff, dash out to my car for one important stop before I head to the airport. Mistakenly, I think it will take me only a few minutes, but because of my own inability to make a quick decision, it takes me well over two hours, but then with everything finished and me completely satisfied, I rush excitedly to the airport and board *JazAir*. When I feel the plane lift, my heart is pounding, my mind is racing, my smile is uncontainable, and butterflies in my stomach are dancing to the happy beat of their wings. Finally, I'm going to see my angel.

As I ride through the streets of London, I wonder a lot of things. Why did Jazmin choose this place? After all, the sun is rare, and she loves the sun. Maybe it was because she knew no one here. Maybe that was the reason. She could start over without anyone knowing her, or her work. No one would have any special expectations. Beyond that, it certainly would have been the last place I would have looked.

All of these thoughts disappear when I pull up to her address in my rental, and before I exit the car, I see her kneeling down over the flowers that she's planting. She looks beautiful in the midst of the various fall colors surrounding her. The wide brim hat she is wearing hides her face, and even though I, too, can tell that she is thinner, there is no mistake. It is my angel. She is a little distance from the front of the house so the slam of my car door does not take her attention away from her task. I walk closer, kneel down on one knee and hold out the diamond ring that sparkles in the sun—the one that took me over two hours to choose. She does not turn. Her hands, at first, are still digging in the rich soil, but I see them when they still themselves in mid activity. The trowel has made its entrance into the soil, but I see her stop, take off her gloves, and with both hands, brace herself on the ground. I know now that she knows that I am there, close to her. She does not turn to look at me but she calls out my name.

"Zack...Zack."

She still does not turn.

"Jazmin, look at me." I feel my tears and hear them in my voice; I know she feels hers too.

"Baby, look at me."

I see her steady herself before her head turns and she sees me, there on one knee holding out a symbol of what I hope she will see as a happy future. She stands and while I want her to run to me, she does not. She is still. The only thing that moves is the October breeze blowing her hair—longer hair that now brushes her shoulders.

"Jazmin Grant, love of my life, will you marry me?" I call to her.

I see her slowly walk over to me, and I pray she is coming to take the ring from my hand and allow me to place it on her finger. I see the tears now, her mouth pinched together, and her eyes blinking too fast. When she reaches me, at first, she simply stares as if to make absolutely sure that it's me, then she reaches for my arm and attempts to pull me up from my knee.

"Jazmin, no."

"What are you doing here, Zack?"

"Something I have never done in my life. I'm begging."

"Don't. I don't want you to beg. I told you almost a year ago. I closed the door on us—on all that we could have had."

I stand up now and face her and I wipe her tears with my thumbs. "That was a long time ago, baby. I was a different person then. I know what I want now; I know what I have to have." I try to pull her to me, but she resists. I sigh deeply, put the ring back in my pocket and touch her arm. I have to touch her. I have waited so long, done so many *particular* things, changed in so many different ways—some ways that she can never understand.

"Will you at least spend some time with me? Can I at least be just an old friend who dropped by?"

"Zack, I didn't ask you to drop by. I didn't want you to drop by. I'm trying to get my life back on track and I can't do it with you."

"Are you at least breathing again?"

"What?"

"You asked me to get out of your life so that you could breathe again. Are you at least breathing again?"

"No."

We stare at each other for a moment, both of us knowing exactly what that simple answer, "no," really means, and then I take her hand in mine.

"Zack, you have to go. You have to leave me alone, forget about me, and move on."

"Jaz. Jazmin, I don't want to make you uncomfortable. I didn't come here for that so I'll just tell you this, and you can do with it what you want. I'm staying at the St. Michaels Manor Hotel on Fishpool Street. I'll be there for three days. My number has not changed, so you already have that unless you threw it away with the rest of me."

"No, Zack. I didn't throw it away. Actually, it's engraved on my brain," she says with a hint of sarcasm. And just for the record: I didn't throw you away; you threw me away."

"Well, that was not my intention, Baby. You stopped talking with me, you moved away, you ran and hid from me. Anyway, I'll go, but remember: I'm here for three days. My flight leaves on Monday." I release her hand, and could have sworn that I felt a slight tug before we separated, but I'm not absolutely sure. Actually, I'm not sure about much of anything at the moment except how much I know that I love this woman, and I know that it's my fault I don't have her in my arms. I turn and walk a few paces before I turn around to her again, but she has already gone back to her planting. Not a good sign for me.

—m—

I check into the hotel, and when I have everything wiped, sprayed, dusted, and hung up to my OCD satisfaction, I take a walk outside and sit by the lake. The fall scenery is beautiful, and I watch the ripples in the water, listen to the singing birds, and wonder will I ever have anyone with whom to share this type of life. I'm excelling in my career to an unbelievable height. The money rolls in non-stop, but still, I could not be more unhappy, more lonely, more dissatisfied at the moment. However, somehow, I know that it won't stay this way. Somehow, I have this uncanny sense that something good is waiting for me. Maybe it's my encouraging talks with Papa G, or the Bible studies, or the forgiveness that has lifted the weight of the world from my shoulders. I simply don't know what it is, but I know things are going to change. Something for me is about to change with or without Jazmin.

I walk around the lake, stoop and dip my hands in the cool water. I think about my past—not the horrible stuff, just the stuff I've done that has brought me to this point in my life. In my mind, I interrogate myself. How did I get to a place where I'm making more money than I will ever be able to spend? How did I will myself to and through Harvard Law from my background? How did I get here, able to stay in a place like this with no worries about time or money? How did I escape a terrible life that seemed destined for me to live? I look up at the blue sky and I ask Him. How? Why? Suddenly the words from a third- grade teacher come back to my mind as clearly as the first day I ever spoke them. I hear the words that Mr. Garrison made us repeat at least three times a day for the four straight years that he tracked us: *"If it is to be, it's up to me."*

The words hit me like a lightning bolt. My happiness, my satisfaction, my successes are all up to me. Words from the poem, *Invictus*, that Mr. Garrison taught us in fifth grade ring again in my ears: *"I am the master of my fate, I am the captain of my soul."* I dash inside the hotel with a new sense of determination...a new sense of knowing what I need to do. I hop in the shower singing our song: *"You are so beautiful to me...."* My thoughts exhilarate me, the shower refreshes me, and I feel a sense of happiness that has eluded me for over a year. I dress casually in black slacks, a gray shirt, black shoes, and a gold chain. I check myself out in the full-length mirror and rush to my car. The drive back to Jazmin's is long to me, but when I finally park in front of her home, I feel a sense of nerves pushing their way to the pit of my stomach, but I make every effort to ignore them. *"...I am the master of my fate."*

I ring the bell and hear her moving to the door. When it opens, there I stand—again. This time, however, I have my old smile back, my swagger, but the difference now is that all of it is just for her—no one else.

"Hey, girl," I say leaning up against her door. "I couldn't wait—couldn't take the chance of your not showing up in three days. I need to see you too much—need to be near you too much. I've traveled a long way to see you. I tried, but I couldn't wait another minute. Let me come in." I wink. I smile my million-dollar smile that sells any-thing and everything all—day—long—every day: that smile that has made me a multimillionaire.

She folds her arms and stares at me. I see the hint of a smile touch-ing her lips, and that's all I need.

"Come on Jaz, stop playing. Let me come in."

"Who's playing? Zack, you took my heart and ripped it to shreds, and you think I want to go through that again?"

"I told you I'm a different man from that time and place. I've changed. You could at least treat me like a distant friend and be courteous. You wouldn't make anyone else who traveled thousands of miles to see you stand out here begging to come in for a minute."

She shakes her head at me, pushes the door open, and steps aside. "Now that you're in, what?"

"What? Hmm. Let me see: Let's start with me having a seat," I say flirting with my eyes.

"Have a seat." *She's sarcastic. I have to change that somehow.*

"Thank you." I flirt again, and she ignores it again. I cross the room and sit in a single seat even though I see a sofa that holds at least four people comfortably. I sit, cross my left leg over my right, rest my elbows on the arms of the chair, and steeple my fingers like Papa G does to me—my power play.

"So, what do you do here in England?"

"Whatever I please."

"And what do you please to do, my dear?" I say leaning forward now looking sexy as you know what.

"Zack, what do you want?"

"You." My very short answer stops her.

"I want you, and I don't plan to leave without you. I told you earlier that I was leaving in three days, but I've come to realize it may take three days, three weeks, three months. It may take three years, but I'm not leaving without you."

"Zack, let's just suppose I don't want *you* anymore."

"Well, that would change things quite a bit, wouldn't it?" I feel my swagger excuse itself and leave the room. I get up from my seat and move over to where she's standing. I don't touch her with my hands, only my eyes.

"Jaz, look in my eyes, and tell me that you don't love me anymore, and I'll leave right now, catch my flight, and go home. I won't trouble you ever again because there will be no need. I mean that. Your father refused to tell me where you were living, and I hired a private detective to find you, and the rest is history. You mean everything to me now. I know that now more than I know anything else in the world, but if you don't want me anymore, if you *really* don't love me anymore, it's over, but I need you to tell me. No games. Just what you've always asked of me: honesty."

She moves away from me now, but I catch her hand and gently pull her back.

"No. No more running. No more moving away. We have to face this now. We have to be as honest with each other as we possibly can be. I've stopped my games and come face to face with some real realities in the last nine months, and you have to do the same thing or we both may miss the last chance we have. So, look at me, Jazmin, and tell me that you don't love me anymore."

I see her hesitate.

"Tell me, Jaz. I have to know the truth."

"Well, the truth is when you rang my doorbell, I was about to go out to dinner. I'm hungry. Why don't you join me, and we'll talk about things over a meal."

"Fine, but we will settle this part of it tonight." *If it is to be, it's up to me.*

The restaurant is absolutely exquisite. We are shown to a table on the waterside. Candles light the room and the cozy atmosphere is extremely romantic, but I'm trying not to let my mind go to romance because I have no idea how this all is going to turn out for me. As far as I know, I may be on *JazAir* tonight flying back home empty handed and extremely sad. Whatever the outcome though, I know that happiness awaits me in the future so I take solace in that. *"I will never leave you or forsake you."* Seated across from Jaz is comforting even if she does seem quite distant. I put my mask away: all of the games, all of the swagger, everything that spells phony, and I take her hand across the table. "What's it going to be, Babe?"

She takes her hand away and picks up the menu. "I don't know yet. Let me look."

"No. I mean with us. What's it going to be?"

"Right now, it's going to be dinner. I told you. I'm hungry."

"OK. You can prolong this as long as you want, but I will get an answer to my question tonight."

"Fine, but right now, I'm ordering."

The waiter comes and takes our order, and we do the small talk thing while we wait. I find out about Brooklyn, her new photo shop, and her deals with the magazine company. I tell her nothing much because later I don't want to think that any of the *particular* things that I've done are the reasons why she is with me. I want her to be with me because she loves me, and because she can see my change. When the dinner comes, we eat with less small talk, and I realize for the first time today that I haven't had a thing to eat, so I am very hungry, and I eat like I'm very hungry.

"Zack, when was the last time you ate?"

"Hmm. Actually, it was yesterday at lunch. Last night I found out where you were living, and I immediately jumped on a plane."

"How do you get a plane that fast? Oh yeah, I remember. You borrow them."

"Hmm," I say looking in her eyes.

"Ok. Now that we have finished our dinner, let me answer your very important question with some explanation."

"All right. I'm all ears."

"Zack, I've heard about broken hearts all of my life. I've seen the pictures of hearts drawn with jagged edges. I've watched movies and cried through them with the actors; I've felt their emotions for a minute even though I knew they weren't real, but never in my wildest dreams did I have any idea how much pain there is in the reality of brokenness. I didn't even know I could feel that much pain in my heart. I still feel the pain, even now. I let the pain have its will. I haven't tried to hide it, stifle it, deny it, or disguise it. I've let it have its way. I've let myself feel every moment of it—every deep ache. It's a very dark place, and I have made a little progress out of my depression, and I can't go back there."

"And you won't have to. I told you I've changed a lot. I know telling you is not enough, but if you let me, I can show you a lot."

"Well, let's start by telling me some of your changes."

"Hmm, if you don't love me anymore, what difference will it make?"

"Oh, we're back to that," she says with a bit of sarcasm.

"Well, that is it, Jaz. It's the purpose behind everything else. So, I need to know how you really feel about me now. I have to know."

I sit back in my seat with my fingers steepled in front of me. Not for a power play this time. I just don't know what else to do with my hands. At this moment, they can't reach across the table and take the hand that means so much to me. Right now, in this space that move is off limits. I'm quiet now staring in her eyes. She is quiet too, and she's staring back at me. I almost feel that this is a standoff, but I have to have her answer. I have to know where I stand. She may be thinking about her answer or she may be trying to decide how to destroy whatever little is left of us. At this point, I have no idea the way this will end.

She makes the first move. She reaches across the table for my hand, and I give it to her willingly. She looks down and rubs the back of it.

"Zack, I have never stopped loving you—not for a moment," she says looking directly in my eyes. I have wished a million times that I could, but I have never succeeded. So, yes, I still love you."

I take a deep relieving breath—one that I know she can plainly hear.

"But, my love for you is really not the issue at all, Sweetheart. The issue is if you really love me, and if you say you do then the question becomes do you love me enough? Enough to rid yourself of the Summers in your life? Enough to give me your whole heart? Enough

310

to stop wearing your mask and playing your games? Enough to be a real husband and eventual father. I've proven my love to you a million times over, but you've done very little to prove to me that you love me at all. I think it's your turn now, and I can't come back to you because I have no proof that anything will be different. You couldn't even get rid of Summer for me. Then there was Taylor, Carmen, and a hundred others standing in line. And then there was me. Well, I got out of the line, and I'll never get back in it. Never, Zack. Never. I lost myself for a moment, but I found myself and loved you enough to leave you."

Her words cut like a knife. I rub my bald-head in a desperate act to hold her off until I can find the right words to answer her accusations: the words that will help her see into my soul: words that will clearly communicate what is presently inside my heart; words that will define my raw emotions and words that demonstrate the actions that speak nothing short of veracity. I can't afford anything less than that. I can't mess this up. What I say right now, in this instant, can be the beginning or it can be the end of everything. Even my Harvard education stands resigned in its inferiority to this moment in time. I speak despite my fear.

"You don't have to worry about any of that because there is no line anymore. I'm so sorry I put you through that, but I was lost, Babe—really lost."

"I know all about your past, Zack. You've told me so much, but at some point, people grow up and move on."

"When you've been through as much as I've been through, that's easier said than done, but my psychiatrist has helped me a lot with that. I no longer think that my Mom's death was my fault. He helped me see that I had no part in that mess."

"You saw a psychiatrist?"

"I'm seeing a psychiatrist. Present tense. He says I'm a work in progress," I smile for the first time since she took my hand that she's still holding.

"I'm also a member of a church now. I gave my life to Christ one Wednesday night at our bible study."

"You go to church and study the Bible?"

"I told you. I'm not the same person that you left behind. Sometimes I think your leaving me was the best thing that could have happened. It woke me up. There are a lot of other things about me now that I'm not ready to tell, because you need to see them. Your Dad taught me that telling is one thing, but seeing is another."

Now it's my turn to rub the back of her hand. "I love you, Jazmin Grant, and the last time I told you that I had no idea what loving someone really meant. To me it was just words in a song and a feel-good moment. Fortunately for both of us, I do know now."

We spend another hour talking with me trying to help her understand the difference between then and now. I make some progress, but not enough to think this will all be fixed in three days. That kind of arrogance is gone. I know I have some very hard work in front of me, and I'm more than willing to do the work, but I want her to believe me enough to come home, but she won't budge on that issue.

"Babe, I need you State side."

"Well, that's too bad because I'm here now, and I don't plan to move anytime soon. You know how to get to me. Borrow a plane."

"I'll do that too, if I have too," I laugh.

"Well, you have too."

"Maybe not. Maybe I have my own *JazAir* now, and I don't have to borrow anything."

"Zack, Did you buy a plane?" She slaps her head with the palm of her hand in disbelief.

"I'll tell you when you come home." I wink and smile at her. The time is getting late so we drive back to her place, and I see her inside.

"Can I hold you for a moment—just a moment? I promise: no kissing. Just let me hold you close to me for a brief moment, please."

"I'm sorry, Zack. I'm really not ready for that."

I touch her under her chin instead, and say goodnight.

24

A Sweet Goodbye

Nothing lifts weight with more power than that of forgiveness.

Jaz and I find time to be together every day that I'm in England. We have a ball riding bikes around the area with Jaz pointing out this place and that art and all the things that have caught her eye over time. We play tennis, and I beat her every game with pleasure. We play on the water, dash here and there out of the rain, bask in the sunshine when we can find it, and generally have a wonderful time reacquainting ourselves with each other. I finally get her to giggle a little every now and then, and I love the sound. We go to a movie, sit by the lake at my hotel, and walk around the grounds enjoying the awesome view of nature. We eat together and do a lot of serious talking. One night, we just sit and talk about silly things—nothing serious, and we even have one dance. Even though it was a fast dance, I still enjoyed it a lot; however, on the fifth day, I get a call from my office with both very good news and some bad. I have won a huge contract for the company, but the clients want to talk only to me in a day or two. My team is asking if I want to Skype the meeting or if I plan to return anytime soon. I ponder it for a moment and because of the financial boom of this particular contract, I feel that I have to be present.

In the morning, I slowly pack my bags, and I feel a sadness envelop me. I really want to stay. I think Jaz and I are making some progress, and I don't want anything to hinder that. At the same time this contract will help a lot of people make a lot of money, and I feel a real obligation to that, especially to the laborers who don't make huge salaries. This will certainly provide a fantastic increase for them and their families. I call to ready *JazAir*, and then I make the call that I don't want to make. Jaz answers on the first ring and that, in itself, is very different and great progress. She has been making me wait at least through three or four rings. When she answers this time, there is something different in her voice. It's brighter, more welcoming, and then my heart does sink.

"Good Morning."

"Hi Zack, what's up so early besides yourself?" I hear an old familiar giggle that I have longed to hear for a year.

"Good and bad news, Babe. The good news is I've won a huge contract for the company, but the bad news is I have to leave, and I really don't want to go. The clients want to meet directly with me since I set all of this up, and I need to review the documents and finalize some things before I sit with them. Come go with me. I'll bring you right back."

"You're funny, Zack. You go. I'll be here when you get back if you get back."

"Oh, I'll get back. You can be sure of that, but for now I just want to come over for a minute before my plane leaves."

"What time will your plane leave?"

"When I ask it to leave."

"OK. Your rich friend came through for you again, huh? Does he ever use his own plane?"

"Jaz, I told you, I don't have his plane, and yes, he uses it quite a bit." In our line of work, we get to travel quite often if we need to do so. Anyway, I'm on my way over, ok?"

"All right, but don't expect anything."

"I just expect you to be there, that's all. See you in a few." My trip over is anxious, and I feel nervous again. I want her to believe what I tell her, but I know deep inside of me that she doesn't. Trust is a real factor with her when it comes to me, and I have no idea how to get that back, but I certainly plan to give it my best. The good thing is I know where she is now, and I finally have her new phone number. When I arrive, I see that the door is slightly open so I push it and call out to her.

"Jaz?"

"Hey, I'm back here. Come on back."

That's new. She hasn't let me come any further than the living room for the entire time that I've been here, but I find my way to her voice and see an awesome sight. The room is definitely the home of an artist. The windows bring in the sunshine, and a fantastic view of a lake in the back that I had not seen. As I survey her new place, my eyes catch something that gives me pause. On a shelf, high up, in a very special spot that you can see from wherever you stand in this room, there is the pink teddy bear from our Disney trip and the music box that plays our song. My eyes drift from that corner and meet hers in a silent reminiscence of happier times. We stare at each other in knowing silence, but then I move over and look at the easels with unfinished work in two different corners. She is working on one in the center of the room that is tremendously beautiful. Her watercolors are magnificent and so was that brief moment that neither of us missed and neither of us acknowledged with words. The connection was, without doubt, from heart to heart—a no words necessary kind of moment. I take a deep breath and force my mind back to front and center.

"Wow! How beautiful," I remark standing back admiring the painting in front of me.

"Well, it's not quite finished, but you've inspired me to complete it."

"I inspired you? Really?"

"Yes, because you make me happy, and I paint better when I'm happy," she giggles tapping my nose with her green paintbrush as she playfully passes in front of me.

"I can make you happier all the time if you go with me," I respond wiping a smidgen of paint from my nose.

She turns around to me now and looks directly into my eyes. "Zack, you have no idea how happy that would make me, but I have to be sure that my happiness is not temporary this time. I can't take a chance on you right now. Do you understand that?"

"Unfortunately, I do. Let me tell you this one thing that might help you understand that I am dead serious this time around. Some months ago, I came looking for you at your parents' home, and I ran into your father instead. After he made me feel as guilty as sin, he talked to me and with me. I mean really talked with me, Jaz—like a father to a son—something I've never experienced. He's still talking with me, and he's responsible, to a great degree, for my changes. He took me under his wing because he says he needs to pay it forward. Someone helped him a long time ago when he says he was as messed up as I, and this is the way he is showing his gratitude for that help. When he told me that his life was once a mess, and he was able to straighten it out and have a family, his words and his life gave me the hope that I needed to make some serious decisions to change things in my own life. The one thing he refused to do was tell me where you were living. He says I don't deserve you, and I know I don't, but I want to change all of that too. I want to give you the world."

"And maybe one day you will, but that day is not today, Babe."

"I know it's not. Well, unfortunately for me, I have to run, but I need something from you. I so desperately want to hold you for a minute—just a minute Babe, please. You told me no the last time I asked. Please don't tell me no now." I know that my eyes are pleading, and I know she knows how much this means to me at this moment.

I see her hesitation, but slowly she moves to me and wraps her arms around my neck and the butterflies in my stomach go absolutely crazy. I almost have to bend over in what is a joyful pain. I wrap my arms around her neck and look into her eyes, and an incredible thing happens. She touches my lips with hers, and the passion ignites. We stand together for a lot longer than a minute, and I make everything I know about kissing work for me. All of our days of longing and hurting, waiting and wondering are wrapped in those kisses. When we finally come up for air, I look at her and my words spill out: "Jaz, I love you so much, and I hope you will begin to believe me again."

She simply looks at me and slightly smiles. I let her go, and we walk arm in arm to her door. I bend down and touch her sweet lips again, and when I finally come back to some conscience place in my head, I have somehow found my way to my hanger, boarded *JazAir*, and left England and everything, I really want in my life, behind.

25

Longing

True love is worth the wait.

Back in New York my office is in celebration mode, but I calm them down because the deal is not yet completely sealed and won't be until the clients have signed on the dotted line. I'm cautious like that, and I know that I still have more to do before we meet. My boss has decided to attend this meeting and that makes me a bit nervous, but I'm fairly sure everything will be fine.

By five o'clock all of the questions have been answered, papers have been signed, and the deal is final. Backs are being slapped, congratulations to my team are plentiful, and again, I am the star. I should be very happy. Money usually does that for me, but not this time. I need to share this with the one I love, and she is not here. The only thing I can do is pick up the phone and make the call to England.

"Hey."

"Hey yourself. How are things?"

"They could only be better if you were here. They signed the deal, and I'm in charge of the project."

"Congratulations."

"Thank you, but I wish so much that you were here to share this with me."

"Maybe next time."

"Jaz, I had a great time, and it was so good seeing you, touching you again. What do you think we can do about this? What can I do to prove to you that I'm serious? I know so much more now than before."

"They say that time heals all wounds. Maybe it just takes time."

"Hmm...Time...Yeah, well, I just wanted you to know how things here came out so I'm going to go home now and sleep. I'm exhausted."

"All right. Be careful in that parking garage because I'm not there to rescue you. Look around and be aware of your surroundings, ok?"

"I will. You take care too. Good night."

When I hang up the phone, I realize that Jaz has no idea that I have my own home now, nowhere near that parking garage—a home waiting for her and the babies I hope we will have in time.

—〰—

The project keeps me in New York despite how much I want to return to England. There is just no time. The work is too new to leave it in the hands of my team without my presence. My bonus is staggering, my promotion awesome, but all of it means very little to me because I have no one with whom to share it.

This day was long and hard, but for some reason, I'm not tired at all. I look out of my back glass wall at the snow falling and the scene from the window is beautiful. I decide to made smores for myself for dinner. I know, not a great dinner, but I don't feel like cooking, and I don't want to go back out in the snow, so smores in the fireplace is what I decide to do. I put on some smooth jazz and take out the ingredients to make my smores. I decide on a grilling fork to melt my marshmallows and some sweet crackers. Sitting on some pillows in front of a cozy fire is comfortable and relaxing. I start to play a fantasy game and in it Jaz is in the kitchen getting the chocolate syrup. When my phone buzzes, it startles me out of my dream, and I am overjoyed to see Jaz's face staring back at me.

"Hey, Lady."

"Hi."

"To what do I owe this awesome surprise?"

I was just thinking about you and decided to call to see what you're doing."

"Well, I'm sitting in front of my fireplace all alone roasting marshmallows and listening to jazz that reminds me of you. ...pretty bad, huh?"

"You don't have a fireplace so I know that little scene isn't true."

"You have no idea what I have because you're not here where you belong. I am sitting on pillows, in front of my fireplace roasting marshmallows and making smores for my dinner. From here, I can see the falling snow, and I'm quite cozy in my little adobe listening to my smooth jazz playing *I'll Be Right Here Waiting For You*," I whisper as sexy as I know how. "I'll admit that I am a bit lonely, but I'm handling it."

"What are you really doing?" she giggles.

"Why don't you come and see since you don't believe my description."

"Maybe I will because your fantasy sounds like fun. I love smores."

"Catch a plane. I'll be right here waiting for you."

"Well, you take care. Maybe I will see you soon."

"Do you mean that?"

"I said, maybe."

"Jaz, don't play with me about this. I want it too badly."

"I'm not playing. Goodnight, Zack."

~ Jazmin ~

26

FACING TRUTH

When TRUTH crosses a threshold,
the door slams in the face of Deceit.

No single day has been the same since Zack left. I thought I obsessed over him before, but since seeing him again, he occupies my every thought. He's in my dreams at night, staring back at me in my morning coffee, plastered on my afternoon easel paintings, reflected in the lens of my evening photo shoots. He is everywhere in my thoughts, and Brooklyn is beside herself pushing me constantly with her daily mantra of *"go and get your man."*

When I am completely honest with myself, I admit that my body aches for him, and waiting to make love to him is becoming harder every day and especially every night. When he was here, his kisses were different. They had a more authentic feel. His arms, wrapped around me had an intensity that was not there before, and it has not hurt to hear that he and my father have a close relationship now. I know that wouldn't happen if things had not changed. When Mom calls, even though she doesn't say too much about Zack, she lets me know that he is trying very hard, but she cautions me to be careful not to rush into anything with him again. The problem is that when I hear his voice now, it penetrates my entire being. Despite it all, I love this man with everything inside of me, but as much as I love him, I love myself too, and I refuse to be used again. I question myself constantly: Do I dare give him another chance? Has he really made hard changes? Does he really sit at home alone at night now waiting for me? How much of this is true? Will I ever be able to trust again? What I know is that I must, whether I'm with Zack or not. There are others that I know I can trust, and I have to let my mind and heart recognize them.

I cannot give myself over to distrust for all that might come to my future. But the big question is can I take a chance with Zack again. I think that if I don't give him that chance, I will forever wrestle with my decision. Somewhere in this moment, in this place, I know without a doubt, I have to go back. I have to stop running, and I have to face whatever I decide will be my future. I have to face it. Running is not working. I have to try to give him another chance. There is so much we have shared that cannot just be pushed aside.

I have made a definite decision. I'm going back. I know that all too well now. I won't pack up my house, but I will pack a bag and surprise him for Thanksgiving. Hopefully this holiday means more to him now than ever before, and I can give him something to be thankful for.

—∿—

The plane is crowded, but I'm comfortable in first class, and the anticipation of seeing my parents and Zack for Thanksgiving makes the hassle of travel worth it all. At least this is better than when I traveled to England feeling it impossible to escape my sadness, the betrayal, and an aching heart that had no mercy.

I have told no one that I'm coming home because I want to see the joy on everyone's face when I just show up. I'm going to see Zack first because I feel like I can't wait another minute to touch him, let him hold me, and share the kisses that I have dreamed about for almost a month.

I have a rental car waiting when we land, and I rush to pick up my luggage and the car. Maybe Mom has prepared the usual delicious dinner for Thanksgiving with all the aunts, uncles, and cousins, but I may not make it over in time if things go well with Zack. Maybe the two of us will just have jazz and fantasy smores for dinner since there really is no fireplace. I smile to myself thinking about Zack's crazy sense of humor.

I wind through the New York traffic and the icy streets and finally reach Zack's apartment. I park in the garage even though I feel a bit intimidated since his attack, and I take the elevator to the penthouse and ring the bell. I hear movement as he approaches the door, and my heart is beating so fast, but when it opens, it's not Zack at all. The girl standing in the doorway is young, pretty, with curves in all the right places. My heart sinks instantly lower than the ocean deep. The energy in my body is zapped in a millisecond, and my voice is nonexistent.

"Hi, can I help you?" she asks still laughing at whatever was said just before she opened the door. She is youthful, full of energy and very happy. I stand looking at her smiling face for a moment and then somehow I answer.

"No, no," I whisper shaking my head. In some kind of dreamlike daze, I turn and find my way to the elevator, but once inside, I see the girl approach with concern in her eyes.

"Miss, are you all right?"

"Yes." That's all I can muster as the elevator door closes. I stumble down to the parking garage, get into my rental, and the tears flood. My cry is deep and my heart feels like it's going to burst. *How could he do this to me again? The deceit is unbearable.*

Then I get angry—very angry and make a definite decision for myself. *I can't ever attempt to see or talk with Zack again. The pain is just too great and, like Derek warned, he has no mercy.* I tear out of the garage and head down the highway for the hour drive to my parents' home. I really don't feel at all like company now, and I have no idea how I will get through the day with family and family friends. I know that the house is packed with company, so I will just make some excuse of being tired from my travel. Now that I know it's over with Zack, I'll make plans to go back to England and finish what I halfway started. I never went into anything fully, but I know that there is so much more that I could have done. Now I'm free to do it. Cars whiz pass and scenery is a blur as I travel up the hills to my childhood home. I need my Mom right now, and I can't wait to get that Mom hug that we all need at some point in our lives.

When I pull into the driveway, the lights are on, but the house looks quiet. I take out my key and enter the only place that is really home to me. I call out to Mom, to Dad, but there is no answer. The house is empty. Great! This is all I need. I throw my bags down, take off my coat, and dig out my phone. I'm confused. Do I want to be alone or not alone? I don't know. All I know for sure is that I won't be good company for anyone. I will, however, make every attempt to be as normal as possible because Zack does not deserve to have the power to make me even close to schizoid. I dial my Mom who never answers her cell, but it's worth a try. I hear the ring and then her voice telling me that she can't get to the phone, but leave a message and God bless me. I try my Dad, praying that he will answer. I hear the ring and then his voice.

"Jazmin! What a surprise. Happy Thanksgiving. I guess they don't keep up the American tradition over there, right? He chuckles.

"Hi Dad. No, they don't."

"Is everything all right, Sweetheart. You sound like you're been crying. What is it?"

"Well I was trying to surprise you guys, but it's not working out. I went to Zack's apartment first and he was entertaining some girl, and when I got home no one was here. Where are you, Daddy?"

"We're at Zack's house."

"Zack's house?"

"Yeah, he invited us over for Thanksgiving Dinner so since we didn't have company coming this year, and he was going to be all alone, we took him up on it."

"I just left Zack's house."

"No, we're at Zack house, and he's been here all day with us. Look, let me come and get you because Zack moved, and you'd never find this secluded place. Just stay put. I'll be there in about twenty minutes."

"Zack moved? He's not at the penthouse?"

"No, Jazmin. He's not there anymore."

"He didn't tell me."

"He has some good reasons why he didn't. Just stay put. I'll get you to him."

~ Zack ~

27

SURPRISE, SURPRISE!

True love brings you to a place called Home.

Having the Grants over for Thanksgiving is making me feel like I have a family even though Mrs. Grant has not completely warmed up to me, but I understand that. I still have not told them that I found Jazmin or that we spent over a week together in England. I can't take the chance of Papa G telling me to stay away from his daughter, and I certainly don't want to go through the lecture circuit with him again any time soon. Today has been extremely special for me, and I feel comfortable in my new immaculate home with all of its unusual beauty. The chefs that I've hired are putting together the dinner and trying to get me out of their way. They desperately want me to go away and stop cleaning behind them every few minutes, but I just don't want anything messy. I'm hoping that they can understand that and leave me to do what I have to do while they finish up. You know OCD me. I can't help myself.

My hands are in the dishwater when Papa G calls me to come into the living room, and I don't miss the relief I see on the chefs' faces. I dry my hands slowly and give them a menacing stare so that they understand I will be back. When I come into the living room, I see Jaz's parents seated in front of the fireplace whispering, and it looks as if the conversation is a bit contentious. They are seated close together, and I see that Mrs. Grant is shaking her head violently, and Papa G is slightly arguing back. All I hear is Papa G saying, "it's time for them to settle this once and for all. They need to get it done."

"Excuse me, Sir. Did you call me?"

"I did. I need you to do me a big favor. I'm not feeling well, and I left my medicine in my living room. I need you to get it for me. I hope I won't ever regret asking you to do this one little thing for me."

"Why would you? I don't mind, but do I need to call anyone?"

"Yes, I think he needs to speak with your psychiatrist," responded Mrs. Grant who rarely says anything to me.

"Psychiatrist?"

"Listen Son, take this key, and go and get my medicine. I need it now. When you get back, dinner will probably be done, the chefs will be happier that you are out of their way, and we can all sit down and have a nice little family gathering, and hopefully I can get rid of this ache in my heart."

"Yes, Sir. I'll be right back. Do you want to lie down while I'm gone?"

"No. I'll be fine right here in front of your cozy fire."

"OK. I'll hurry."

"Not too fast, Son. Take your time."

In the car, I go over the conversation again in my head. I can't make sense out of why Mrs. Grant would be so upset about my going to get Papa G's medicine unless it's more serious, and she wants him to go to the hospital instead. The thought of it being serious makes me hurry, and I speed down the highway and around the hills a bit too fast, but I'm cautious too.

At the house, I see the lights are on, and I rush out of the car, digging the house key out of my pocket. I enter the foyer, move quickly to the living room and look around trying to see where he might have put his medicine. I hear a slight noise and look up when I see her slip into my view and I into hers.

"Jazmin!"

I immediately feel my knees buckle and my heart picks up the rhythm of African drums. Like in the movies, she runs to me in slow motion and fills my arms, smothering me with kisses in a passion that I have never before felt from her. The surprise is overwhelming to me, and I know that I need to find the nearest seat, but she is holding me, and I don't ever want to move from this place. In the midst of the kisses, all I can do is whisper her name.

After a few minutes, we just look at each other—almost like examining our faces to make sure that this is real. She's touching me, and I'm touching her, but somehow it all still seems like a fantasy. Finally, we sit and find words that have been bottled up inside of us for months.

"I didn't know you were coming."

"I know. I wanted to surprise you."

"You did. Big time." I can feel that my eyes are open wider than usual.

"Come here, baby. Let me just hold you," I say after I find my voice again. She moves over closer to me, and for a few minutes, we sit in a comfortable quietness, but I break the silence.

"What brings you home?"

"You. I got to a place where I just wanted to touch you. I had to touch you."

"Does that mean that you love me?"

"I told you. I never stopped loving you. It's just that I want to be sure of your love. That's what holds me back. I know that I love you, but I'm not so sure you love me."

"You know, Baby, for a while I didn't know. I didn't even know what it meant to love someone, but today, thank God, I do. I've practiced on your Dad," I chuckled, "and I'll explain that later. I've done some very hard work in the past year, Babe, and I've actually found out a lot about myself. I've learned how to make things in my life better. You really don't have to worry about the old Zack resurfacing. I know what I want now, and I told you in England, I'm not going to stop until I get it. I want you, and no one else will do. I know that now."

"Well, you might have to help me now, Zack because I've been through so much. You'll have to help me trust you more if we're going to try to get this back together. After you left England, I had to make a decision to forgive you, and I did. That's why I'm here. I need to let you know that I forgive you, but something happened today that lets me know that I'm really not there yet—that I need your help to reassure me that you love me."

"What happened today?"

"I flew into town, rented a car, and headed straight for you. I went to the penthouse where I thought you were."

"Oh, no. What happened?"

"A pretty young lady opened the door, and I thought you were with her. I was so hurt and speechless that I just walked away in a daze."

"She didn't tell you that I don't live there anymore?"

"I never asked for you. I just assumed that this was still your place, and you were entertaining another woman after all that you said to me in England. Zack, I couldn't take it. I don't know how I made it here without having an accident. God was with me."

"Oh Baby. I'm sorry. I didn't really tell you about my new home because I didn't want you to think that I was trying to buy your love. I wanted you to come back to me just because you love and trust me again, and for no other reason, and that is what has happened even if there was a little drama."

"But don't you see what happened? Even though I didn't ask any questions, I made the assumption that this was another one of your ladies. I don't want to be in that place again."

"And I don't want you in that place either. I think that both of us have had to grow up some, and it's going to take time for me to build your trust again, but in my study of Jesus and now in my experiences with Him, I know that all things are possible to those of us who believe. Finally, Jaz, I'm a believer. God has had to take me through a lot of twists and turns, but He has brought me to a clearing—a landing, and I see some daylight. I see some of what He wants me to do in my life. I was just making money and looking for myself in all the wrong places, but now, I understand what my Grandma meant when she told me a long time ago to hold on to the Rock and never let Him go. I get that now. I don't carry that stone around with me all the time anymore. I don't need it because I have something far greater and more permanent. I pray every night that your trust in me will grow stronger, but I'm not foolish enough to think that this will happen overnight. I know it's going to take time."

"Zack, stop—please, stop talking." She puts her fingers to my lips to hush me. "Right now, I can't tell you how happy I am, and all I want is for you to hold me and never let me go." I look deeply into her eyes and our lips meet spontaneously. The kiss is a kiss of longing, of love, of released pain, of fulfillment and neither of us wants to let the other go, but suddenly, I remember the medicine that I came for, and I stop in my tracks.

"Wow, your Dad sent me for his medicine, and I totally forgot. Let me call him."

"Medicine? He doesn't need medicine. Baby, he knows I'm here. I talked to him. He sent you here on purpose."

"No, not him. He didn't do that. He has no idea that I found you and came to see you in England. He'd kill me if he knew that, and he'd kill me if he knew I was with you right now."

"Well, he may not know that you came to England, but he certainly knows that I'm here in this house, and if he sent you here for anything, it was to find me—not for his medicine. Besides, my Dad is healthy as a horse. He doesn't take medicine." She's giggling now and falls over on me like old familiar times.

"Well, I'll call him anyway and see what he says while I'm a distance away. I think he's going to kill me. He told me to never ask him where you were."

"Did you ask him?"

"No, not today."

"But he told you. Zack, he wanted you to find me here."

"I'm calling anyway."

"Suit yourself."

I dial his cell, and Papa G answers on the first ring. "Sir, I can't find your medicine."

"Is Jazmin there in your arms smiling?"

"Yes, Sir."

"Then you've found my medicine. All I want Zack is for my baby girl to be happy. If you can make her happy then all is well. I just hope you never make me regret what I've done."

"I promise you, Sir. I promise you. You will never ever regret this—not ever."

"Great. Now, the two of you get over here so we can have some of this good smelling food. We're starving."

"Right away, Sir, and Papa G, thank you so so much."

"Thank me by your actions, Son. Do some more *particular* things. Take good care of my baby girl."

"I promise you I will. We'll see you in about forty-five minutes."

"It only takes twenty to get here."

"Come on, Man," I whine. I know. Give me a minute. We're coming."

Jazmin

When we drive up to Zack's house the beauty of it is unbelievable. It's like nothing I've ever seen in my life, not even in magazines. It's seated on a beautiful rocky hill overlooking the majesty of the ocean. We drive around a lighted curvy path to the entrance and the landscaping is nothing short of award winning. There are double doors that, even in the semi darkness, display the glitter of decorative glass and expensive wood. When we enter the foyer, we step on to a shinning marble floor that moves seamlessly up a spiraling staircase. The living room, just off the foyer, is from where my parents rush to greet me. Through all of our hugs, kisses, and tears, I see the place where dinner smores are made, and I smile a secret smile to myself. I see the glass wall that displays God's creation of sky and water, stars and moons, mountains and snow- covered trees that only He commands. A back wall opens the room to a beautiful water fountain that in summer will cascade down sloping steps into a pool where aching bodies can be refreshed. It almost looks like a monument. To my surprise, near the fireplace, I see the painting that I gave Zack so many months ago. It's the one I refused to allow him to buy—the one that reminds him so much of his childhood place of freedom, the one that was inspired by God and more than special to me for that reason. It is the one that my hands moved over almost automatically, and I had no idea where the images were born, but now I know, and there it is, hanging in all of its glory in its own special place of honor surrounded by a frame far more expensive than the one in which I first housed it.

The four of us stand close with grins that can't stop. My mom can't stop crying, my dad can't stop smiling, and Zack can't stop staring at me. Me? Hmm. I can't stop this heart of mine from loving. This is Thanksgiving, and I couldn't be more thankful. Zack finally goes to check on the food, and it is ready. He ushers us into a formal dining room that takes my breath away. The table is a dark mahogany and the high back chairs are upholstered in contrasting white linen. The chandelier overhead is crystal and sparkles in its own light. A fireplace heats the room, and the candles and roses on the table add a touch of romance. The table is laden with all kinds of food and Zack must not have eaten in days because he stops talking completely, and all I see is my man stuffing his mouth with far too much food at once. I smile with the joy of watching him, and I see him watching me.

After dinner, Mom and I sit at the table talking and laughing about silly things that we have said and done in the past, and I see Dad and Zack move back into a den area near a television. The Thanksgiving game is on. We hear them shouting at the players and loving the joy of this game where the players throw a ball, chase each other for that one little ball, fall down, and try not to hurt themselves.

Zack

I see Papa G enjoying the dinner and the game, but I also see him eyeing me every now and then. Finally, at halftime, he lets me know what's on his mind.

343

"You know what I did for you today, don't you, Son?"

"Yes, Sir, and I couldn't be more grateful."

"You know that this is no game, right?"

"Yes, Sir. I know that very well."

"You're not going to make me regret this day are you, Son?" "

No, Sir, not if I can help it."

"Well, I asked you to talk with me after you'd done some *particular things*, and you have done some very hard things. I truly respect you for what you've done and what you're doing. All I ever wanted was for my daughter to be happy with someone who respects her heart and her life. I think you're getting there now. You've passed a lot of tests. What I've seen you do this year proves a lot to me. The day I went with you to Mt. Hope to seal the deal with your Dad was a day I'll never forget. That was the day you gave your life back to you. You see, Son, it takes a lot to forgive especially what you had to forgive, but since that day I've seen a weight lifted from you, and I know you can feel it. You're so much happier."

"Yes, Sir. I do feel it. In a way, that was one of the happiest days of my life. You could have made it even happier if you had told me where Jazmin was.

"You weren't ready for that on that day, Son, or let me say, I wasn't ready.

Papa G, I want to marry your daughter, and I know I'm ready. There is no one else in this world that I love like I love your Jazmin. I know that now. Will you give us your blessing?

"What makes my Jazmin different from all of the other women you've had in your life, Zack?'

"That's easy, Sir. She's the only one I see as a partner, one who gives more than she gets. Most of the women I've known want money. They love the life style, but Jaz is different. She wants my heart. She's the only one who will feel comfortable growing old with me watching the changes in body and mind. She is my forever...my no matter what life throws lady. She really loves me, not what I have or what I can do for her."

Papa G leans over in his chair, and again, with his elbows on his knees, steeples his fingers in front of him. The fingers touch his lips.

"Zack, a father walks his daughter down an aisle to an altar, and the minister asks a question. He says, 'Who gives this woman to be married to this man?'" Papa G pauses in his same positions, and his look in my eyes is extremely serious. "Do you have any idea, Son, the responsibility I will have on my shoulders if I answer, I do? Those two little words mean I trust you with her... that I believe as much in you as I believe in her...that I honor this marriage—that I believe the two of you belong together—that I believe you will treat her with dignity and respect—that the two of you really love one another as God commands us to love. So, I'm going to tell you, Son, I have a huge responsibility if I say I do and hand my precious child over to you knowing that the words say that from this time forth, she is to forsake all others, including me, and cling only unto you for as long as you both shall live. That's a lot to give over to someone, Son, but because of all that I've seen you do this year, all that we have shared, and the consistency of what you're doing...the PARTICULARS... I do trust you and you do have my blessing. Take your bride, Son, and love her, respect her, love your children that will come in due time. Always make your wife and children your priority, and love yourself. Most of all, to make it all stand firm and good, continue to love the Lord. Congratulations, Son."

Tears are in our eyes, and I get up from my seat and slowly cross over to where my future father-in-law is seated. He stands up, and we seal this deal with a hug and his hard slap on my back. I know he meant for it to be hard because he's always sending me some message one way or another.

"I want to show you how proud I am of all that you've done, Son. I've grown very close to you through all of this; I love you. I know you're a very rich man, but I'm not so bad myself, and I want to give you something that you and Jazmin will never forget. I want you to tell me something that you want that will make you both happy. I know you can get it for yourself, but I want to give it to you. You can think about it if you need to do so, but if not, tell me now."

"How about a wonderful romantic honeymoon? I have a very good friend that I would like for Jaz...Jazmin to know and he lives in France now. I'd like to take her to France."

"You've got it. I'm so happy that I can do this for you because you have met all of my demands, and you deserve to be completely happy."

"Thank you, Sir. I can't tell you how much I appreciate all that you've done for me and it's a lot."

After a little more conversation, I excuse myself, and go into my bedroom, and take a moment for myself. I thank God for His goodness and His mercy. I will have my angel after all of the turmoil, all of the distrust, all of the agony. Derek's voice comes to me. *He will never leave you or forsake you.* I can't count how many times he told me that one scripture over the years that we spent together, but the words never meant much to me until now. When I finish my prayers, I get up from the side of my bed, open a drawer and pull out the ring that I once offered far too soon. I look at its beauty, and turn it around in my hand much the same way I did during the two hours it took for me to choose it. I put it in my pocket, stand still for a moment and take a lot of deep breaths before I join my company again. When the game is over, and we are all sitting together again, I stand up and look down on my Jazmin. I take her hand in mine, bend on one knee in front of her and her parents.

"My sweet Jazmin, my angel, my life, the one who helps me breath, we've been through a lot together and there is no one in this world I want to spend my life with but you. I know that now more than ever. On the inside of you, I've experienced beauty that I didn't know was real, and on the outside, your beauty is incomparable. You are the light in my eyes and the beat of my heart, and I know that I am your breath of life. I want you near me, Baby, with me, beside me for as long as I live and even beyond. With you, I'm home. Will you marry me, Jaz, and make me the happiest and most blessed man in all of this world?" I kiss her hand.

Her left hand has covered her mouth through my entire little speech, and tears have fallen, but now she moves it and slides to the floor with me. She gathers me in her arms.

"Yes...Yes, Babe, I'll marry you, and you'll make me the happiest woman in the world."

In the background, I hear applause and congratulations as I slip the ring onto her finger. Jazmin and I get up from the floor, hug each other and move over to her parents and hug them.

"There's one more thing I have to do now. I have some family I need to share this moment with," I say. I reach for my cell and dial Chad. When I tell him, even on the phone, I hear the smile in his voice.

"You finally decided to grow up, huh? Finally decided to let me go."

"Yeah, 'cause staying a kid gives you too much right to almost kill me," I chuckle. "Will you come back here to be my best man?"

"You know I will. All four of us will be there. Tell Jazmin she's got a good man."

"What? Did I hear you say a good man? I'll tell her that for sure. Look, Chad, thank you so much for my life. I know you gave up a lot for me, and I can never thank you enough. You were hard on me, but you were my Robert Frost urging me always to 'take the road less traveled.' You had 'promises to keep and miles to go....' I totally understand that now."

"Yes, I did. Together, we kept the promises to Mom. Go be happy, Little Bro. Finally, Mom is smiling down on both of us. Colin is helping me become the architect that I've always wanted to be, and I am so happy out here with him. There are a lot of pretty girls out here too," he laughs."

"I couldn't be happier for you. You deserve every moment of this time in your life." I hang up with Chad, and I smile at my soon to be in- laws.

"I've watched you carefully this year, Zackary, and I don't know anyone who has worked harder to go after what he wants. I admire that. I think my daughter is as blessed to have you as you are to have her." Mrs. Grant puts her arms around me, and for the first time, she gives me her love. In my ear she whispered, "Jazmin told me you searched for her until you found her. You made her very happy. We'll keep that our little secret."

That moment will forever be very special for me. A mother's hug and confidence are things that I've longed for and needed for quite a while. My soon to be in- laws leave my home with the promise that I will drive Jazmin back home TONIGHT. The words weren't spoken verbally, but I know they still expect her to be a virgin in the morning, and she will be. Alone, we hold each other, gaze in each other's eyes, kiss, and I take her up the spiral stairs to show her one more surprise. We stop at the white door, and I push it open.

"Zack, why are you showing me an empty room?"

"Because it's not going to stay empty. One day we'll have a roomer in here that will probably stay for about eighteen years," I chuckle.

"Do you think our roomer will be a boy or a girl?"

"I have no idea, Babe. All I know for sure is that I'm ready for this too." I pull her close to me, and she giggles with her lips kissing my neck.

"Are you sure about this, man?" She asks playfully attempting to mimic my voice.

"So very sure," I look directly in her eyes, and respond in the most serious voice that I can muster.

She spreads her fingers, and looks at the brilliant diamond sparkling on the fourth finger of her left hand. She grins a wide grin that shows her deep dimple, and in the midst of her kisses, she whispers to me.

"We'll take one day at a time, Baby—one day at a time." Standing, at the nursery door holding Jaz, I wish a thousand times that I had not promised to bring her home tonight, that I didn't care what Papa G

thought, but that is no longer the case. I care a great deal what he thinks, and, in reality, I don't want that to change.

"I promised to bring you home tonight."

"I know."

"Do you want to go?"

"No."

"What do you want to do?"

"Keep your promise. Staying here is too risky. Yes, I have the ring, but I don't have the vows. I need the vows, Zack, in front of God and company. That's very important to me."

"And that makes it very important to me," I say swaying in her arms. "I'm so ready for all of this." I peck her nose and we walk down the spiral staircase arm in arm, and I drive her first to meet JazAir that will take her to gather her things in England and then close to morning, but not daybreak, I drive her home to her parents.

~ Zack ~

28

NEW LIFE

Our God specializes in doing the unexpected.

We decide immediately not to prolong the engagement because we both can't wait to be married. We plan a Christmas wedding and that is perfect for my little Christian. To make sure that everything is beautiful and exactly what Jaz wants, her Mom hires a wedding planner who assures them that for the money being paid, she can make everything happen in record time. I don't believe her until I see the stacks of invitations being mailed in record time, the place booked, the food paid for, the orchestra hired, and all of the other things that will create a life of dreams coming true for my angel and me.

I opt not to have a bachelor party because the last thing I need is for "the girls" to surprise me and do something to mess all of this up. Instead, Derek and my brothers take me out for what they call my "last supper." The place is elegant. It's a Derek kind of place with all of the amenities, delicious food, outstanding jazz, and a very few great drinks. Papa G is invited and present with a watchful eye, so my evening is very safe, and I like that. My friends and family are around me and for the first time in my life, I feel really loved.

We all end up at my house later, shooting a little pool with everyone taking a turn trying to beat Papa G at the game he claims he's mastered. Derek and I have a chance to catch up on a lot of missed time, and Chad can't stop talking about how close he is to becoming a real architect. I'm more than excited for him, but my real excitement is for the morning of my wedding day. Before it's too late, I call my angel and we speak too briefly for me. I hear the music and laughter around her, and I can tell even on the phone that she is happier than she has ever been.

"I can't wait to see you tomorrow."

"And I can't wait to hold you in my arms as my wife. Have you been practicing your new name?"

"No, silly. I don't need to practice that. I did that when we first met," she giggles. "I wrote it a thousand times to make my dreams come true."

"Call me before you go to sleep tonight?"

"Why, I may be too tired, Zack."

"Jazmin, call me before you go to sleep tonight," I say more emphatically.

"If you insist."

"I do. I need to hear your voice before I fall asleep. All right?"

"All right. I love you. Good night for now."

"I love you more. Call me."

When everyone has gone to bed, I feel very good having so much family around. For the first time, I feel like my beautiful house is a home. Derek is here with Arianna and the baby, but tonight Ari and Chase are at Jaz's house for the night. My brothers are here, and so is Papa G. I clean up a few things that were left out, vacuum a large area, and dust before I decide to find my way to bed. I slip down into my cool clean sheets, my phone buzzes, and I know exactly who it is.

"I'm just checking in to say goodnight again."

"Thank you, Love. I just want you to be the last person I talk with tonight."

"Ahh, that's sweet." I hear her giggle.

"You're silly. I hope you enjoyed tonight as much as I did. Just think, tomorrow night this time you will be lying here next to me in our bed. Baby, I can barely wait."

"Me too. I know how comforting that is because I remember how I felt lying next to you in the hospital."

"Well, it will be much better this time around because you will be under the covers with me, not lying on top scare to death that I might touch you," I laugh.

"I wasn't scared."

"You were scared."

"...Was not."

"...Was so."

"Goodnight, Silly. See if I'm scared tomorrow night."

" I love you more than words can say, Jazmin Grant, and tomorrow night, I promise you that I won't let you be scared. Good night." I hear her giggle and the phone disconnect. I turn over and I'm sleep in seconds.

—m—

The morning is a bit chaotic. There is definitely far too much testosterone in one spot. At breakfast, my brothers and I playfully argue about everything. It looks like all of us want to be the most intelligent, know all the right answers, and tell the funniest jokes. Most of the time Derek is sitting at the table looking totally lost and missing his wife and son. He talks to them briefly, but is hurried off the phone by Jazmin and the rest of the bridal party. Even I'm a lot more quiet than usual, but, true to form, intimidated as I may have been, I still get in my share of digs for a youngest brother, even if I did have to be on the receiving end of too many punches to my chest.

Around three o'clock we start to dress for the wedding and Derek tries to pay me back for how I acted on his wedding day. Even though he is not my best man in name, he knows that he will always be my best man. I am sitting in my bedroom just to get a quiet moment before the wedding, and Derek knocks softly.

"Yeah, it's open."

"Hey man, you look great, so why are you hiding out in here?" he asks peeking inside.

"Not hiding. I just needed a moment. Come in."

"Can I get you anything for you? Maybe some water...a cigarette? ...a drink?" "You're funny. I remember when I did that to you," I smile.

"Yeah, asking me if I wanted a cigarette when you knew I didn't smoke," he chuckles and we just look at each other and let our unspoken memories fill the room. For a minute, we are both very quiet.

"Zack, I want to apologize to you. I didn't make this wedding event easy for you to get to, and I'm sorry. I just never believed that you could change."

"To be honest, D, neither did I. It took a while before I even tried. I've learned so much about myself this year, and I understand what you were thinking and why you told Jazmin to stay away. It was good advice then. I put her through a lot, but like you told me a thousand times God never leaves. He didn't give up on me even when I was ready to give up on myself."

Well, I just wanted to let you know that I'm sorry, and that I see the change in you. I hope nothing but the best for you two. I mean that, Z. Well, I'll let you have your moment in here to think, but I had to let you know how happy I am for you and for your bride. Be blessed, man."

"Thanks, D. You're a good man."

He moves over close to me, and I stand up and receive the love from him that he has always been so willing to give to me. He is truly my best friend.

—◇—

When Derek, my brothers, and I drive up to the front of the church there is no possible way that I could ever have imagined that Jaz and her mother could have planned something this beautiful in the four weeks and few days that they had to put all of this together. But here it is, in full view. Flickering in the darkness are steps lined on both sides with different size jars holding lighted candles that create a path of fascinating romantic beauty leading to the doors of the church. I am unaware that my mouth is open until Chad breaks my fantasy spell.

"Close your mouth, Little Bro. Get some dignity here. Don't act like you're not used to stuff. You're a rich man. You got to expect things like this." He slaps me on my back and guides me up the steps. When we open the door, the sight of the church takes my breath away. At each pew are tall lighted candles enclosed in slim glass tubes, and each candle holder is finished off with mistletoe and red satin bows that stream to the floor. The altar is flanked by four candelabras holding six candles each and the floor is covered in a beautiful white satiny cloth pull tightly. It shines in the glowing light of the church chandeliers. Flowers deck the altar, and the Christmas colors are mesmerizing.

Rev. Hyland greets us at the door and ushers us to a small waiting room in the back. Derek and my brothers are dressed in black tuxedoes with black vests, white pleated shirts and small red carnation boutonnieres. My formal suit is white to match my bride. At some point, my ushers get very busy and only Chad, Rev. Hyland, and I are waiting in the back. I can hear the beautiful organ music, and I can't wait to see my bride. I force myself not to pace back and forth, and I try to pretend to be perfectly calm, but everything changes for me when Colin comes to the back and tells us that its time. At that point, I'm a nervous sweating wreck.

The six o'clock evening atmosphere is stunning. We walk to the altar, and I watch my brothers and Derek escort beautiful bridesmaids down the candlelit aisle in their flowing red dresses with short white fur wraps. Each is carrying a bouquet of red and white roses. Jaz's best friend, Brooklyn, is her Maid of Honor. She's wearing a dress that is slightly different from the others because she has a short train that flows down one step. When each of the bridesmaids is in place lined up the steps with the men on the opposite side, I see the double doors in the rear open and for a moment no one is there, and then I see her... my angel, and she is more than beautiful. Her flowing white gown fits every one of her curves perfectly, and I see the wedding planner adjust her train for that fairy tale look that all brides aspire to when they come down the aisle with their father. Her dress sparkles in the candlelight, my heart pounds, and only very deep breaths control it as I watch her come to meet me at this sacred place. When she reaches me, our eyes meet through her veil, and we stand for a captivating moment that I know will be stamped in my mind for all eternity. Even through the veil, I see those gorgeous long eyelashes that captured me so many months ago in a church in Virginia. Finally, I hear Rev. Hyland clear his throat, and he brings me back to my wedding day.

I hear the Dearly Beloved part and how we are gathered together today in the sight of God and this company for the marriage of Zackery Tyler Belford and Jazmin Taylor Grant. I hear him ask who gives this woman to be married to this man, and I see Papa G step slightly forward and answer, "I do." I remember the power of those two words and even in this moment, I wonder if I will be willing to hand my own daughter over to the love of her life one day. My thoughts flitter here and there, capturing images of my life with Jaz. All of our experiences together flash before me...those things that have brought us here to this spot ...in this blessed moment, and my heart is leaping with joy. Despite my exhilaration, I still feel the perspiration trickle down the side of my face as Papa G places Jaz's hand in mine, and I really know now what he is doing and what a gift he is giving me. When we turn together to face Rev. Hyland, my mind comes back to the present.

"Is there anyone in this company who can show just cause why these two should not be joined together. Speak now or forever hold your peace."

For a second there is a nervous complete silence, and then, from a very dark corner in the back of the church, we hear a rather soft but firm voice. "I do speak now," travels the voice to the front as Jaz and I turn with our eyes peering into the distant darkness. I hear the rustle of the audience turn and the mummer of their voices asking questions in shock. I hear her heels click on the tiled floor in the back and fall soft on the white cloth lining the carpeted floor. Summer moves to the front and stands in stiff arrogance looking directly at me. I look at Jazmin and see the beginning of tears forming in her eyes, so I immediately hold her hand tighter and wrap my arm around her waist to symbolize our strong bond that will not be broken by anyone.

"Don't worry," I whisper in her ear. "Everything will be fine."

"What do you have to say, child?" asks Rev. Hyland, his own voice shaking in surprise.

The look in Summer's eyes is untamed and beyond anything I am used to seeing from her. I am almost unsure how to handle this situation without using extreme force and my wrath on her. When she finally speaks again, it is in a tone that matches her wild eyes.

"This man is my man. He belongs to me, and he knows it as well as I do. He has spent the last two weeks with me pouring out his love for me, but today he makes this feeble attempt at marriage. This is a mockery, and I won't stand for it."

Still holding tightly to Jazmin, I refute her statement with everything inside of me. "That's a lie, Summer. That's a vicious lie!" I exclaim in disbelief that she would actually do this. "I haven't seen you in months. Why are you saying these awful things?"

"Because I love you, and you love me. You know you just left my bed in the early morning hours of this very day."

A loud audible gasp from the audience fills the entire sanctuary, and then another hush falls on the room.

"Summer, that's a lie. Why would you do this to me?" Before I can say another word, I hear the voice of the only father that I have ever known. Papa G comes to the altar and turns to address the audience.

"I have no idea why this young lady would come here today to try to disrupt this beautiful moment for my daughter and my soon to be official son, but I can tell you that this woman is a blatant liar. Because of her, Zackary asked me to stay at his home with him to protect him from this woman's harassment. I have been at his home for the past three weeks." Papa G is speaking loudly so that everyone in the audience can hear, but he is not taking his cold eyes off of Summer as he moves very close to her and continues his defense. "I

361

KNOW where this man has been for the last three weeks, because I have been with him, and I have never in my life seen this woman. She is a desperate liar, and I suggest that we dismiss her and continue with what will now be even a more meaningful wedding because we see that no man or woman will break this bond. Young lady, I suggest that you leave here immediately and leave this man and this woman alone to finish the beautiful life that they have started."

We see Papa G, Derek, and Chad take Summer firmly by the arms and together they start to walk quickly and with a bit of force down the aisle. I see Summer look back at me with tears in her eyes, but they do not move me or anyone else in this company.

When everyone is back in place, and Summer is safely locked outside these church doors, and more importantly securely locked out of my life, Rev. Hyland continues the ceremony, and begins the vows that ask us to promise to love and honor each other for the rest of our days. When it becomes my turn to speak, I speak from my heart.

"Jazmin, thank you for standing with me through all of that disruption. In that one selfless moment, you've shown me again how much you love me. ...so much that you are willing to sacrifice for me. For the rest of my life, I will try to show you how much I love you. *Jazmin Taylor Grant, you are my life. Without you, I cannot breath. You've taught me what it really means to love and for that I will forever be grateful to you. God has taught me what true love is, and I memorized it so that it would forever be available to me. I know without a doubt that I love you with every fiber of my being, and I know what that means: 'Love is patient; Love is kind; It does not envy; It does not boast; It is not proud; It is not rude; It is not self-seeking; It keeps no record of wrongs; Love does not delight in evil but rejoices with the truth; It always protects; Always trusts, always hopes. It always preservers; Love never fails.' Because of Jesus and you, I have a different heart, a different perspective on life, and there is a different person behind these eyes that look into yours. Jazmin, you cover me with your love, and I love you more than words can say. As God is my witness, I will spend the rest of my life proving that to you."* I bend to kiss her unveiled face, but Rev. Hyland stops me abruptly.

"We have not yet come to that part, Son," he quickly whispers. I straighten and Jazmin finds my eyes and smiles her rather shy smile.

"Zack...Zackery, I know your struggle to reach this point, and I love you for your determination to be a better you. We have experienced so much apart and so much together. With each event, we have drawn closer and closer to this point where my heart is yours and your heart is mine, and they beat as one. From you, I have learned not to run away from problems, but to stay and face them with the man who, I know now, will be always by my side. I have learned to discern truth from jealousies, and to be patient when things don't go my way. I promise that I will love you in our joys and in our sorrows. I will love you when we are in that peaceful place that life affords and also when problems come in our midst and trouble the waters. I will love you in sickness and in health, in times when you make me so proud that my heart could burst and when, like all of us, you make the mistakes that disappoint. I know that Love is patient, Zackary, and I love you enough to keep no record of wrongs. I know that it preserves. ...that it never fails. I believe that God has walked with us this far, and that He will forever be our guide helping us through all that life has to offer. I believe this in the name of the Father, the Son, and the Holy Spirit."

We exchange rings and vow that the circle will never be broken. Then Rev. Hyland says the words we both long to hear: "For as much as Zackery and Jazmin have consented together in holy wedlock, and have witnessed the same before God and this company, and thereto have pledged their faithfulness each to the other, and have pledged the same by the giving and receiving each of a ring, by the authority vested in me as a minister of the gospel of Jesus Christ according to the laws of the State of New York, I pronounce that they are husband and wife together, in the name of the Father, and of the Son, and of the Holy Spirit. Those that God has joined together, let no man put asunder. Zackery, you may NOW kiss your bride." We hear the laughter from the audience as we exchange a shy and nervous kiss. We turn to face our family and friends who we see wipe happy tears away as Rev. Hyland booms: "To this waiting company, I now present to you Mr. and Mrs. Zackery Tyler Belford." The orchestra strikes all the right chords, and we rush together down the aisle to the limo that waits to take us on a short ride around the block and bring us back to take the pictures that will seal our memories for a lifetime.

Later we find our way to the reception. In elegant and breath-taking beauty, we celebrate with family and friends. We dance, listen to speeches, make speeches, eat delicious food, and enjoy every moment of this very special day. Jaz has to even share her special day with little Chase Wellington watching me bounce him on my knee to his squeals of delight and my grin from ear to ear. When it is time to go, we leave to begin our lives together that will commence with a fantasy trip to France in a few days.

During the blissful night of our wedding, we sleep...resting from the excitement of our beautiful and miraculous day; however, somewhere in the dawn of morning, at the inception of day, we meet and moments stand still. For the first time in my life, I know the exhilaration of making love. With my angel, my once virgin in my arms, we lay and sweep together the shattered pieces of our lives and mold them into each other without flaw. In these moments of perfection, we truly become one.

"Trust in the Lord with all thine heart; and lean not unto thine own understanding, In all thy ways acknowledge Him and He shall direct thy path." Proverbs 3:5-6

ABOUT THE AUTHOR

Doris H. Dancy is an accomplished and award-winning educator, writer, speaker, playwright, novelist, a church officer, and a member of the Lambda Omega Chapter of Alpha Kappa Alpha Sorority, Inc. She received her BA Degree in English and Spanish Education at North Carolina Central University in Durham, North Carolina, and her MA Degree in English Education from Hampton University in Hampton, Virginia. Dancy has been a Teacher of English, High School English Department Chairperson, English Teacher Specialist, and Supervisor of English K-12 for Hampton City Public Schools. She is the author of the Redemptive Love Series: *Jagged Edges, And the Word Became Flesh* and *All Other Ground*. Each novel has received numerous awards.

Mrs. Dancy is married to Willie Dancy, Jr. and they have two daughters, Monica Dancy-Hayes and Tara Dancy Abaya. They have three beautiful granddaughters: Cadence, Tali, and Zoey.

To learn more about Doris H. Dancy,
please visit: www.dorishdancy.com

ADDITIONAL TITLES
By Author, Doris H. Dancy

The Redemptive Love Series

All Other Ground

My website:
www.dorishdancy.com

Awards

1. Readers' Favorite Five Star Award
2. USA Best Book Awards Finalist
3. International Book Award Finalist
4. 3-in-1 The Voice Book Award for Christian Writers
Available At: www.dorishdancy.com

www.ingramcontent.com/pod-product-compliance
Lightning Source LLC
Chambersburg PA
CBHW060928030726
47503CB00003B/515